BREATHE WITH ME

AMANDA KAITLYN

AUTHORS' NOTE

Previously released as two titles, Breathe With Me is a romantic suspense that deals with some issues that could be triggers for some readers. Please read a sample beforehand if you think you may be upset by these triggers.

For the girls out there that are still looking for Mr. Right.
Breathe.
I have a feeling you'll find your Hudson, too.

ACKNOWLEDGMENTS

When you, the reader, purchased a copy of this book, you took a chance on characters that intrigued you and an author that poured her heart, soul, everything between its pages. So, thank you. Thank you for choosing this book to occupy your lazy Sunday morning or late Friday night. You'll never know how much your support means to me.

PROLOGUE

EMBERLY

Age 10

The bottom of my stomach dropped as I was awoken by a sharp cry coming from downstairs. Curling my blankets around me even tighter, I shivered in dread and laid perfectly, completely still, awaiting what would come next.

At least once a night, I woke up like this.

My mama was downstairs with my daddy, though I didn't think of him that way. All he'd ever given me in my young life was sadness and fear. The longer I laid here in the darkness of my room, the higher the fear inside of me rose.

A sharp, broken gasp left me when I heard her sobs, loud, anguished sounds that tore into my heart, leaving only hopelessness in their wake.

My mama was so strong.

She loved me so much.

I saw it in her eyes when she looked at me, even when they were too swollen to see anything.

I could remember a time when she was happy and my parents were crazily in love. They would cook together, dance together, laugh together.

Before my nightmare began.

Before everything changed.

Before I lost hope that true love was real.

I tried in vain to smother the sounds of her pain with my pillows and a sob burst from my heaving chest. Hot, stinging tears slid down my cheeks and I tried so hard to stop them.

I hiccuped as quietly as I could, knowing that if he was mad enough, he would come up here and start in on me.

My mama always took the brunt of his anger.

She said it was her way of protecting me.

We couldn't leave because it would make him mad.

But I think she is just too scared to try.

Sometimes I wonder if we'll ever get away from him.

She says we will and to trust her.

But he hurts her so much, what if...

A shudder wracks my body at the thought and I jump as the sound of the front door slamming reaches my room.

I always leave my door open so I can hear when he leaves.

He always leaves afterwards.

He'll say he has work to do, but I know the truth.

He can't stand to look at my mama after hurting her.

He'll come back in the morning and beg and plead with her to forgive him.

And a part of me hates her, because she does forgive him.

Every time.

Slipping out of my bed, I pad quietly down the stairs, holding my breath just in case he comes back.

He almost never does.

"Mama?"

"Oh, baby. Go back to sleep."

Reaching for the first aid kit I keep on the top shelf of the linen closet, I shake my head gently, knowing I couldn't do that.

She's my mom.

I always take care of her.

"How bad?"

I whisper the words, still afraid he'll return and catch me tending to her injuries.

Once, he did and I'd never seen him so angry.

"B-bad, baby. I burned the chicken. He wasn't happy about that."

I bite down on my lips to stop the words wanting to slip free at her softly spoken excuse for him.

My mom's an amazing cook.

She learned from my grandmother and my grandmother learned from her mother.

She says it's an Italian thing.

You have to know how to cook because that's what's expected from a wife, a mother. I don't bother telling her that it's the 21st century and men can cook, too. She'll always make excuses for him, just like I'll always let her. It's our way of coping. *We don't know any other way.*

"You need stitches, Mama. Do you want me to get some aspirin?"

"No, baby. It's okay. Just fix me up."

"Ma-"

When one of her shaking hands grabs mine, I nod.

I quickly fix her up as best I can and then help her to her bed, where I cover her up with a thick afghan my grandma made.

"I'm so sorry, Mama."

"Shh, Em. We'll be safe soon."

Her warm, loving arms come around me and though I know her words are a lie, I believe them, anyways.

EMBERLY

The warm summer air gusted over my face as I rushed into the hospital in my typical late fashion. My stomach was in knots when I saw my administrator, Linda sitting at the desk just inside the doors. My nerves seemed to intensify when her brown eyes narrowed at me, the sharp tips of her blue painted fingernails rhythmically thrumming against the desktop.

Shit. I was in serious trouble this time.

All my life I've been falling behind.

My eyes snagged at the clock that hung above the wall behind Linda's head and I grimaced when I read that it was well past eight in the morning, when my shift was scheduled to start.

It wasn't that I wanted to be late, time just got away from me sometimes.

I could see in my boss's eyes what she thought of me. I felt her judgmental stare upon my face and I knew what she must have been thinking of me.

I was careless, irresponsible maybe even rude. But that wasn't true, not even a little bit.

I was a neonatal nurse and it was the most fulfilling job- at least in my book. *It was why I woke up in the morning.* Caring for the little munchkins in the wing upstairs filled my days with warmth, with light. The excitement of the next milestone I had the privilege of sharing with the families that trusted me with their little ones made my shifts fly by in a rush of smiles, laughter and little miracles.

Even my worst days were worth it because I had them.

"You are on thin ice with me, Ms. Logan. You have been late every day this week." Nodding, my head dropped below my shoulders.

I really didn't want to lose this job.

"I know, Linda. I'm sorry." She nodded, but the frustration in her eyes didn't falter.

"You need to try to be on time, Emberly. We need you here on time."

Shifting on my feet, I knew she was right. I was without a car right now and I had a fifteen minute drive as it was to work. Now, having to commute by bus, I was lucky if I got here within the hour.

Though lately, I hadn't been having much luck.

A few minutes later, I was walking up the third flight of stairs and toward the nurses desk just outside of the Ni-cu. The smell of baby powder littered the air and the scent calmed me instantly.

A head with long, wavy hair was tipped down as I approached and I smiled. Ashlee was a nurse, just like me but she was also more. She was the head nurse of this floor and a damn good one at that.

She was also my best friend in the world.

"Hey, girl." Her head lifted and her face lit up with a smile.

"Hey, back."

I was grateful that she didn't mention my lateness as she handed me my rounds sheet for the day.

"We're down one nurse today so I may need you to work for an extra few hours today, is that okay? I'm sorry to ask but-"

I shook my head, scanning the page for my first patient. Jenna James, the newest mother on the floor.

The young woman had given birth to a beautiful little boy that had yet to be named. Her and her husband had trouble conceiving their first child and it was a treat for us to see them with their little boy. He was so damn cute.

"Don't worry about it, Ash. I don't mind. I'm going to start my day."

She nodded, smiling in the way that she always did, brightening the whole room with just one smile. The air around her seemed to lift when the happiness spread over her face and inwardly, I warmed at the sight.

She was such a happy person.

Sometimes I wished I could be more like her.

Moving away from the nurses desk, I headed down the hall toward my first patient's room. We had placed her as close to the nursery as possible at her husbands request.

"Good morning, Jenna. How are you feeling this morning?" Jenna was sitting up in bed when I entered and her husband looked up from where his sights had been obviously set on her.

"I'm good, thank you. When can I see my baby?"

I smiled, moving to her side and lifting her thin wrist in one hand in order to check her vitals.

"I'll bring him in as soon as I check your vitals." My fingers applied pressure to her pulse point and I listened to her deep, even breaths as she excitedly recounted the birth of her son, her eyes going to her husband when he whispered something I didn't quite here.

These moments were so important to their little family and stepping back, I was careful not to intrude on them.

"I'll go get your boy, now. I'm sure he is eager to see you" She smiled and the expression takes over her whole face.

"Hello, sweet pea" I gently crooned down to baby joy James as I carefully slid my hand behind his head and lifted him against me, my hands cradling his tiny body as he awoke.

"Your mom and dad are very excited to see you today. They have waited a long time for you, do you know that?" He looks at me, so innocent, so beautiful.

As he clenches his tiny fists into my hair and tugs with surprising strength, I pulled back, shock and amusement filling me.

Damn, this boy was strong. I opened the door to Jenna's room gently with my shoe and heard her audible gasp when she saw the little boy in my arms.

"Oh, Scott, he's so beautiful."

"He is." I heard her husband mutter, quietly, as if he was speechless at the sight. With care, I lowered him into her arms and smiled softly, watching the lovely sight of her holding her baby for a moment.

Time lapses as they shared their moment and checking her vitals, along with the baby's once more I silently left them to enjoy their morning together.

Would I ever have what they had?

As I walked toward the nurse's desk where I'd find Ashlee, I couldn't help the fleeting thought that gave way to a flutter of hope that loosened my chest from the loneliness I lived with, day after day. It was easier this way or at least, that's what I'd been telling myself for years now. The problem was, I wanted more. My heart was mended from the pain of my past and a part of me wondered if it was time to open up, again. To let love in, if it found it's way into my seemingly empty heart. On a heavy sigh, I shook my head at myself, knowing that I wasn't ready to open up, again. Not yet.

"Want to go on your break now?" I was pulled from my saddened thoughts at the sound of Ashlee's voice and at that same moment, my stomach decided to rumble loudly. Nodding, I stopped at the desk only long enough to retrieve my purse from the drawer and thank her before heading toward the elevators, leaving my melancholy thoughts behind.

I was having a nice, peaceful lunch, sitting outside the front entrance to the hospital when I noticed a sleek, shiny car pull into the parking lot of the hospital and for some strange reason, my eyes were pulled to the drivers side door as it opened and a dark head of hair emerged from behind it. My heart begun to race as I wondered who it was, since this lot was mostly used by the nurses and doctors here, not patients or anyone else, really. He could have been a security guard, but I doubted it since it was well past noon and the rest of the security team Linda hired were long gone, by now.

My wandering thoughts were hushed, though, as a man unfolded from the car and I gasped as I caught my first glimpse of him. I wasn't sure if you could call the mass of muscle and tanned skin I saw before me; a *man*. He looked to be more of a beast of a man, to me.

For some reason, my desire to *people watch* disappeared into thin air. The man standing on the side walk only ten or so feet from me intrigued me immediately, causing my skin to lift with goosebumps and my heart to fasten in it's pace within my heaving, erratic chest. He was built like a truck, large, broad shoulders meeting thick, muscular biceps and forearms covered by the black tee shirt he wears.

His sun kissed flesh moved as the muscles in his shoulders tightened, then released and my eyes became transfixed on the sight. My wandering eyes continued their search of him, my wide, curious stare finding his hands, clenched at his hands and I gasped, audibly.

What a man like that could do with those hands of that size...

I felt the surge of energy coming off of him, the agitation painted over the hard features of his face telling me something has angered him, that much was obvious to me. My teeth sunk into the skin of my lower lip as I continued to look at every inch of him. This man was nothing like any other man I had ever, encountered and that fact causes a sharp pull inside of me.

As if he felt my eyes on him, the man suddenly whipped his head in my direction and I froze, caught, like a deer in headlights. I had no idea why I was looking at him like I was or why I had this longing to step closer to this beastly man.

He could hurt you. My inner voice said to me, urging me to look away.

The voice of the girl I once was.

Meek.

Scared.

Afraid of taking a risk or jumping into the deep end.

But for once in my life, I don't listen to that voice. I'm too curious about him. But as he approached me slowly, surely, like a predator eager for his next meal, I stilled my body, unwilling to wield to the sudden urge I had to go to him.

He was a stranger. So, why was I suddenly eager for his brand of trouble?

"Hey," His deep toned voice fell between us and unconsciously, I leaned forward in my seat, not wanting the distance between us to exist. The massive hands at his sides reached between us and I found myself holding my breath, as if every molecule in my body was awaiting his touch. *A strangers touch...*

When strong, thick fingers wrapped around my shoulders and pulled me slightly forward, I let myself be pulled from my seat and into his personal space. My skin tingled deliciously at his touch. I had the fleeting thought that he shouldn't ever stop touching me.

"Hudson," He rumbled, deeply, his voice once again broke the silence between us. My teeth dug into my lower lip again and I tried to remember how to speak as he assessed me with eyes as blue as the clear sky above us.

"I-I'm Emberly. Em."

My voice comes out in a tumble of words, the sounds ragged and disjointed and clenching my eyes shut, I felt my face flame.

Stupid, stupid girl.

"Emberly..." He said my name like it was so much more than a name, like it was something to be treasured. My lips tipped up and my eyes opened, only to be met by the heart stopping smile he gave me.

I hardly knew the man, no, I knew *nothing* about him but when he smiled like that, my heart seemed to stop in my chest.

I'd stayed away from men as much as I could and for good reason. My father was a bad man and after realizing that fact, I knew I could never trust another man.

I learned early on that everyone has something to hide.

A secret.

A lie.

A hidden agenda.

An insecurity that no one can understand but them. I have a few of those.

Daniel Logan had a truckload of them, making it his life's work to lie and steal and barter with even the worst of people this world had to offer.

You would have thought that being his only child, I would have been somewhat shielded from that side of him, but no.

He had no shame of the man he was.

He was a liar and a snake and the one lesson he taught me was this:

No matter how hard you try, you cannot force someone to love you.

I had tried for basically, well, my whole life to get him to do just that and in the end, I lost myself.

That was many years ago and since then, I've learned a few more lessons along the way. I look away from my hands that have knotted themselves together against my side and shrug my pensive thoughts of my father away, not wanting to dwell on the past I'd rather forget. Because in this moment, I felt alive.

My heart was beating so fast that I could hardly catch my breath.

My eyes feast on the man before me and for the first time in my life, desire coiled low and thick inside of my belly.

I hardly know him but I want him.

I see something dark pass over Hudson's face and though I can't decipher it, it erases the smile across his striking face, the lines of his jaw forming a hardened look that causes worry to curl into my veins. I don't know what I did to erase that beautiful expression he'd graced me with just now, but I instantly regret it. I wanted to ask what was wrong, what had upset him but my trepidation in the presence of another large, intimidating man; one that was probably used to using his size and strength to hurt those around him, just like my father...

No. I thought to myself. He wasn't him. Even just the few minutes I'd spend regarding him told me that. Not all men were as dark and disturbed as the man who raised me had been and reminding myself of that, I let my body slowly relax, the man in front of me somehow calming me with his presence. He moved forward, his large combat boots that he wears coming closer and closer until he is only an inch from me, his hands coming up from his sides and he cups the back of my neck in one of them while the other slides deftly down the length of my arm to grasp my hand beneath his much larger one. The way he rubs the pad of his rough, callused thumb over my nape made me edge closer to him, as if my body was drawn into the orbit his heat creates. I don't know what I am doing but one thing I do know for sure is that for some crazy reason, he makes me feel safe. He caused warmth to center inside of me and I don't want to let go of that just yet.

"What's wrong? It's written all over your face, *Emberly*. Tell me what's bothering you."

For some reason, I liked that he didn't call me Em. The way his deep baritone curled around my name sent shivers up my skin, as if he was touching me. I wanted to hear it again.

He's luring me closer and he smiled softly, subtly raising his eyebrows, black and thick just like the lashes that surround his pale blue eyes.

"It was nothing." I half whispered, confused as to what the hell was going on with me at the moment. Hudson just pressed closer, and the fabric of his denim jeans brushed against my knees as he boxed me in to the wall closest to where we stood. My heart beat begun to race.

Not from fear, which should have been my logical reaction to a man I didn't know cornering me outside of my place of work but no, his closeness excited me. I wanted him closer. *So much closer.*

He was intriguing the hell out of me and I needed to know more about this man. *Was he real?*

"I want you to tell me."

He repeated his statement and this time, I weakened, wanting to open up to him. His eyes were stark and beautiful and focused, right on me. I wasn't sure what it was about me that had him so invested, what pulled him to me enough to approach and talk to me just now; but I was thankful he had. As his thick, dark brows lifted, I remembered his question and nodded my head.

Though I didn't know him, I had a feeling that denying him wasn't an easy feat. Everything about Hudson screamed confidence and I wasn't about to deny him such a simple thing, especially when he was looking at me with those round, intense eyes. It wouldn't surprise me if women made a habit of throwing themselves at his feet with just one look from him.

My head dropped just slightly and a heavy sigh left me and I told him.

"I wasn't expecting you. I have a hard time trusting men and with you so close, like... this... I can't think straight."

My words were just a whisper and when he takes a large step back and frowns deeply, my heart dropped to my feet instantly.

I shouldn't have said anything.

I watched his every step as he retreated from my space and

lowering my head, shame filled my veins with what felt like lead.

I thought that was the last time I would ever see him.

What I didn't know was that Hudson would come to mean much more than a mysterious stranger to me.

2

EMBERLY

*O*ne of my favorite *Linkin Park* songs played through my headphones and the deep, gritty sound of the voice as he sings motivated me to move faster, push myself to work harder. It was Saturday morning and as I had the day off, I decided to get in a much needed work out to start the day.

My whole body ached from the long week at the hospital and all I wanted to do was sleep. Thankfully, after I finished up here, that's exactly what I'd planned to do. I loved my job but sometimes, I wished I could have a life outside of the hospital and all that encompasses it. I often worked twelve to twenty four hour shifts and it wore me out, physically yes, but emotionally too. The work I did was so damn rewarding but it took a toll. The infants I cared for were the most precious things I had ever laid eyes on and it was humbling to know that I was helping them and their families during times of need.

But standing between life and death each and every day wasn't what I expected when I signed up for nursing school. I imagined all of the people I would help and the good I could do to those that needed it. Working for the hospital had its ups and its downs but, to be honest, I cherished the days I didn't have to go in. The time to regroup was much needed, especially after the long, week I'd had. I didn't tell Linda any of that, though.

A warm bath, a glass of wine and a long nap were in order. *God knew I needed a day to relax.*

I inhaled through the slight discomfort caused by one too many lifts of my arms and kept going, knowing I could do more. *Keep going, keep going.*

The mantra fueled my aching limbs as I finished my third set and gratefully setting the weights back down, my arms reached over my head to test my sore, slightly over worked muscles. I shifted forward again, toward the weight set that was placed just above the one I had just set down. This one was much heavier, one I had never pushed myself to lift but today, I felt strong enough.

I could do it. And then my phone rings, sounding off loudly in the otherwise silent area of the gym.

"Hello?" I answered, not bothering to check the caller I.D. before answering the call.

"Hello, Emberly, this is Linda. How are you?"

My stomach dropped in dread at the sound of her voice.

"Hi, Linda. I'm good. Just getting in a work out. Is everything okay?"

"There was a power outage on the second floor last night and we need all hands on deck. When can you be here?"

"Um, today is my day off..."

I cradled my phone under my ear as I pulled my gym bag together and quickly made my way to the locker rooms just inside the entrance.

I didn't even have to ask if she really did need me.

I knew I had to come in. Thankful that I hadn't unpacked my bag from the night before, I pulled yesterday's pair of navy blue scrubs over my head, my eyes snagging on the way the fabric fitted over the prominent curves of my stomach and love-handles.

Ugly.

The thought whispered through my head and I dropped my eyes to my feet, wondering if there would ever come a day when I wouldn't doubt my self worth, my body. I'd been seeing a therapist up until this year and I think those sessions helped me see that beauty isn't only skin deep. That it was about who I am, on the inside that mattered and that if someone truly loved me, they would look past my curves and my ripples. As I finished getting dressed, I wondered if there would ever be more for me than just a passing interest. I didn't want a man to have to *look past* my short comings. I wanted him to see me, for who I was.

Curves, and all.

Was that even possible?

Hudson sees me.

As suddenly as my self deprecating thoughts had come, they were diminished as I reminded myself that one man did look at me that way. *Like he desired me.*

Hudson. The stranger I'd met outside of my work place. The stranger that all but ran away from me when I'd opened my mouth and admitted how much he frightened me; just not in the ways I thought he would. It wasn't the sheer size of him that scared me. It wasn't even the way he radiated power and confidence, a self assuredness I never truly mastered for myself. No, it had been a completely different kind of fear. The way he looked at me...

No one ever looked at me like that. Not even the few boys I dated during school.

I couldn't help how I ached for that look from him, now. Two weeks had gone by since that first, fateful meeting. I'd been right when I thought he worked at the hospital that day. Except, he wasn't the security hired by Linda. No, Ashlee's dad had hired him. He worried about her working so late at night and it eased his mind to always have eyes on her. She couldn't really blame him, though. Wherever Ashlee went, so did her brooding, mysterious body guard. *Hudson.* He'd barely looked my way over the past weeks. But when he did, God, was it worth the wait.

"I'm leaving the gym now, I'll be there as soon as I can get there" I rushed to pull a light jacket over my shoulders and hurried from the gym, hopeful that thoughts of a certain security guard would be left behind. The warm wind hitting my face cooled my heated skin as I jogged toward my car outside and placed my gym bag on the passenger seat. The engine of my 1969 Mustang convertible revved to life underneath the pedal and I smiled.

I loved this car.

"Oh, I'm so glad to see you, Em. I'm sorry to have to pull you in today, it couldn't be helped, though." Linda had met me by the entrance of the hospital and when I saw how worried she was, my disappointment for my lost day off disappeared.

They needed me here.

"It's okay, Linda. What happened?"

Her thin eyebrows creased with that same worry I saw before as she leads me to the desk in the center of the room.

"I can't tell you much, honestly. At two this morning, the hospital was locked down. There must have been some sort of security breach."

All the blood drained from my head at her news and I stopped short, looking up at her for some sort of rhyme or reason to what she had said.

"There was a break-in?"

My stomach turned against the harsh wave of fear that pushed its way under my skin, leaving goosebumps over the surface.

What happened?

"Is everyone okay? God, the babies..." My voice trailed off as

I thought of the small, innocent souls that slept just upstairs, unaware of all that was wrong in the world.

I jumped a bit when I felt the contact of Linda's hands encircling mine and her soft smile, full of endearment and worry, calmed me.

"No, honey, everything's fine. Why don't you head on upstairs? I am sure Miss Lewis will fill you in"

I nodded, even as a dark, sinking feeling rushed through my bloodstream telling me that she was definitely leaving something out.

Why else would an intruder go through all the effort of coming here?

What had he wanted?

The second the elevator of the hospital stopped on the floor I worked on, I grabbed my bag from the floor beside me and hoisted it high on my shoulder as I practically ran toward the nurses desk. As I approached I spotted my friend standing behind the white countered desk, her face blank of the happiness she seems to always exude. Her bottom lip trapped beneath her teeth, she gnawed at it in a habit of worry. It was her tell.

"Shit, Ash, what happened?"

When she saw me, she shrugged her shoulders, lightly, as if all of this wasn't as big of a deal as it was.

"Ash," I repeated, and she pulled her gaze up to mine where I saw the reflected fear I was feeling. I quickly pulled her small frame toward me and wrapped my arms around her slender shoulders in hopes of taking some of her worry away. She leaned against my hold, the tension leaving her body at the contact.

"He had a knife, Em." The words she spoke were muffled into the fabric of my sweater but I heard them loud and clear, the nickname she always called me shook with emotion. Dread coiled in my gut as I pushed back from her and shook my head, unbelieving this would happen *here.*

This was a hospital.

A safe haven.

Why the hell had someone wanted to harm it?

"Were you here?"

Shaking her head, she pulled me to the bench beside the adjacent wall and I grabbed her hand, watched her head fall into her hands.

"Hey, everything is okay, now right? We're safe."

She moved her head from her palms after a few seconds and nodded.

"He wanted to know who was working the desk here. Leila called out last night, her son apparently had an emergency at his school. I didn't have anything going on so I told her I'd be happy to cover for her."

I nodded, squeezed her hand in mine in a show of faith, the ball of worry that had formed in my stomach growing larger as time went on.

Leila was our newest nurse to come on staff here and she was amazing. She hadn't missed a day of work since coming on almost three months ago. If she'd needed coverage yesterday, it had to be an emergency.

"It was dead all night so I just had to check in on the baby unit one last time before clocking out for the night. The phone rang and Linda answered from downstairs."

My heart was in my stomach as I gripped her hand tighter, a mixture of worry and abrupt fear spreading through me.

"He asked for you?"

Her eyes closed and she began to gnaw on her bottom lip again.

"That's what Linda said. She thinks he was the man that's been stalking me..."

I hated that she was going through this. *God, it shouldn't be happening.*

This is a safe place.

"But didn't you say he had a knife? If it wasn't you..."

Understanding cleared my fogged mind and I instantly felt

horrible for being annoyed with Linda when she asked me to come into shift, today.

If only I'd known...

"She's okay. She was a little shaken up yesterday, but she seemed fine when I came in early this morning. You know Linda. She's tough as nails."

It had to have rattled her, though. A man with a knife obviously had intentions of hurting us, at least *scaring* us. But, why?

My mind wouldn't stop wandering to that question. It was on a continuous loop that would probably never stop, not until we knew what was going on and who wanted to hurt us.

Ashlee pulls the color coded shift schedule from the shelf above the desk we stand behind, skimming her hand down the sheet until she reaches today's date. I briefly let my eyes wander the hallway, wondering if my own overbearing man was nearby.

Get it together! You barely know the man, so how could he be yours?

"You wanna be with the babies today?" Ashlee's voice pulls me from my irate thoughts and raising my head to her gaze, I grinned.

"I would love nothing more, Ash."

3

HUDSON

There was a break in, Officer Lennox. No one was hurt, but the intruder left this behind. Taking the note from Linda, the administrator at Cedar Park Hospital and ironically, a close friend of my mothers I clenched my eyes shut, trying to rein in my control. I had only been on Ashlee Reed's detail for a while now and I already knew it would be best if I pulled myself off and let another fitting cop take my place. Not because I thought I couldn't do the job or protect my sergeant's daughter as if she were my own. And not because I was unworthy or unfit for the job. No, it was because of *her.*

Emberly. Jesus, even her fucking name was like a punch to the stomach.

Short, pixie cut hair that just barely grazed round, slender shoulders and smooth, blonde locks that framed a pale, freckled face that damn near brought me to my knees. Meeting her wasn't supposed to be some sort of cosmic moment that I would become infatuated with, thinking about it at all hours of the day even dreaming about it on the off nights that I found sleep. But it had. Emberly was so kind, down to her core. Sweet and soft and beautiful, in the simplest and most complex of ways. It was the way her eyebrows drew together when she was met with a

22

problem in her work and how her front teeth came down to worry her bottom lip until she figured it out. It was the cute as fuck way her eyes would sparkle with mischief whenever she caught me staring or saw me adjust the always present hard on I had whenever she was near. The smell of her vanilla scent and minty breath when she would hug me goodbye at the end of her driveway. Almost as if she didn't want to let go.

Was I just dreaming it up?

Did she feel it too?

"*Fuck...*" Pulling my angered, agitated hands through my hair, I dropped my head and read over the note the bastard had left in his wake, as if we'd want to hear his side of the story. I didn't care what his motives were or why he thought it was okay to not only endanger the lives of Emberly and Ashlee but of Linda and a whole hospital of innocent, struggling civilians.

It was wrong. Every damn bit of it. *I had to get this son of a bitch before he strikes again.* The thought was a mantra, a belief, a promise to myself and those I'd promised to protect. The note was cryptic, if anything ever was.

She wasn't here, but I'll be back. Keeping her from me will only end in more pain, I promise you that.
Until next time.
Bx

Tracing my finger over the signature, my frown deepened in utter confusion. B. It was a clue, one that was as cryptic as the rest of his note because with only a first initial to go on, I had nothing. There were fingerprints, fibers, even to be processed but with how smart he had been with all of this- I doubted he'd leave any trace behind. I had nothing.

"Hey, anything?" Tristan stood beside me, stripped of his blues as it was his day off and I shook my head, angry all over again that this was happening and with all of my training, my instincts, my badge- I couldn't get a break.

"Nah, man. He left this shit behind, but it's all just BS. Nothing to fucking go on." Handing him the note, I watched as he read it over and his face masked with the same muddiness I felt, too.

"There has to be some sort of clue, Hudson. Has to be. And we'll find it, alright?" I nodded my head, but for once my partners assurances didn't settle me. This wasn't just some case. It was Emberly. I *had* to protect her. There was no choice. No plan B. She was the priority. Number 1.

His strong, always assuring hand gripped my shoulder and pulled me from my deep thoughts of the case and mainly, Emberly.

"Whatever it takes, yeah?" There was no sway in his conviction this time, no self doubt or reservedness of the case that had me so messed up. He was there with me, no matter what it took. And he always had been.

"Yeah."

4

EMBERLY

"*O*h, there's my boy." I cooed to little baby Lee as he suckles his mouth around the tip of my thumb as I lift him from his crib. I slide my palm beneath his head, smiling as he wiggles against my hold, trying to move already. Beginning to gently rock him as I walk with him, warmth bursts in my chest. There is nothing that quite explains the sensation of holding a little life in your arms. To know that his life has just begun and you have the pleasure to hold him in his earliest moments in the world.

A hopeful feeling of joy curled underneath my skin as he popped his oval eyes open and I saw the flecks of color developing in his irises. The little man is only a few months old and he's sadly had a rough go at the start, but look at him now. God, he's so darn *cute!*

"Let me get you a new diaper, okay? Then we'll go find your Mama, does that sound good to you?" I cooed to him, my voice soft and low and he blinked a few times, his eyes squinting at me.

Taking that as a good sign, I pressed my hand under his bottom making sure to cradle his head as he's lowered to the changing table in the corner of the room.

Kicking his feet, excitedly, I moved them down to the paper underneath as I changed him to make sure he doesn't get too excited. In my first days as a Neonatal nurse, I had a few accidents with excited babies and slippery hands.

A shiver at the memory.

Bodily fluids I could handle, in small amounts but having baby poo covering my hands and most of my forearms was something I never wanted to experience again. Thankfully, I was a fast learner and those were my only *shining* moments.

A gentle knock against the unit's glass has my head popping up from the little man's freshly changed diaper and I smile when I see Tristan, uniform and all, standing behind it.

Gently placing baby Lee back into his crib, I placed a kiss to my fingers and pressed them to his tiny hand, getting a cute as hell smile in response.

I pushed the door open quietly, not wanting to wake anyone from their afternoon nap and grinned as I approached Tristan.

Him and my best friend were dating and ever since meeting him a few weeks ago, she was so much happier, lighter, filled with excitement. It made me happy that she was happy. Because of that, he'd had my stamp of approval for a while now.

Intersecting the white coffee cup from him, I moaned as the taste of my favorite caffeinated beverage hit my taste buds. White chocolate and cinnamon was my weakness and he knew it.

"Thank you." I mumbled, taking another grateful sip.

"It's no problem."

Nodding, I took another sip, leaned against the glass for a moment.

"Thank you for looking after my girl, Tristan. This whole situation scares me."

His usually stoic face softened at my words and he nodded, bumping my shoulder playfully.

"One, she's my girl. We've talked about this." The tease in his voice helped ease the tension that had taken root in my stomach from this mornings events and I was grateful for it.

"And I have had my partner on her since I heard about this shit with her stalker. I am not about to take any risks when it comes to her. It's not an option, Em."

I gasped, surprised and then as if two mismatched puzzle pieces had clicked together in my mind, I nodded.

Was Hudson his partner?

The sexy as sin man had been everywhere I looked lately. I had caught myself on more than one occasion feasting my eyes on him from the corner he always stood in, close, but not too close.

For some reason, he had kept his distance. No matter where I was or how I enticed him to talk to me, he stayed put and worse, he stayed quiet.

In those moments of silence between us, I *craved* him. Wanting him closer, closer, *nearer*. I wanted him to grace me with that roughly sensual voice once more. I wanted to *know* him and that fact scared the shit out of me.

From the first day my eyes caught on Hudson, I had an inkling that he was a protector. I just had no idea he was an actual cop. *The fact that he was didn't surprise me.*

"Hudson?" I asked and Tristan nodded, tilting his head in curiosity.

"You've met him."

He didn't ask me, he knew.

Nodding, I shrugged my shoulders as I attempted to make light of the fact that I had met him. But the truth was, it was *everything*.

He was an impenetrable man, with haunting sky blue eyes and a map of ink that covered his skin that I yearned to *uncover*.

"Yeah, he stays close to the desk. I work there most of my night shifts."

Standing up a bit straighter, he quirks a brow at me.

"He say anything about me?"

"Uh, no. He isn't exactly *chatty.*"

Stepping back and taking a long sip of the iced coffee in his hand, he makes a weird face. As if he is perplexed by what I had said, or he just thinks it strange.

I'm not entirely sure but when he shrugs his rather large shoulders and waves a hand, retreating down the hallway he had come from, I'm sure I have the same look of confusion on my face.

The afternoon seemed to drag by after I fed the babies. I begrudgingly returned baby Lee back to his cradle after a happy visit with his mother, his always kicking feet resting in my palms when I heard the in unit telephone ring with a phone call from the main desk. Pointing at the little man, I smiled when he scrunches up his nose in the cutest damn way.

This baby is gonna be a heart breaker for sure.

"Hello, this is Nurse Logan," I answered.

"Ellie is on her way up to cover you, Emberly. You can take your dinner break."

"Sure, sounds good. Thanks, Linda"

"No, honey, *thank you.*"

She hangs up before I can respond and I move the phone back to it's cradle.

My stomach's grumble comes at the perfect time because, damn, I'm hungry.

I'm tidying up the baby changing area when Ellie comes in and gives me a soft smile, taking her sweater off and placing it by the hooks outside the door.

I have worked with her ever since coming on to this job and she has been a gods send whenever I have needed someone to talk to that could understand the demands we faced at times. Working with the fragility of life and death of these babies took a

toll on a person, especially when the sweet first moments experienced became the most painful to bear.

"How was your weekend, Ellie?"

She smiles again, a tint coming to her cheeks that looks like a
blush to me.

"Oh my gosh, something happened with that man didn't it?
Do tell"

Okay, so I was a bit of a gossip. It wasn't my fault really.

When you worked this closely in this line of work, you
became not only colleagues and friends but *family.* I had listened
to Ellie worry that her date a few weeks ago had fallen flat and
she was sure he wasn't going to call her like he had promised.
Inevitably, he didn't and my happy friend was crushed.

She had explained that he was busy, something about a big
promotion.

It seemed to me that he had come around to her, though.

"Shit, how did you know?"

I smirked at her, waiting her out and with a soft sigh, she spilled.

"It was so nice, Em. He showed up outside the hospital last
night and took me out to dinner and then we headed to the local
pub to have a drink. He's funny and charming and damn, I
could feel his muscles through his shirt! He is toned, girl"

Now a deep, almost cherry blush had taken place on her
cheeks and I shook my head at her excitement. It was nice to see
after her worry filled week.

"Oh, you should go. Linda said there is some big meeting at
seven and she wants the shift to be in order before then."

"Sure, let me just grab another package of warming blankets.
We just ran out of them."

Nodding, Ellie turned on the water of the faucet by the door
and I slipped out to get what I needed from down the hall.

We kept all of our supplies, medication and necessities in a
supply closet a few steps down the hall and it was only opened
with an employee code. We each were given one. As I typed the

six numbers into the code reader beside the wooden door, I felt an acute awareness cover me, as if someone was watching me. A shiver rushed over my skin in response.

Shaking my shoulders and the weird feeling away, I opened the door, leaving it slightly opened behind me.

Now all I had to do was find the blankets I kept in here for inventory of the units. Finding anything in here could deem a hard task since there wasn't a rhyme or reason to where things were stored, it bugged the hell out of me, honestly.

Before I could quite reach for the shelf in front of me where surprisingly, I found what I had been looking for, I heard the audible click of the wooden door closing behind me and I froze.

Someone had been following me.

Oh, no, no, no...

"Who the hell-" My voice fell away as I took in who had followed me inside.

Hudson.

My skin pebbled with goosebumps at the sight of his large, seemingly intimidating frame blocking the entrance of the room, effectively locking me in the small space with him.

What was he doing here?

"I- What are you doing in here?" I asked, unconsciously taking a step back from him. He exuded heat, power, *fire* and I wasn't looking to get burned.

Even as that thought raced through my mind, I had an inescapable urge to step closer to the force that was this man. My body was at odds with my mind and God, I didn't know what to do. I remained still, instead.

Massive, tanned arms moved to fold across his broad chest, the defined muscles flexing at the movement. My eyes followed him, as if in a trance. I just couldn't stop myself from looking at him. From *watching* him.

Shit, I was in over my head in his presence and I hadn't even kissed the man. I couldn't help wondering what it would be like to experience it, though.

Would it be soft and gentle or rough and intense?

Would the kiss be filled with pent up need or with passion that would explode between us? Would my toes curl in exquisite pleasure or would my heart race in excitement of what he'd do next?

Thoughts I shouldn't have been thinking flooded my mind and for a moment, I forgot about all the reasons to avoid this hulk of a man.

I wasn't ready for a relationship.

It was only when I lifted my gaze to his icy light blues that I realized he hadn't answered me.

"Hudson," I breathed, just wanting to say his name.

Hudson. It fitted him.

Strong.

Resilient.

Beautiful.

"You're not supposed to be in here."

His shoulders, tense with tightly strung muscles, just like the rest of him, lifted in what looked like a shrug.

"Yet, here I am, Emberly."

He stepped toward me, his movements slow yet precise and it felt as if he was a predator as he advanced on me, one large step at a time.

"*Hudson-*" I spoke his name once more, this time in warning.

I wasn't sure what I would do if he touched me now.

Heat had pooled low and wet between my legs and the affliction only worsened the closer he got to me. Then he was only a step away from me and I panted in a breath, my chest tight with the urge to reach out to touch him and feel the electric shock I knew I'd find at the contact.

"I think you should leave." I said, but the words held no power behind them. They were the complete opposite of what I wanted to say. My head over ran my heart and I wanted to listen to its reason.

What I truly wanted slowly thrummed through my veins, heating me from the inside until I couldn't ignore it.

I didn't want him to leave.

I wanted him closer.

I just wasn't going to admit that to him.

"I watch you, Darlin'. You have had your eyes glued to me since I found you just outside this building and they haven't left me. Why do you think that is?"

My heart sped up as the easy endearment fell between us and I found myself wrestling my bottom lip between my teeth in an effort to alleviate the ache he had caused in me.

The reactions my body had to him were crazy.

I had never felt anything like it before.

"I don't know what you are talking about." Hudson took another painfully slow step into my space and my breath was caught in my throat. His closeness had my body buzzing with energy and it's only a matter of time before I'd fall into him and the connection that buzzes, full and bright, between us.

"Wrong answer, you want to try again?"

Swallowing the lump in my throat, I move my hands over his large, rough ones that are covering my curved waist and gasped in a shaky breath of air.

"I mean, it's normal to be curious about a stranger." I reason, nervously twisting my hands in front of me to avoid his assessing, inquisitive gaze.

He nods, strands of his short, dark hair falling over his face.

"That could be true. At first. But there's more. You are *attracted* to me, I feel it, right here, between us. Do you feel it, Darlin'?"

The word once again, steals my breath and cautiously, I push the few pieces of his hair away from his eyes, he has the most intense eyes I have ever seen.

I could get lost in them.

"I-" Grasping my hand in his, Hudson flips it over in his own and presses the flat of my palm to his chest, directly above where his heart is.

The pounding of his heart against my fingers feels strangely intimate, because even with not only his white button down shirt but his leather jacket too covering his heated skin, I could feel it.

"This is what you fucking do to me."

I bit even harder down on my poor bottom lip and watched as Hudson's pupils honed in on the action and the muscles of his face tightened as if it was taking every ounce of his control to stay where he was, with my hand pressed to his as it was.

"Tell me." He muttered and my eyes widen, hesitation stopping the words wanting to roll off my tongue.

If I told him what was racing through my mind right then, I would be in even more trouble.

"W-what?" I breathed as his roughly skinned fingers rubbed against my jaw and he skated one hand to my lower back to hold me right where he wanted me.

Hudson's hands on me gave me a rush of anticipation that pooled low in my stomach and sparks, actual sparks of attraction flew beneath the surface of the skin that he touched.

"Tell me what you are so afraid of, Emberly."

I attempted to back away from him but just as I knew he would, he kept me there, my body wedged between his parted knees and my back pressed tightly against the wall behind me. He was *inescapable*.

"I told you-"

I stilled as he dropped his head to my neck and breathed in my scent, nose pressing to the skin behind my ear, effectively causing a shiver of awareness to skate up my spine.

I didn't dare move in fear he would move away, instead I slid my hands from the wall to his shoulders. The muscles I felt beneath my fingers clenched and moved as I held him there, the rough feeling of his stubbled jaw drawing up the length of my neck eliciting a moan to escape me.

"You smell so fucking good, what do you wear?"

I blinked at him when he lifted my chin with his hand, forcing my eyes upon his.

"I don't wear anything, it's my shampoo. It's vanilla." His mouth quirked up in a smile at that and he nodded, but didn't step away from me. Inwardly, I was grateful he didn't.

"You gonna tell me now? Or should I keep torturing you?"

Frowning, I sighed in frustration when he didn't budge from me as I tried to slip past him. Hudson was a large man and there was no way of me moving him if he was content to hold me here.

Crap.

"You weren't torturing me." His large hand lifted again, this time dragging painfully slow down my arm and tracing a line of fire against my already heated skin.

"Hudson," I breathed heavily and when he raised his eyes back to mine, I know he had me. His touches, his voice, the slow advance on me- it's all torture for me.

"Why are you doing this?" I asked, once again attempting to get past the beast of a man. Again, he shook his head at me and keeps me put, only tightening his hold on my hips. My head falls back to the wall behind me with a thud and I groan inwardly. His warm, mint laced breath covered my cheek as he lowered his head toward mine. I heard his whisper, rough in my ear.

"What are you afraid of?"

"*You.*" I finally whispered.

His head pulled fractionally away from me and his hands slid into place to take hold of my face.

"You should be."

Before I know it, Hudson's mouth was covering mine. He presses his full, dominating mouth over mine and swallows my startled gasp, his teeth coming down to torture my lower lip with soft bites and licks meant to tease.

And God, he does tease me.

"*Hudson,*" My voice fell between us and on a hungered

growl, he took full advantage of my plea as he delves his tongue between my lips and claimed my mouth, completely.

My body came alive for him upon the contact, my hands covering his against my cheeks and my mouth falling open to him in a plea for more.

"Fuck," He gritted against my mouth, drawing away once he's had his fill.

"Hud-" I breathed again, this time in a craving for more.

His head falls next to mine against the wall and as our foreheads touch, he muttered my endearment once again.

"Darlin'."

5

HUDSON

I grasped the handle of the entrance as I took in the sight just inside the glass door. My skin prickled with a keen sense of awareness. I watched her silently, from afar. It had become a past time that I thoroughly enjoyed. *Watching her.* As I looked inside, I saw her.

Emberly.

She sat in one of the patient lobby sections with her blonde hair curled into a pony at the back of her head, her bright, expressive eyes smiling as she talked to a young girl sitting beside her. I guessed she was probably about six years old. The easy affection she had with the young girl made my heart race like a fucking teenager.

She was so fucking beautiful.

I had been patrolling all major entrances of the hospital all afternoon, even working with the security department here in order to help get an idea of who the assailant had been last night. I shook my head as the anger I felt this morning when I heard of what went down in my absence flew back to the surface. My fists drew together, my heart slowed in concentration and my vision filled red as the anger took hold. The idea of someone hurting my girl hit me deep in the chest and caused an even deeper pain to attack me.

She was filled with beauty, light and such a poignant innocence she glowed with the strength of it. She was adorable and fierce, beautiful and complex. She was a jigsaw puzzle that I craved to unravel one piece at a time.

Emberly Logan was mine. She just didn't know it yet.

But she would very soon know the depth of my craving for her.

When she did, I feared she would run.

I could be a lot of things, but patience had never been one of my strengths.

When I found something I wanted, I took it. I wanted her and if it was the last thing I did, I would take her. Not only did I want her lush, curvy body that had my dick hard in a matter of seconds from meeting her, but I wanted to claim her heart and when I did, she would have a claim on me, too.

I just had to prove to her that she could put her safely guarded trust in me.

I just had to give her time.

My fists clenched together, the harsh movement causing a bite of pain I appreciated as I swore to myself I would wait for her. Fucking this up was not an option.

I was going to earn her.

A sense of peace washed over me a moment later and my mouthed tipped into a grin as I felt her always curious eyes on me. I didn't need to see her to know that's what was happening. She was watching me, just as I had been watching her.

I lifted my gaze to meet hers and leaned my back against the wall just inside the waiting room, my chest moving quickly in an attempt to get my reckless heart beat back to a somewhat normal pace.

Raising an eye brow, I challenged her to look away.

She blinked once then dropped her gaze from mine as the girl at her side asked her a question and a deep blush covered her cheeks.

Fuck.

My dick was a fucking steel rod under my jeans as I stood there, ravishing my gaze on that blush I had caused in her.

Palming the front of my jeans, I dropped my head and forced a deep, agitated breath from my lungs in order to calm the fire that was licking up my veins with the need I had for her.

I was so fucking screwed.

I stalked away and toward the nearest bathroom to alleviate the affect she had on me and I swore I could feel her gaze on me as I left.

If she kept that up, I would have her under me tonight.

I wanted that.

A part of me wanted to just say fuck it and take her home with me, not giving her a choice in the matter of what we had. To make love to her slowly, fast, rough then gentle, giving her all I had to give but shit, I didn't want to rush with her.

Because she was different.

I was going to do it right with her because she deserved more from me than a casual fling or a quick fuck.

Emberly deserved to be ravished, enjoyed, cherished and then and only then, would I fuck her like I craved to do now.

But first thing was first, I had to get some relief.

I pushed the door to the second floor bathroom open with the toe of my boot and closed it with a push, locking it for good measure. It was seven o clock at night but I wasn't going to have some scraggly old doctor walking in on me jerking off.

That shit was not happening.

Not ten minutes later, I found myself back at my post, where I could watch over both the main entrance and the desk that sat directly outside of the main areas of the floor. My eyes scanned each face that entered and left the elevator, my focus solely on protecting the nurses that stood just behind the barrier of the desk. Ashlee stood beside my girl, heads down as they spoke quietly to each other, low enough that I would have to strain to hear their conversation.

It unsettles me but I remembered that to them, I'm intruding on their privacy, their lives so I stepped back and kept my distance while I could.

My eyes landed on the clock as it hit nine at night and heard her footsteps as she reached the elevator. I'd told her to wait for me after her shift but had she listened? *Of course not.*

Stubborn woman.

"*Wait.*" I told her, and her frown greets me but thankfully, she waited for me.

I placed my hand to the small of her back as we stepped inside the car and I hit the button along the floor panel that would take us to the ground floor. Emberly's bright, violet eyes fluttered up to meet mine and an indulgent smile tugs at my mouth. She has the most beautiful eyes I had ever seen and I can't help looking at her, losing myself in her warm yet oh-so defiant gaze.

Every day since having her under my protection, we've done this silent dance. Emberly, the bullheaded woman I learned her to be, tries to sneak off from the hospital without waiting for me and I have had to chase her.

"How was your day?" I asked her as I took her hand in mine inside the elevator and rubbed my thumb over hers. Her eyes meet mine once again and she smiles softly. My heart stops and my legs fucking shake from the force of that softly given smile.

How the fuck does she do that to me?

"Long, a bit exhausting. Glad it's over now. I just want to have a quiet night at home"

I nodded, though my idea of a quiet night at home was filled with hot, wet, dirty fantasies of her and I had the idea that if she came home with me tonight, we would be anything but *quiet.*

"You good to drive, Emberly?"

Her violet and blue hued gaze sparked with something I couldn't decipher as she simply nodded her head.

"Let me take you home."

Her eyes, guarded and curious, met mine and narrowed.

"You don't have to do that." I grabbed her hand and tugged her close, heard her soft gasp in response.

"Yeah, I do." She nodded, folding her fingers together in what I guessed was a nervous habit. We stepped outside and I led her toward where she told me her car was parked in the lot to the right of the building.

"In you go, Darlin'."

"You can't drive my car."

Frowning, I grasped the door before it shut and looked down at her in confusion. Fuck, why did she have to be so difficult?

"Yeah, I can. You need to see my license?"

I smiled wide as she shook her head at me in exasperation.

"No. I mean I don't want you to drive my car."

"Shit, then we have a problem." I bent closer to her and slipped my hand into her hair, unwilling to go another damn second without having my hands on her in some way. This girl was like a drug to me and touching her was the only way I'd get my fix. Her body tensed up at my touch but as I trailed my thumb over her lower lip, she melts for me, just like the last time I had my hands on her.

Jesus, she's perfect.

"You're exhausted, Emberly. Let me drive, alright?"

After a good minute of looking at me, she nodded.

Closing the door gently, I shook my head in bewilderment.

What the hell was I getting myself into with this girl?

40

6

EMBERLY

I watched as the sun sunk lower into the Texas sky from the window. I have always loved watching the sunset, always thought that the sparks of color that blend together across the sky are too poignantly beautiful to be ignored. As I raised my head and watched the black night turn bright yellow, hued orange and red I smiled.

When I was little, I watched the sun set with my mother. The fuzzy memory comes to me and unconsciously, I close my eyes in hopes of seeing her face. I had an amazing job and a safe place to rest my head and for that, I was grateful. I hadn't grown up in what you would call a *happy* household.

At one time, my family had all been together and though I could hardly remember days that we were happy, I was sure we must have been.

After my mom passed, everything changed.

My father was a hard man. I used to wonder if the ruthless man my fathers business associates knew him to be would surface when he was with us and inevitably, he had. My eyes squeezed painfully shut as one of the darkest memories of my childhood flew to the front of my mind and I remembered.

My eyes flew open to the pitch black night as I abruptly woke to my fathers booming voice as he and my mother fought.

He was always angry with her, for one thing or another.

"You are useless to me." He would say. And then I would hear it.

The horrible sounds.

The sounds I never wanted to hear again.

First came the snap of my fathers wrist, the sound of a smack as it landed across my mothers cheek and then as I pressed my ear to the bedroom door and sniffled back the sobs that always came, I listened to my mothers cries.

"Please- no!"

He would crack his fist again, and by the sound that reverberated off the walls of the otherwise silent house, it would be even harsher than the first.

"You disrespected me, Mary. This won't stand."

Though I knew what would come next each of those nights, I listened.

Eventually, my father would grow tired and the tell tale sound of his belt hitting the floor would sound, followed by the retreating foot-steps as he left her there.

I ran down the steps to the first floor where I found my mom laying across the hardwood floor of the kitchen, her face hidden in large, yellowing bruises and as she blinked at me, fear filled her eyes.

"Oh, Mama." I whispered, tending to her face as best as I could from what I learned in school and from the television father always kept on the medical channel. The fact that he did was our saving grace because otherwise, my Mama would have bled out on the floor long ago.

But I helped her and then, when she was able to sit up by herself, I would tell her about the funny things that I hoped would make her laugh and sometimes, they did.

I blinked back the moisture that gathered in my eyes as I relived that night and each night that came before and after it. Sometimes, at night, I would stay awake and wait for those sounds to come. Like clockwork, I would wait. Until it was midnight and they never came and I could finally allow myself to sleep knowing that I was safe now.

He couldn't hurt me anymore.

I sighed as I lifted my head and felt a rush of warmth fill my chest as I spotted a man sitting against the wall directly across from where I sat behind my desk. *Hudson.* He had his eyes set on me all night though now, they were closed peacefully; his face a wash of calm vulnerability that I hadn't been expecting. The thought that he had fallen asleep watching me was a sweet one and shaking myself from the sudden hope fluttering within me, I stepped toward his large, folded frame a mere few feet away. No matter what I was doing, where I was? He was always close, watching, waiting, *guarding* me.

Why did that fact make butterflies take flight in my stomach?

I bit my lip as I knelt down next to him until my knees touched his. His body tensed for a moment, as if he was only then aware that he'd fallen asleep. When his ocean blue eyes flew open, meeting mine I smiled softly. He was constantly on high alert, ready to protect me at a moment's notice. I was coming to love that about him.

More than one month ago he'd been detailed to protect my best friend but yet, he was here, with me while Ashlee was safely at home with her own man that protected her, just like Hudson did me. I had hid from it but it was true.

He had been protecting me all along.

"Hey," He murmured, his voice deep and rough with sleep still. I smoothed my fingers through his left hand and tugged at it gently.

"Come with me?" Hudson's thick fingers tightened around mine as I pulled him, or at least tried to- to his feet.

"Darlin'," His raspy voice next to my ear causes my heart to stop and then speed up as the pull of energy between us becomes almost too much to ignore. It's the first time he'd called me that and I tried to tell myself it didn't mean anything but it was a lie; it did. The feelings I felt for him weren't going away and if the affectionate names told me anything, he was feeling it, too.

It's always there. I reminded myself. No matter how hard I tried to ignore the connection we have, it was always there between us. Like an impenetrable force, it lay in wait for us to finally act on it. I just didn't think I was *ready.*

I'd been running from emotional attachment and relationships for so long, I wasn't sure I knew how to stop, to stand still. *I wasn't sure if I knew how to let him in.*

I pulled him towards the end of the hallway that housed both the Nicu and the row of pediatric patient rooms lining it. I heard the husky, temptation filled sound of his chuckle from a few steps behind me and I looked back at him from over my shoulder. His smirk widened as he sees me watching him but his eyes, two pools of the palest blues, held so much more.

Hunger.

Need.

Curiosity.

It's all there and my teeth begun to worry my lip as I realized that it was all caused by me. *How was that possible?*

"Where are we going?"

I blushed as those wide, assessing eyes of his roved over my face, the hunger and stark desire in their depths undeniably potent.

"You'll see."

It was as clear as day that he wanted me.

It should have scared me, the way he made me feel. Sometimes, it did. But, as I shut the door to the on call staff room behind me, my blood heated with excitement and I knew, Hudson caused yet another crazy emotion in me. Pulling the bed sheet back on the bottom bunk placed against the wall, my eyes raised to meet his only to find them already trained on me.

"You can sleep here for a bit." Nodding once, those sky blue eyes still silently watching me.

Plopping down on the mattress, Hudson kicked off his shoes

and I found myself wondering what it would feel like to lay next to him.

To sleep in his arms.

I was achingly familiar with the sensation of sleeping alone at night and the longer I was around this man, I was realizing that I wanted more and I wanted it with him.

I watched, entranced as Hudson's arms lifted above his head and he shed the white, button down shirt he wore. Each tantalizing inch of his tanned skin that was revealed hiked my breathing and stole the heart beats straight out of my chest, causing me to stand there, my mouth parted open as I stared at him.

At his now naked chest.

At his all-too-confident grin.

At him.

Holy hotness.

Hudson's messy, dark hair fell over his eyes while he lowered his large frame to the bed, his head hitting the pillow with a low *thump.*

Watching him, my stomach pulled with the urge to go to him but instead I leaned my back against the wall behind me and lowered my eyes to the floor as the all-too-present blush covered my cheeks. Seeing him half naked was doing things to me and though I wanted to say that it didn't affect me, I couldn't. I was a quaking, shivering mess of feelings and unrealized desires, having him so close, tempting me to act on these feelings that scared me down to my core. I could feel his eyes on me, hungry and curious and I lifted my own, my mouth watering at the sight of him.

"Stop looking at me like that, Darlin'."

His deeply spoken voice makes my eyes fly up to meet his again and my cheeks to blush knowing he's caught me staring. *Again.*

"I don't know what your talking about, Hudson."

Before I know what he's doing, he was off the mattress and

stalking toward me at a relentless pace. I froze, the breath knocking out of me as I was pushed up and against the wall while large, assertive hands trapped mine against it.

Hudson's eyes were full of that same hunger I saw in them before. I realized that I've lost all function of my voice to tell him off and my feet to walk away from him, like I probably should have.

"Do you know why I was put on your security detail?"

His question stopped my efforts to push him away and I blinked a few times, trying to recollect my fragmented thoughts.

My security detail?

"You mean-"

His hand covered my mouth before I could say much else and I gasped against his flesh.The smells of peppermint and beautiful, sinful man invaded my nostrils and I found myself pressing my body an inch closer to his, so that I could keep his scent with me.

This man was temptation personified and if I thought before I was in trouble, I was most definitely screwed then.

"I have been protecting you from the very moment I laid my eyes on you, Emberly. I haven't been able to tear my eyes away from you ever since."

Arousal rose between my legs from his roughly spoken words and my body, once rigid from his hold was now putty in his hands. I just looked at him, my breaths coming faster as the heat in his eyes threatened to consume me.

My fingers flexed beneath his, testing to see if I could shake them loose.

"Do you feel this?" Hudson's voice, next to my ear now, whispering slowly against the heated flesh of my blushed cheek. I pressed my hands against his once more and the soft bite of his teeth meeting my earlobe tingled my skin.

He bit me.

"Did you just bite me?" My voice was nothing but a careless whisper against the onslaught of sensation his proximity created.

The hum of his mouth against my cheek had goosebumps covering my skin.

"Answer the question."

Gasping in another breath of air, my fingers tightened against his and his mouth ventured further down the slope of my neck to the tender spot just beneath my collar bone. When his lips grazed over it, a moan of protest escaped me.

"You scare me."

Hudson drew away from my space the moment the words slipped past my lips and inwardly, I cringed. Rough, callused palms reached my jaw and I look up into his wide eyes and softly smile. The way he looked at me felt intimate, almost sexual and it scared me even more.

Somehow he saw right through my defenses. *Somehow, he sees me.*

"You aren't afraid of me."

Gently, he brushes away the thick strand of hair that fell in front of my face and his large hands cupped the back of my head.

"You're afraid to trust me." He said and that's when I realize just how deep our connection ran.

The walls I have tried to put up to everyone around me had been knocked down by his intense, blue eyes and heart stopping smile and somehow, I was thankful. Because when I looked deep into his gaze, I knew I was safe with him. My head lifts and Hudson tilted his head to mine and I felt the beat of my heart fasten within my chest as I waited for him to kiss me.

"You're safe with me, Darlin'. Believe that."

As he spoke against my lips, I melted. Moving my head to his chest, I buried my face into his neck and nuzzled my nose against the smooth skin there.

He smells like home.

The thought scared me but I shook it off and sighed the moment large, muscular arms wrap around me and he just *held* me.

I took a full breath of his musky scent, trying in vain to calm the effect he's had on me.

"I know." I whisper, but he just held me tighter. Minutes passed between us, maybe more before Hudson's body drew partially away from mine and he stifled a yawn against my hair.

"Lay down with me."

He wasted no time before hauling me closer to his warm, hard muscled body and laid down across the mattress without taking his hands off of me.

It's as if he was afraid I'd slip away if he does and on a soft sigh, I caved.

For just this one moment, I'm *his*.

7

EMBERLY

*M*y eyes fluttered open and my body instantly tenses as I felt a pair of thick, powerful arms bound around my waist, a possessive hand hidden beneath the fabric of my scrubs.

I am in a bed with a man.

A man who makes me feel these crazy feelings.

A man who calls me his Darlin'.

"Hudson," I breathed. His hand rubbed a gentle path over my hip, lifting the fabric of my shirt higher to better gain access to my skin.

My teeth come down to worry my bottom lip as sparks fly beneath the surface of my skin and he must have seen it, because he rose up on his forearms and loomed over me, his tanned chest spanning my vision as he drags his hand higher against my stomach until he reached my rib cage and I shuddered beneath the tender touch. When his index finger brushed against my upper stomach, I shook with the effort not to cover up. *Ugly.*

The word rushed through my head on repeat and unknowingly, I'm scooting away from his gentling touch.

"Get back here, Darlin'."

He begun to advance on me from my spot at the edge of the

bed and I stilled, having the fleeting thought that I would want to be caught by him.

I was so tired of wondering what it could be like if we gave into our connection.

I wanted to fall because I knew in my heart that he would be there to catch me.

He wouldn't let me go.

"Hudson, we shouldn't-" I protested but as the knowing smile covers his devilish mouth, I knew they were empty words.

"You like pushing me away, don't you?"

My mouth opened in surprise by his words and then my head was shaking viciously. That couldn't be farther from the truth, he had to know that.

"*No.*" The word merely a breath as I placed my hand to his bare chest, his skin hot and pulsing beneath my fingers. I itched to touch him everywhere and I tell myself going slow with this man was the only option.

I have a feeling *fast* to a man like him could only mean one thing.

He would devour me in an instant and I would get help-lessly, crazily, indecently lost in him. And that fact terrified me because it's what I wanted more than anything.

I craved to get so lost in him that I forgot everything else and all that remained would be us.

"You're fucking beautiful, you hear me? Don't you ever shy away from my touch like that. Get it through your head, sweet girl. I want you."

His large palms encompassed my face as he took a breath in order to calm himself and then his intensely blue eyes were boring into mine.

"The moment I kissed you, you were mine. Fuck, even before that. I laid my eyes on you and everyone else seized to exist. You were all I could see."

Hudson shook his head once, grabbed my hand laid against his chest and pressed it firmly to the front of his jeans where I felt the unmistakable hardness of his cock. My stomach pulled in arousal and hot, thick moisture gathered between my legs, making it impossible to ignore the ache resonating in my core from the contact.

The room we were in felt entirely too small, the air surrounding us thick with desire and *hot* with anticipation. My face flamed as he granted me with a devilishly beautiful smirk, his hand pressing mine against him as he become rock hard beneath my palm. *Holy fuck.*

"Hudson, God-" My lips parted on a deep, ragged inhale.

"Have dinner with me." His next words quickly stole my breath, all over again. They were so completely unexpected, knocking all coherent thought from my otherwise clear head.

He wants me to have dinner with him. Why?

I blinked up into his hunger filled gaze and instantly knew the answer to my internal question. *He wants more.*

"*Yes.*" I let myself utter and raised up and into his hard muscled chest, my urgent hands curling around his neck and settling against his skull as my fingers urgently tangled in his hair. It met his neck and I thanked God for the leverage his smooth strands created as my mouth folded against his.

Hudson stilled above me, either surprised or wary, I couldn't tell but after no more than a moment, a deep, possessive growling sound resonated from his throat and his tongue was pushing between my lips.

Tasting me.

Devouring me.

Marking me.

Claiming me.

My short, gasping breath was the only thing between us as he took a long pull of my taste and pulled marginally back and peered down at me.

"I'll walk you to your car."

I nodded, standing on shaky legs, his arm the only thing tethering me after the onslaught his kiss just created.

"See you tonight, baby."

The engine of my car came to life before I wrapped my hand around the wheel and reversed out of the parking spot, all the while feeling Hudson's watching gaze on me.

"You took me to a buffet?" I asked, annoyed at the crazy, gorgeous man I hadn't been able to get off of my mind. He smirked at me, the dimple in his chin coming out to tease me and I inwardly groaned. I couldn't count the number of times I imagined leaning forward and pressing my lips against that exact dimple, just to experience how it would feel on my tongue. But, just like every other time my mind ran away from me, I denied that urge.

"Come on, baby. You remember who's been watching you for the past month or have you forgotten?" His deep, playful tone rushed over me in a wave of excitement and sinful thoughts and I nodded, trying my best not to kiss him like I wanted to.

I purse my lips in an effort not to smile back at him, shaking my head.

"I don't know what you're talking about." I leaned against the door jam of the quaint, little chinese buffet Hudson had driven us to. It was just off of the highway and I hadn't even noticed it until he pulled into the parking lot. I was guessing he had been here before.

I felt the hairs at the back of my neck stand up and a slight shiver to shake my body as he stepped toward me, his lean, large body boxing me into the wall and his rough, callused hands slid over my cheeks so I was looking into his eyes. The intensity in his gaze stole my breath all the while the nearness of him made my heart stutter in my chest.

"I can't believe you took me to a buffet for dinner."

Chuckling in my ear, he kissed my temple, causing my chest to warm and my hands to come up to take hold of his strong, oh-so-broad shoulders. Drawing away just an inch, his eyes met mine again, this time filled with amusement.

"Oh no, Darlin'. I took you to a Chinese buffet. All you can eat."

Pushing his shoulder, I laughed with him. *I loved his laugh.*

It was husky, deep and full- warming my hollow heart and filling my belly with frantic, little butterflies.

"You asshole. I don't eat that much Chinese."

It was a total lie. I had an incredible weakness for it and indulged whenever I thought I could get away with it.

That didn't mean I wanted to admit it, though.

"It I get fat it'll be your fault, you know that right?"

He threw his head back in laughter, and I watched, rapt as he chuckled loudly.

My head knocked gently against his chest and I was still shaking my head at him when the young girl that sat behind the hostess stand called our number.

"Come on. I want to watch you stuff your face."

Taking my hand in his, I was tugged into his side but I didn't complain.

I loved how physical he was with me. Hudson always made sure that I knew how he liked me and I loved that, even if I wouldn't admit it to him.

"I'm sorry, but the only seats we have open are upstairs by the windows. Is that alright?" The hostess asked as she led us up the stairs of the restaurant and I shrugged when Hudson's gaze darted down to mine.

"That's fine with me."

As we walked, my eyes took in the surroundings of the restaurant Hudson had taken me to. The walls were painted red, the bright shade of red seemed a stark contrast of the dark floors and black topped tables and chairs. The buffet was placed in the center of the floor and surprised how busy it was, I wondered how long we'd have to wait to eat. My stomach growled as if it sensed my thoughts and I blushed.

"Let's get you fed." Hudson muttered, helping to remove my jean jacket and purse before he placed them on one of the chairs. I nodded, this time I took his hand before he could re-claim it and I followed him silently.

"Holy shit, this is good." I moaned as I chewed my first bite of crab Rangoon, the taste of it delicious on my tongue. I heard a groan from the other side of the table and raising my eyes to see Hudson's eyes set on me, narrowed and filled with amusement and hunger. I swallowed thickly, embarrassed.

"Sorry."

Leaning forward, his face came to only an inch from mine and I watched his smile widen until that damn dimple revealed itself to me again.

"Don't be, Darlin'. I like that you love food so much. I would hate for that to change just because your embarrassed."

"Okay." I felt his hand reach over the table cloth toward mine and mine met it halfway, my fingers locking with his much larger and thicker ones.

"So," He said, a few minutes later and I looked at him, my napkin pressed to my mouth as I wiped away the crumbs on my lips from the meal.

"So," I said back and his mouth twitched in a smile.

"Tell me something about yourself."

It sounded like the most typical date question and I cringed.

What did he want to know about me?

What could I say?

Nerves curled deep in my lower stomach and made it clench in something other than hunger. His eyes narrowed slightly and his thumb brushed against my hand, causing a calm to wash over me.

I took a deep, calming breath and nodded.

"What do you want to know?"

He moves his other hand to our joined ones that rested across the table and I sighed at the contact. His touch did crazy things to me and I craved more of it.

"Anything you want to tell me."

I looked down at my plate, now empty besides the napkins on top of it and one lone piece of chicken I hadn't had room for. I rubbed my thumb against his and decided to start simple. I hadn't done this before and was afraid to mess it up. Dating had never appealed to me before him and I wondered if there was a reason for that.

Maybe I had known to wait for him.

Maybe it was meant to be.

Him and me.

I shook my head to rid of my strange thoughts before they took hold of anything meaningful. Anything I wouldn't want to admit.

"Emberly." His voice was deep and filled with worry and a need I was becoming familiar with and my gaze rose to his once more.

"I have this craving to know you better and I have tried to squash it, to forget it, to ignore it. I have tried everything in the book to rid of these feelings that you cause in me but it's no fucking use because I want you."

Every concern for what came next vanished as I heard his softly spoken confession and I didn't care how hard I had tried to keep him at arms length.

I wanted him just as much as I was sure he now wanted me.

Why the hell was I denying it?

The man was infuriating and sexy as hell but he was also everything I wanted.

My heart knew what it wanted as I moved from my seat and walked into the circle of his arms, my hands going down to his as he held my waist securely.

"I want you, too"

"Fuck, thank God."

Hudson stood to his full height, grabbing my face in his callused palms before he dropped his head to mine and his mouth whispered over mine in a soft, feather-light kiss.

It was a stark opposite of the kiss we shared not long ago but just like the last time, my body melted into it and his name was on my lips when I came up for precious air.

"Hudson."

He moved away, pressing a kiss to my temple in the same gentle press that he kissed my mouth. My arms wrapped around his hips tightly as he continued to press light kisses on my upturned face.

"Yeah, Darlin'."

"Take me home."

HUDSON

"You want me to open the door for you, baby?"

Feeling her nod against my chest, I deftly moved the key-ring in her hand and turned the first key in the lock until we heard a faint *click*.

Yes.

My hands molded to her hips as I pushed her gently into her living room and heard her drop her purse and keys at the coffee table placed in the middle of the room. She had been avoiding my eyes ever since our talk at the hospital and her admission had been bothering me the entire time since.

I couldn't fathom why a woman as fucking beautiful as she was wouldn't know that she was beautiful. Anyone with eyes could see that.

As I stalked toward her, I smiled the smile that I knew made her blush and when she did, my chest tightened at the sight.

If I wasn't careful, I would get lost in this woman and it surprised me that the possibility of that didn't make me run the hell out of bound.

Instead, I quickened my pace and gained the distance between us in a matter of seconds. Emberly begun worrying her lush bottom lip with her teeth as her bright, violet eyes watched me.

"What are you doing?" She whispered.

I leaned my head against hers in an attempt to calm my breathing.

She caused the craziest fucking things in me.

Just having her this close in proximity made my spine ache with the need to claim her, once and for all.

I knew from the way her cheeks flushed pink anytime I looked at her that she was unclaimed.

That simple truth drove me crazy with need for her.

But I held back.

It had been over a month since meeting this girl. This shy, kind hearted, *beautiful* girl and I knew it was fast, my attraction to her.

I dipped my mouth to hers and pressed my hands roughly against her lush ass, needing to feel her there, too.

"Hudson, what are you *doing?*"

She asked me again and I licked my tongue against her full lips, begging for her to open that perfect mouth for me.

When she did, I all but growled at the sweet taste of strawberries that hit my tongue. Fuck, she tasted like heaven. But I wanted more.

"Show me where your bedroom is, Darlin'."

Feeling her gasp against my mouth, I drew back, expecting her to tell me I was going too fast. She had only agreed to be with me last night and here I was pushing her for more.

I wanted to be good for her.

Patient.

Tentative.

But I couldn't, not with her.

This gnawing hunger I had to taste every fucking inch of her never waned and I hoped it never would. Because I wanted us to be more than a passing attraction. Even a passing fling.

A few weeks of sweaty sex and meager conversation

wouldn't do. I needed *more* and I damn sure was going to push her if that's what it took.

Her face was flushed in a deep blush and her mouth was parted as she licked her lips as if she wanted to feast on me.

"Upstairs," She whispered, pushing her hands in my hair again.

I'd never admit to it, but I loved that she was always touching me. Her fingers, her hands, the little ways she would find to brush against me when we were in the same room. She had this unique way of making me feel like the center of her universe and I fucked soaked it up.

I wanted that. To be her center. Her anchor. Her safe place.

It didn't matter that I didn't know the cause for her distrust of men.

Her shyness in even the simplest of situations. Her instinctual self blame whenever something went wrong in her life.

Whether it was the copy machine at the hospital or a rather rude patient in the waiting room she always seemed to find a way to blame herself.

One day, she would tell me.

There was no way she wouldn't because one way or another, I was going to imprint myself so deep inside of her that she would never shake me.

I couldn't wait for that day.

"Put your hands around my neck."

Her gorgeous, wide eyes snapped to mine as she nodded and did what I told her. I reached my hands under her knees and with a quick tug, I had her legs wrapped around my waist and my hands filled with her lush ass.

Fuck, how was I going to keep my control in place with her?

I was so fucked.

"Oh, Hudson," She breathed and as I carried her up the long, winding staircase she laid her head on my shoulder and dug her fingers into my shirt.

She felt perfect in my arms.

I cleared the second floor and reached over one of the small tables in the hallway to flip on a lamp, bathing the space in faint light.

There were four doors and a large, bay window with a small window seat covered in all kinds of fancy pillows. Briefly, I imagined taking her over there and stripping her bare of the clothes she wore. I would wrap her legs around my shoulders and eat her perfect pussy until she begged me to stop. And then I would do it again.

Emberly lifted her head from my shoulder and swept her hands over my chest as she steadied herself in my arms.

"Its the first door."

I guessed she was just as eager to get inside her bedroom as I was.

8

EMBERLY

*P*ressing my house key into the lock the following day, I heard my cell phone ding with a text from my purse, causing a smile to tip my lips.

Today, Just Now: You up for a girls night?

I sipped a small glass of my favorite White Zinfandel and typed back a message to Ashlee.

Bestie: I have plans tonight

Me: Coming over. I expect details girl!

I stared at the screen, shaking my head at her though of course, she couldn't see me.

Last night hadn't felt real to me. It was beautiful and perfect and so, so right. Going to work this morning was difficult, with that hulk of man still laying peacefully in my bed. I'd told him to take the day off and let Tristan cart me around for the day. He deserved a day off and though I doubted I would ever be able to give him the peace, safety and kindness he'd given me- I could give him a day off. Thankfully my shift at the hospital went by relatively quickly. On my way home from there, Hudson texted me. He wanted to have dinner again.

So, here I was, waiting for him to pick me up for yet another date.

Except this time, it wasn't trepidation that filled me as I waited in anticipation. It was excitement to see him again.

I was dressed in a comfy pair of yoga pants and a U of H sweatshirt by the time I heard someone knock against the front door of my house. I padded on bare feet to the door and pulled it open only to be caught in the gaze of a pair of pale blue eyes. I audibly gasped, stepping back a step in surprise.

Shit! I was so not ready for our date. Hudson crossed his arms over his large, leather clad chest, a smirk toying at his full mouth. His eyes darkened as they rove over me slowly, as if he had all the time in the world. It made me hot all over.

"Hudson, I-"

He pushed forward and took my hand in his, then, guiding a callused finger over my palm. His touch was gentle and on contact, it calmed me.

"My sergeant canceled our meeting. I thought I would come and get you early, if it's alright." His tone was gentle and sincere but the bite of his control still lays there in his voice, reminding me that he does anything he wants.

That fact makes me hot all over again because I know that what he wants in this moment is me.

"It's okay, I just, need to get changed."

Feeling the vibration of my phone in my pocket, I turned away from the sinfully, sexy man standing in my kitchen expecting another text from Ashlee awaiting me.

An unknown number popped up on the screen and for some reason, my heart begun to beat faster in concern. I had all of my work colleagues saved in my contacts so I knew it couldn't be someone from the hospital. As I opened the message, I became increasingly worried about who the sender could be.

Today, 5:30 PM: You're mine.

Today, 5:50 PM: He doesn't deserve you. Do you remember me when you're with him? I don't care if you think you love him, Em. I'll never let you go.

Today, Just Now: I'm coming for you.

I felt all of the blood drain from my face as I read the words displayed on the screen again and again, hoping I could make sense of them.

But none of it made sense.

"You okay, baby?"

Hudson's callused thumb brushed over the soft skin of my lower lip, causing a sharp, shiver to wrack my body in the affect I always felt when we were together. I didn't know what we were, but I really wanted to find out.

I wanted to let him into my heart and see what we could become and not even my worry about Ashlee's stalker was going to stop me from doing just that.

Why would I rock the boat for a few weird text messages?

Letting my head rest against his shoulder, I nodded.

I was okay.

Because of him.

"Are you ready for dinner?"

Nodding, I leaned against him, loving that all the hard parts of him fitted against my soft curves. I often looked in the mirror and despised my curvy body and loose hips and stomach. When I was with him, I didn't feel that way. I felt completely and utterly... wanted.

As we walked out of my apartment and across the parking lot where he parked, Hudson told me about his day. It's a mundane thing actually, small talk. With any one else, it would be normal. Boring, even.

But with this man it was thrilling.

Exciting.

Interesting.

Riveting.

When he spoke, his voice penetrated deep inside of me, as if it was trying to find a home there. He tells me about how his mother called while he was coming to get me and how he could hear how excited she was for the barbecue his family is throwing in just a few weeks. I heard the softness bleed into the tones of his voice and it made me smile.

He told me about the accident on the freeway earlier this morning and how he *fucking hates traffic*. His words, not mine. I've noticed that when he swears, his voice grows gentle and his eyes narrow as if he is angry with himself for swearing with me.

Hudson's eyes shifted to me as I watched him and tipping his head to the side, he grinned that sexy smile; my heart stopped all together.

"You staring at me, Darlin'?"

I looked down to my feet, a blush covering my cheeks and felt his callused fingers press beneath my chin, lifting my face upwards.

"Don't be shy when you're with me."

Nodding, my face pressed to his palms as he held me there, looking intently into my eyes.

My eyes went to his full mouth, his bottom lip trapped between his teeth. God, I wanted to kiss him.

The kiss we shared earlier today was branded into my mind and the craving for another was stronger than the fear of risking my heart again is.

I'm scared, too.

But more than anything, I want him.

"Okay." I breathe and then his mouth is on me and my breath is stolen. Taking my bottom lip between his teeth he tugs and an ache penetrates my core.

"You okay, Darlin'?" Hudson asks, his hand sliding over my thigh in a gentle yet possessive grasp. I have no idea how a man like him can lay claim with just a simple touch but he does it effortlessly.

"Y-yes. Where are we going?" I ask, cringing when I hear the shake in my voice, giving away the obvious effect he causes in me.

How did I ever think going out with this man would be a good idea?

He possesses my every thought and it has only been a few minutes into our date. If he is making me feel this crazy so quickly, I can't even imagine how I'll be feeling by the end of the night.

I can't wait to find out.

The thought makes my teeth come down to worry my bottom lip and my pussy to contract in a heady feeling of anticipation.

"My place first. I want to show you where I live."

My heart races within my chest at the thought of seeing where he lives. Excited, I move toward him in my seat and press my fingers over his as they lay against my knee.

"I would love that."

We passed the welcome sign as we leave my small town of Cedar Park and enter the tree lined city limits of Austin. The skyline was lit up against the stark night sky with white, bright light. My eyes wandered below to the buildings lining the bustling downtown streets and I was riveted. Never having been inside the city in the three years I had lived here in Texas, I wondered why I never ventured out. Austin was brilliantly beautiful, the skyline offsetting the harsh edges the skyscrapers gave it while the busy city streets hummed with energy and excitement. I couldn't help thinking how I could barely hear myself think as my gaze slid across the landscape just outside the window my cheek pressed against. I felt Hudson's fingers clench against the fabric of my thigh and I moved my gaze to his as he drove. One hand rested on the steering wheel while the other gently held mine, our fingers interlocked in a way that felt intimate. He squeezed my hand gently as if it was his way of making sure I knew he was here with me.

"Is this your first time in the city?" He asked, his eyes filled with curiosity as they turned to me and I noticed softness I was coming to love there in his gaze. I nodded, resting my cheek against the leather head rest so I could keep looking at him.

The city bustled and hummed around us, something I knew I could become addicted to. As my gaze ventured to his full mouth as he drove, unaware of my attention, I smiled around the sigh that left me.

I could become addicted to him, too.

I think I already was.

"You love it, don't you?"

"Yeah." He murmured, tipped his head back as the truck came to a stop in a parking spot next to a large, blue plated building. I looked up through the window and noticed it was a apartment complex, though a small one.

"I love this city. I have always lived here, so maybe that is why. Even when I went to college, I never ventured far. Austin is my home"

He pierced me with his intense blue eyes and the small small he gave me was almost shy as he squeezed my hand once more and left his side of the cab.

I took the chance to take a full breath of air before he was opening my door and taking my hand in his much larger one.

"Hop down."

Hudson secured his arm around my waist before opening the glass door of the building and we entered a warm light filled room which I guessed was a lobby of some sort. I didn't get much time to wonder, though because the door man to the elevator was awaiting us as we entered and before long, Hudson had me in his arms while the elevator rose to the top floor. The entire unit was made of glass and as we rose higher and higher, my gut clenched in quickly firing nerves. I bit my lip as I tried to be calm, but I could feel the beginning of a panic attack coming as my body jolted in shivers. Even with Hudson's strong, never wavering arms around my waist, his chin resting a top of my shoulder, nothing could stop the panic from rising within me.

"Em?"

His voice covers me and I nod shakily, the units subtle vibrations heightening the anxiety heating my blood. I feel his fingers gently grip my chin and then he turns me toward him, his hand cupping the side of my face as he looks me over.

"Fuck, Emberly, look at me. Look at me."

It takes me a few minutes to get up the courage to do just that but when I do, a wash of calm covers me.

"Hudson..." I breathed, my head leaning forward and my cheek falling to rest against his chest as my body goes lax and the onslaught of panic that had risen wanes.

"You're okay, now. I have you."

His words are whispered in my hair and I nod, thankful for it.

"You should have told me you are afraid of heights."

Hudson says as he brushes his thumb over my cheek, his touch awakening my senses as my body leans into his.

"I wasn't thinking. I didn't know this elevator was glass."

I'm led out of the unit and finally being able to breathe normally, I lace my fingers through his at his side and smile shyly when he looks down at me.

"I'm sorry."

My hand is lifted to his lips and his head lowers enough so that he can place a kiss to the skin of my palm before he whispers in my ear, low and oh so sexy that I'm sure my knees are weakening at just the sound of his voice.

"Don't ever be sorry. Everyone is afraid of something."

My mouth parts in surprise at the honesty of his words and I find myself wondering what a man like him could be afraid of.

Hudson's large hand warms me as the aftershocks of my panic attack ebb away and we step out of the glass unit and onto a red, carpeted floor. The hallway he leads me down is large and spacious, but becomes more narrow the further we go. I notice the room numbers are going up as we walk and I count them.

1108, 1109, 1110, 1111...

Then we pause in front of a white door with a black door knob and two deadbolts at the top. There is a large plate at the top of it that reads *Room 1112, Penthouse.* I gasp audibly and then my chin is gripped gently as Hudson turns my face to meet his gaze. When our eyes lock, I see a nervousness in them that does nothing to set me at ease.

I know this is one of the moments in my life that a *fight or flight* instinct should be kicking in. I am about to walk inside his penthouse only knowing him a few short weeks. He could be nothing but trouble for me. He could want me for all the wrong reasons. I mean, *he could have any woman he wanted. Why would he want me?*

Ugly. The word whispered through my mind again and I bit down gently on my lower lip, halting its trembling as his narrow, blue eyes trained on me.

Assessing.

Pulling.

Calming.

His eyes were something I couldn't shy away from, no matter how hard I tried. Because as deeply as my flight instincts were ingrained in me, they didn't take notice when I was in Hudson's presence.

It was as if my body knew that he was safe.

He was good.

He wasn't going to hurt me.

As that thought whispered through my mind, a low sigh left me and my nerves began to calm.

"Need you to stay out here for a bit. My place hasn't been kept the way it should be for guests. I have been working a lot and I haven't found the time to clean properly. Give me ten minutes. I'll let you in soon."

Everything in my tensed body softened as I heard the worry his tone held.

Was he seriously worried about the state of his home when I saw it for the first time?

I wouldn't have cared if there were clothes thrown on every available surface.

Any time we were alone together, my entire body buzzed with the effect he had on me. My attention was constantly trained on him.

I realized that it wasn't one thing that drew me to him.

It was the package that it came in. It was what laid underneath the layers of hot, smooth skin and ink that I craved for.

It hit me then that he was humble. Hudson worried about how I felt about his place of living and it warmed my heart and made it stop all together.

I didn't care. I just wanted to spend time with him.

"Hudson." I said, my voice raspy and shaking from the emotions he had pulled from me with his quiet admission.

"I don't care if your place is messy. Let me in."

I tipped his head down toward mine and with the five or so inches he had on me, he had to bend his knees a bit for us to be at the same height.

"Are you sure? There may be-"

I pushed my fingers over his full mouth and shook my head at him, partly in amusement and partly in exasperation.

"Don't care, Hud."

His head nodded and as it did, some of his hair fell between where our faces were only inches from each other.

I laughed lightly and pushed the thick, smooth strands through my fingers.

The sound of his soft growl against my cheek stirred the dormant desire within me and I felt hot moisture pool between my legs.

"Don't know how I'm ever going to take it slow with you."

My head drew back from his as I frowned, unsure if he meant to say that out loud or if he was talking to himself.

"What?"

He grabbed my hand in his and shrugged my question away.

"Come on."

9

EMBERLY

I sat at the breakfast nook of Hudson's spacious, brightly lit kitchen as he moved about the room. His tightly toned shoulders and arms rippled and flexed as he pulled a large crock-pot from the top shelve of a cabinet above the stove and greedily, my eyes took him in.

He dominated the space without much effort, his presence creating a thick aura of energy in the air between us.

"Can I help?" I asked. When his stark blue eyes met mine over the top of the island counter tops, the hard lines in his face softened and he nodded.

"Can you chop these vegetables while I start the Chile?"

Nodding, excitement buzzed through me at the thought of *cooking* with him.

Silence settled between us as I took the long, kitchen knife from his hand and set into the task of cutting up the tomatoes, green pepper and potatoes placed on the cutting board. The smell of spiced Chile hit my nose and wafted over my taste-buds as I took in a deep breath of the heavenly scent. I wasn't exactly a *good* cook. Having never been taught how to prepare a proper meal, I settled for simple, fast food when I was home and take out the rest of the time. It sufficed, I guessed. But now I was craving this home cooked meal we were making and hoped it was the first of many to come.

My mind must have wandered as I focused on what I was doing because when Hudson's smooth hands clasped my shoulders from behind, squeezing gently a gasp leaves me.

"Sorry. I didn't mean to startle you. The sauce is ready."

Smiling softly, I nodded and looked up where I saw approval once again dancing through his gaze. My chest warmed instantly.

I didn't know why, but knowing that I made him happy, even in such a small way, warmed me up. I diverted my gaze as I cut the last couple of potatoes in front of me. His warm breath washed over my neck as his head lowered closer to mine. I felt his jaw rub against my cheek as he spoke again.

"I'll put these in and then start the bread."

I expected him to pull away from me then, but again, the rough whiskers of his beard rubbed against my over heated skin. The sensation of it enticed a shiver to dance up my spine.

"O-okay." I shakily said and I swore I could feel his sinful smile against my cheek.

Hudson moved to the oven and my eyes followed him as he went to the stove top and tipped the white edged cutting board, using the steak knife grasped in his hand to sweep the array of vegetables into the sauce.

"You want to see the rest of the house?" He asked, his back pressed to the brick wall adjacent to where I sat and his muscles flexed as he placed his arms across his chest in the ultimate *bad boy* way.

I licked my lip unconsciously and nodded, moving toward him until I stopped a foot in front of him. The pull radiated through the room as he stared at me, those wide, intense eyes raking over seemingly every inch of my body before he settles his attention on my eyes again.

"Fuck, do you know how beautiful you are?"

A blush covered my cheeks at his praise and my gaze dipped

to the floor, unsure of how to take his words. I had always had a problem feeling beautiful.

Maybe it was because of my father.

Maybe it was because every time I looked in the mirror, all I could see was the extra skin on my middle and the curves that lined my body.

The space between us diminished as he moved toward me, his thumb and forefinger taking a gentle hold on my chin lifting my gaze away from my feet and to his softened gaze.

"One day, you are going to see yourself the way I do. I'll make sure of it."

My mouth dropped open slightly, my mind fumbling for words to say back to that, but none came. I wasn't sure what he was telling me was possible but I knew that if any man could do it, it would be him.

He was a demanding man. If he demanded me to look at myself, I would.

"Do you know how Beautiful you are?" He repeated, his voice gentle this time and I bit my lip, unsure of the statement but with the way his eyes rove over me in hunger, I was started to believe him

He moved closer, his hands moving to my shoulders, sliding down ever so slowly until he took my hands in his and moved his thumb over each of my knuckles. I stepped back from him, my heart racing at his proximity but he didn't let up on his hold on me, caging me in until his brown leather couch hit the backs of my knees and his hard lined body pressed to every soft curve I had. I felt the heat rise to my cheeks as he moved closer and the bulge in his black jeans pressed against my belly. An undeniable heat licked through me then, like liquid fire. It pulsed through my chest, causing my heart to beat faster until I was sure he could hear it. My veins fired with it while my skin pebbled with the need for his touch on me again.

"Hudson, what are you doing?" I breathed, feeling his hands travel down the front of the blue blouse I changed into after work today. My body swayed impossibly closer, every line of my body melting to his as he reached the bottom of the fabric and his blue eyes, dark with a mixture of hunger and something else I couldn't decipher.

"Touching you."

His head dipped and his mouth pressed to my throat roughly as he spoke again, his words engraved in my skin.

"Kissing you."

He drew his head back and took hold of my blouse once more, his gaze turning serious as he slowly lifted it over my stomach and rib cage.

A heavy breath left my lips in the wake of his touch and I nodded.

He would take care of me.

Hudson lifted the fabric higher up my body and I moved my arms above my head so that he could take it off of me. He moved back to me instantly, his roughly skinned hands roving over my waist, my curved hips and higher, still.

My breaths came faster and shorter the higher his hands traveled and soft moans fell between us. I felt hot, too hot. Like my body was being burned alive by his heated stare and his hot skin against mine as his fingers reached my shoulders. A finger traced a line down one shoulder, his touch achingly slow. It ventured lower, tracing against the thin, black strap of my bra. My breath caught in my throat and I looked up at him, hoping he could see how much I wanted, no *craved* him in this moment.

I had thought of this and nothing but this since he first kissed me yesterday and I knew it was right.

It was fast and maybe a bit crazy for me to want him this much in such a short amount of time but in this moment, I didn't care.

I trusted him.

I reached behind my back and undid the clasp at the back of my bra, allowing it to loosen around my arms. Heat bled through the pale blue color in his eyes as he watched me and his mouth laxed in what I thought had to be desire.

"Fuck, look at you."

His hands went to my bottom, both hands pressing firmly to the denim covered flesh and then he was lifting me up his body until I had no choice but to wrap my legs around his waist and my hands grasped his large, wide shoulders as he sat me on the couch behind us. The sensation of the cool leather and his mouth sucking at my exposed throat caused a whimper to leave my mouth and he chuckled.

"Does my Darlin' need something?"

I nodded, loving the way he spoke to me.

Like I was special and that he couldn't stop himself from wanting me like he did. My hands wrapped around the long strands at the back of his head as he placed wet kisses along my jaw, behind my ear and further down my body until his mouth was pressed to my collarbone. I had never been kissed there but I arched up into his mouth at the sensitivity I felt. The whiskers of his beard trailed over my heavy breasts as he ventured lower and I felt him smile against my skin.

"Hudson, please." The plea fell from my lips easily. I wasn't sure what I was begging him for, though. Was I begging him to stop the torture of his mouth on me? Or did I want more?

His mouth caught one of my nipples then, his teeth scraping against my areola and I moaned his name louder, fervent need curling through my stomach and down to where I was aching for relief.

Take me.

The words were on the tip of my tongue but I was afraid to say them. My hands clenched against the leather cushion under me and my fingers slipped against it as he moved over me, his body caging me in.

"Lay back, Darlin'. I'm going to take care of you."

My body melted at his promise and pressing my shoulders and head back against my cushions, I bit my lip as hot need pooled low in my stomach and my pussy clenched around nothing.

God, I wanted this.

I wanted him to claim me.

And it scared me, but still, I craved it.

He moved on to my other breast, his fingers latched on to both of my pointed nipples then tortured them with slow pulls of his hot mouth. When I felt his tongue come out to tease them, my hips moved off of the couch and pressed to the front of his pants where I felt the undeniable hardness of his cock and a damp spot against the fabric there. My body was so hot and sensitive and I needed something. I needed *him*.

I never liked asking for what I wanted from people but as I laid there beneath him and his hot gaze traveled over my bare body, I did.

"I need more."

Hudson's mouth tilted into a sexy smile and he nodded, his mouth bruising mine in a kiss before I could get another word out.

"Open your legs, baby."

I parted them for him, my knees falling over the edge of the leather as he reached under the fabric of the white flowy skirt I wore for our date and finding the lace panties that lay beneath.

"You're fucking drenched, Em. Is this for me? Have you been thinking of me?"

I nodded hurriedly, my body coming alive with desire as he dipped one thick finger through my folds and against my clit. Sparks flew beneath my skin and I heard my panting breath grow faster as he strummed the aching bundle of nerves.

Once.

Twice.

On the third time, he hit a tender spot within me and I arched my back, my hips raising toward him.

"*Oh*, please..."

He moved down my body and I heard a rip and then the

sound of my lace panties tearing. I gasped, ready to protest but didn't get the chance before his full, sinful mouth was on me.

Licking over my clit and then inside me, his hands held me in place with a strong hold and he controlled my pleasure as his mouth moved over my heated flesh, his tongue licking up and around before he added one, then two digits inside my walls.

"Oh god, oh god, Hud..."

I tried to hold back the onslaught of sensation that curled into a ball in my belly, sending sparks flying through my veins and sounds of pleasure fell from my mouth. My orgasm built impossibly fast and there was no stopping it.

"Hudson, oh god, I'm going to come."

At my words he bit my pulsing clit, scraping his teeth over the swollen bundle of nerves and pulled my lower lips between his lips before moving faster, adding yet another finger to my core until I felt full of him. I began to tremble as the waves rocked through me at lightning speed and my thighs shook as he took one more long, slow pull of my juices before moving back up my lax body.

"You feel beautiful yet?" His raspy voice was against my ear as he spoke and my eyes opened, the effects of my orgasm leaving me sated underneath him.

I closed my eyes again and nodded, not bothering to hide the deep blush that I knew was visible on my face as he looked at me.

"I think so." I whispered.

10

EMBERLY

*H*udson swiped a wet bath cloth between my legs with gentle, smooth touches as he takes care of me and my chest warms at the sensation his tender care brings me.

"You didn't have to do that." I said as he tugged me up to stand and slides a warm hand around my hip to hold me close.

His lips tipped up in a small smile, his head shaking at me.

"I told you, I'll take care of you."

I took his hand and nodded, my heart faltering when I saw the evident affection that bled through his gaze as he looked down at me.

"I'm not used to being taken care of." I confessed, letting him lead me toward the dining room table set just beside a large window. The curtains were drawn up and the only light filtering in the room were from the stars of the night sky.

His hand tightening over mine caused my eyes to returned to him and I saw a darkness in his stoic face I didn't expect.

It confused me.

"Did I say something wrong?"

"No, Darlin'." His softly spoken words were against my ear and a shiver licked up my spine, having not realized he was so close.

"I need you to know that's gonna change. I know you are an independent woman and I don't want to take that from you but I also won't let you feel alone ever again. You've got me now."

My heart quickened in my chest as I took in what he had said. I felt the squeeze of my hands within his, telling me he wasn't going anywhere.

I didn't want him to.

The thought that I wanted what he was eluding to so deeply terrified me.

I took a step back from him, but as I expected, I didn't get far.

"Hudson, you can't possibly think this will work."

One thick eyebrow raised as he silently questioned me and I shook my head, exasperation replacing my fear. I welcomed it. I could deal with annoyance at his stubborn ways. What I couldn't handle was the hope that I could have found someone to trust, to love, to believe in.

Could Hudson truly be that person in my life?

"I don't know what you thought this was, but I'm not spending time with you because of some passing interest. I am here and *you* are here because I want much more from you. I want *you*, Darlin'."

The fingers of his left hand moved to my cheek then and I gasped, my breath stalling in my throat as that stupid hope fluttered through my stomach again.

I want you, Darlin'.

God, I wanted him, too.

As if by gravity my body pressed closely to his much larger one and I pushed my fingers through the collar of his shirt to feel the heated skin of his chest, just over his heart. Touching him calmed my erratic heartbeat and enhanced the hope to bloom. In that moment I knew there had to be a reason he made me feel this way.

We fit.

The thought filtered through my mind and I tipped my head

back to see his eyes and they were assessing me, just as I was him.

It was as if we were waiting for who would pull away first.

"What do you want from me?" I finally asked, my voice coming out unsure because I honestly didn't know what his answer would be.

His head dropped lower to mine and our foreheads touched.

The action reminded me of our kiss in the supply closet of the hospital earlier today and I closed my eyes so he didn't see where my mind had drifted.

"I want to see where this goes. I want to *be with you*, Emberly. Can you do that with me?" His voice was softened with caution and hope and it was a dangerous combination for a man like him.

I sighed, knowing that in some way, I had seen this coming a month ago when I felt the connection between us for the first time.

He grasped my jaw in his hand that was holding my cheek and with a gentle tug, my eyes slid over his again.

There was no denying the emotion laying in his stare and if I turned away from it, I knew I would regret it.

I had dreamed of the day that I could find my happily ever after. I had a strange feeling that this was it.

Hudson could be the one to give me my happy again.

If I didn't try, I would be a coward.

"I want this, too. I'm so scared to let you in, but this- this feels so right. Like this is where I have belonged all my life and I'm only now realizing it."

He curled one thick arm around my waist and another under my bottom and then I was being hoisted into his arms and against his hard chest.

I sighed at the heavenly feeling of being in his arms again and my head pressed gently to his neck as he spoke roughly against my ear, an affection bleeding through his tone that warmed me all over.

"I know your scared, baby. I'm scared, too, I just hide it better."

There was a haunting vulnerability in his deep voice that had me drawing my face away from his.

"What are you afraid of?" I whispered and he just shook his head before ghosting his hands over mine on his shoulders and lifting one to his lips for a kiss. The loving gesture had my heart racing and my chest warming and I loved every second of it.

"You have the unique power to hurt me and that scares me. I'm a strong man but if you told me you didn't want this, didn't *feel* this? I don't think I could take that."

I would never hurt you, Hudson.

How could I when your the one making me feel things I never thought was possible for me?

I never thought I was lovable after the way my father treated us.

After watching him slowly come to detest my mother for no other reason but that she existed.

I had learned that love and hate are very similar and in one wrong turn, those emotions can bleed into one.

"I won't." I whispered, hating how small those words sounded against the gravity of his fear. But I meant every word.

I would never want to hurt this man and even if I had to hurt myself in the process, I would make sure I never brought him the trouble my life seemed to always bring whenever I had something good in my life.

After moving out of the house I grew up in and taking the short flight from Georgia to Austin I was afraid the terrors of my child hood years would follow me here. It was the reason I shied away from any sort of relationship in the past five years. I didn't think I was worthy of someone else' love when the one person who was supposed to love me unconditionally did everything in his power to hurt me and my mother.

I hated him for a very long time and inevitably, with years of therapy and Ashlee's support, I learned to let go of the anger I felt for my father.

I was free from it all and I thanked God for that as I leaned closer into Hudson's strong, unwavering hold and placed a kiss on his neck to reinforce my promise.

"I won't, Hudson."

He dipped his mouth to mine then, and I sighed against his lips as he softly, reverently kissed our fears and worries away.

I was going to take a chance on this.

As he swept his tongue softly into my mouth and took a long pull from my mouth, I calmed and pulsed with want for more, my indecision long forgotten as he loved me with his rough and tender mouth.

He could do the most sinful things with it but for now, he was reassuring me and I soaked up every ounce of the tenderness I found in our kiss.

One large finger dipped under my chin and dragged over my cheek until it reached my lower lip where he tugged gently. My mouth fell open wider for him and as it did, he deepened the kiss sending my toes curling and a soft mewl to escape from my lips.

"Hudson, we should eat before we get carried away."

I breathed and a low growl left him as he nodded, his mouth begrudgingly retreated from mine on a hiss of displeasure.

"Yeah."

I watched him move away from me and go to the stove up where we had left the Chile simmering on a low heat setting.

He moved with sure, dominating steps taking two large white dinner plates down from the cabinet above the kitchen sink and he dished out our dinner along with the garlic bread we had made earlier before stalking back over to where I sat at the head of his long, pine wood table.

"What would you like to drink?" His voice was raspy and sexy as hell as he spoke and I bit my lip as my eyes looked over him looking all domestic and homely. I loved seeing him this way and I craved to see more private sides of him he only showed the people in his tight inner circle. As he raised an eyebrow at me and a small, playful smile covered his face I realized I was one of those people now.

He wanted me.

It still seemed crazy to me but I was going with it.

"If you have wine, I would love a glass." I murmured and he nodded, placing my plate in front of me. A light kiss feathered over my cheek before he was moving away again.

Once Hudson had poured us each a glass of my favorite white wine, we settled in to eat our dinner. I took a small bite of the heavenly smelling sauce and sighed in contentment. It was perfect. Not too hot, with a few spices to heat up the sauce while keeping the natural flavors of the vegetables.

"Stop looking at me like that, Em".

My eyes dropped back down to my plate and a blush rose in my cheeks as he caught me looking at him. I just couldn't seem to help myself.

I took another bite of the crisp garlic bread and shrugged my shoulders.

"Why?"

He moved forward in his seat, his gaze turning heated in a matter of seconds.

"Because it makes me want to kiss you."

My skin pebbled in goosebumps and I moved closer, my eyes watching the hunger move through his face.

"I'd like that."

"Eat and then I'll kiss you."

His voice came out all growling and rough and it was the sexiest thing I'd ever heard.

I went back to the meal we'd prepared, but felt his gaze on me still.

"You're staring now."

A low chuckle came from his full lips and the sound caused

warmth to rush through me. I was coming to love the sound of his laugh.

"Can't help it. Your just too fucking beautiful."

My plate was clean by the time he stopped staring at me, but that was only because his hands had reached between us and sought out my face, his mouth on mine in a matter of seconds, doing what he'd promised he would as we ate. I had learned quickly that he was a man of his word.

He would tell me the truth, even when it hurt. He would never lie to me, unless it was for the cause of protecting me. I had a feeling he was keeping something from me when I had asked about the hospital break in a few nights ago and he had told me not to worry about it. He knew who was responsible, or at least had an idea as to who it could be. I knew when it was right, he would tell me the truth and he would protect from it, too.

That was just the kind of man Hudson Lennox was.

His tongue traced the seam of my lower lip as he pulled away and I reached out to grasp the collar of his shirt before he moved too far.

"You make me feel crazy."

My breaths were fast and panting from his rough kisses. A slow, sexy smile widened over his other wise hard edges face and the inked fingers of his hands brushed over my cheeks in the gentlest way. The gesture was a complete opposite to the way he kissed me and I soaked it up.

"I like making you feel crazy."

I laughed and so did he, a quiet laughter that meant we were in this together and I loved that, too.

I rested my face against his chest, the sound of his quickened heart beat calming my racing one and a feeling of safety rushed through me. Binding one arm around my waist while the fingers of his other hand smoothed over my hair, he whispered into my ear.

"Your safe with me. I won't ever hurt you, Em. I need you to believe that."

I curled my hands around his neck and pressed my head against his as I whispered a confession I needed him to hear as much as I needed to say it.

"I do."

It was close to midnight by the time we pulled into my driveway outside of the city. Hudson took my hand in his large palm and skated a kiss gently over my knuckles.

"Thank you for coming out with me."

I leaned into his hand as it glided over my cheek, my body craving the sensations it brought upon contact.

"Can you walk me up?" I asked, a hesitant excitement in my voice.

Depending and trusting in another person, especially a man I had only known for a matter of weeks was both terrifying and liberating. I knew he was one of the good, true men in the world and I found myself wondering how I had gotten this stroke of good luck to have him in my life, even if it was for a short amount of time. I knew from experience that life was unexpected and scary at times so when good things came around, it was hard to let myself trust in it.

The more I was around this man and learned about him and who he was, down to his core, the more I realized he'd be worth the risk.

His long, thick fingers slipped through mine and I slipped my house keys out of my purse to unlock the door. I felt his heated gaze on my face as I did and a small smile tipped my lips.

I don't think I have ever smiled as much as I do when I'm around him.

I felt another piece of my heart fall into place as he took my face in his hands, his hold on me gentle and his wide, pale blue eyes took me in. He didn't move in to kiss me like I had expected him to but he didn't move away to go back to his truck, either. He just tipped my head back with a hand on my nape and looked at me. I wiggled slightly under the intensity of it and then he lowered his mouth to mine in soul mending kiss.

"Goodnight." He growled against my lips and a sigh left my lips at the sound of it. I was coming to love when his voice would go all husky as he kissed me.

"Thank you." I whispered and felt his sexy smile against our kiss.

As his head drew apart from mine, I captured his hand before he strayed too far.

"Stay."

EMBERLY

"Em, baby I think you got some mail." Hudson's deep voice carries from the bedroom as I attempted to tame the frizzy and curly mess that was my hair the following morning. Putting my brush back on the bathroom sink, I stepped through the open door to my room and smiled as I saw him in all his glory, thumbing through my mail- shirtless. God, I could get used to this.

Slow down, girl.

Marriage and babies is a long way off...

"What were you just thinking about?" He was suddenly much closer than before, with his large, cullused hands cupping my cheeks and his wide, blue, piercing eyes adoringly on my face. Pulling back a fraction, I smiled and leaned into his touch; as I always did. He was my one and only addiction; a man I could never get enough of.

"Nothing, Hud. I'm fine." I assured him, letting my hands rest over his toned as all hell chest. He met my gaze for a long moment before grinning wide, again.

"Yeah, you are." Crushing my mouth under his after his teasing words, I laughed beneath his kiss feeling my soul light up with the warmth being with him like this always gave me. I didn't know something so good and so right was possible after the life I'd lived but with Hudson, it was.

I was like a love sick actor in one of those musicals my Mama always loved, singing gleefully about how anything is possible.

"What did I come in here for?" I asked almost an hour later, as we lazily laid over my bed, a mess of tangled limbs and hot seeking mouths, eager for just one more taste.

Laughing loudly, Hudson slid his hands down my back and grabbed my ass in his way before smirking and kissing the top of my head as if he thought I was cute.

Knowing him, he probably did.

"Mail, baby."

"Oh. If it's a bill, I don't need it." I teased, pushing him away when he begun to kiss down my neck again. He was a walking, talking distraction, this man.

"Funny. No, it's a letter." Huh. That was weird, I thought to myself. I hadn't read a real, actual letter since before Nursing school and it was only because it had been my acceptance letter. It's much easier to send an email or text now a days.

"Let me see." Taking the letter from where he picked it up, I skimmed my eyes over the return address. Atlanta, Georgia.

No, it couldn't be...

Reading it again, I realized it had to be from my father, if he wasn't in jail or dead by now. From what I could remember, he'd had a lot of friends and some deep pockets, too. There was no way that even if someone did find out about his shady business or the fatal assault on my mother, he wouldn't atone for it.

Grasping Hudson's arm for more support than anything, I looked up at him hoping he didn't see how much I was freaking out right then.

"Could I read this alone?" His eyes, crystal blue and laced with concern narrowed ever so slightly before he nodded, dropping his head to mine and kissing my cheek with a gentleness I'd come to crave from him.

"Only a few minutes, Em. If you need me, I'm right outside. Yeah?"

I did need him. But it was my father. I had to deal with it on my own.

"Okay." With another slight nod of his head, he closed the door behind him, leaving me effectively alone with the words of the man that made me the woman I am today.

Sometimes scared. Sometimes weak. Sometimes tainted. And I hated him. I would always hate him, down to my bones.

Dear Emberly,

His letter began the same way almost every other does and as I continued reading, I hated every single word that came after it.

HUDSON

Leaving that room was probably the hardest thing she could have asked of me. But Emberly had her own mind and if I denied her that, I wouldn't deserve her. So I let her have her space. Sitting against the door of her bedroom, I listened like a hawk, ready to burst inside as soon as I heard anything that told me she was upset by the letter.

It was from Atlanta, a place I knew she was born and grew up in. What I didn't know was who would take the time to mail her a letter or why she didn't want to share it with me.

Was my girl embarrassed?

Did she think that whatever was in that letter would somehow change the way I felt about her?

How I loved her?

"Hud, baby I need you." Her words came from the other side of the door and stumbling in my frantic need to get to her, I turned the door handle and opened my arms just in time to catch her when she fell, right into me, where she belonged. Her hot tears bathed my neck and her warm, heaving breath blew over my skin and I held her, so damn tight I was sure she couldn't breathe but at that very moment I didn't care.

I would be her damn breath.

"Tell me, Em."

"M-my dad." She weakly whispered.

Fuck! I should have never let her read it before I got my hands on it. Of course she'd wanted to read it alone, her father was reaching out to her and she didn't want him to touch us. Where I was protective of her in spades, so was she. She was my little fighter, unwilling for her past to taint us. Eventually, it would and when that day came, we'd deal with that. But, until then she wanted to protect me from the vile words he'd most likely written for her and if I knew her as well as I thought I did, she wouldn't tell me all of them.

She was protecting us.

"Come here." Sitting on the edge of her bed, I laid down and took her with me, letting her rest her head on my chest in hopes that the sound of my heart beat would calm her as it normally did when nightmares plagued her dreams.

"Before I left for school, my father did something bad-horrible, really. I didn't want to be involved in what he was doing, shady dealings in his business that I knew would take everything from him- his house, his cars, his money. The only thing he truly had to lose was me and I was already gone. He said I'll be sorry..." Before she continued, she peered up at me, her tear stained cheeks so pale it had my heart stopping in chest.

How was I supposed to fix this? Fix her?

"Look at me, Darlin'." When her big, wet eyes met mine, I grabbed her face as gently as I could and made sure she saw the honesty in my own.

"His wrongs aren't yours. Whatever he said to make you sad, don't be. Please, baby. You know what these tears do to me."

Smiling shakily, Emberly nodded and leaned into my touch as I tried my best to wipe her tears away with my thumbs.

Fuck, was she beautiful.

"I know. I'm okay, Hud. He's just...he's my father. I don't want to hate him, but I do. Does that make me a bad person? That I hate my own blood?" She peered up at me pleadingly and even though I couldn't have ever imagined having hatred for my family, I knew her childhood wasn't even close to mine. The man had hurt her, body and soul. How someone who was supposed to love and protect her could do that, I'd never know. I just had to be here for her if she needed someone. And right then, I was.

"You're so damn strong, Em. You know that, right?"

Nodding her head, she smiled big and bright, lighting up the whole damn room.

"I want to be. You make me believe I can be, Hud. Thank you."

Shaking my head at her in exasperation, I kissed her forehead leaving my mouth there as I admonished her.

"Never have to thank me, Darlin'."

HUDSON

I stepped inside the hospital entrance the following day with a hot, paper cup in my hand from the café.

I was a simple man.

I liked my woman strong willed and beautiful.

I liked my coffee hot and black.

And I liked Emberly a hell of a lot more than I should.

But fuck if I cared. I knew with a sad clarity that life was too short.

Some people went their entire lives without really living. Yeah, they may have gone through the motions of their lives.

They may have been married, had a bunch of kids. Maybe they went on a few vacations from their boring old jobs, too.

But they didn't live. Life was all about taking chances. *Risks.*

Taking the leap and hoping to God that you would land on your feet. It was about loving the ones you could and taking advantage of the time you were given because it could be taken away in an instant.

And when it did, all you were left with were regrets and enough *what ifs?* To last you a fucking lifetime.

I looked down at the red coffee cup in my hand and shook my head in disbelief.

That wasn't me, though. I was going to live every second like it was my last because in my line of work, that was a very real possibility.

I turned the corner towards the nurses desk where I'd last seen her and a chuckle fell from my lips.

This girl.

"Oh, is that for me?" Her sweet voice asked and she turned from where she stood next to the tall and large glass windows across the room. I stalked toward her, my boots eating up the small distance between us. The moment I reached her, I slid one hand behind her head and pulled her in for a quick kiss.

"I know you need your caffeine, Darlin'. Drink up." A big smile lit up her face then and my damn chest warmed at the sight.

How the fuck did she affect me this way?

"Thank you." Her eyes lifted to the windows behind her again and that smile somehow brightened as she looked at the array of stars across the night sky. I swept my arms around her waist and she leaned into me almost instantly. My chin pressed to the top of her head and my arms held her close as we stood there. As always, I felt the quiet hum of electricity between us and I forced a breath from my mouth in an attempt to calm my craving for her. As the minutes past, her body begun to press deeper against mine and one of her small hands covered the fingers of one of mine. Moving my hand on her waist up to the slope of her neck, I pushed her long, golden blonde hair away from the side of her face and placed my lips to her neck in a reaffirming kiss.

"It's beautiful, isn't it?" She whispered and I smiled against her hair.

Yeah. She was fucking gorgeous.

But I was pretty sure she wasn't talking about *my view*.

I knew from the many long nights we spent together at the hospital that she loved looking at the night sky. She believed if she looked at just the right one and made a wish, it would come true.

Emberly saw the world through the brightest glasses and the hope she had for the future made me want to make it happen.

The world could be a scary place but with me by her side, I vowed that she would never have to know that.

Because I would go to the ends of the fucking earth to protect her. As she looked up at me with those wide, lavender eyes, my heart stopped.

I was so done for.

Inching closer to her, my hands slid over her cheeks and as I ran my thumb over the rose blush there, my chest tightened and my damn heart kicked into over drive again. I lowered my mouth to hers, softly brushing my lips over hers in hopes of calming the need I had for her with a kiss.

"Hudson," She moans my name. The sweet, raspy sound of her voice stirring my cock to life between us and causing me to kiss down her neck, knowing that her scent would help ease my ache for her.

Her vanilla scent wafted from her lips as she whispered my name again and it alleviated my need for her only slightly.

This girl would drive me crazy if I let her.

I placed my mouth over her earlobe as I descended back up her neck and felt rather than heard her gasp of surprise.

I trapped the skin between my teeth and gave a slight tug, causing her to whisper my name again. Her head rocked against my shoulder and her body leaned even closer to mine as I continued my assault over her heated skin.

"I would rather look at you than the night sky."

I curled my arm around her stomach, holding her to me and I felt the moment she realized what was pressing against her through my pants.

A shuttered sigh left her as I laced one hand with hers against her hip while the other trailed up to her shoulder.

"Then why aren't you looking at me?"

I chuckled against her hair, the sweet scent of her shampoo enveloped me.

Feeling her body lock up against mine, I move back a step, taking her hand in mine. When she turned to face me, I could see a darkness in her eyes.

Fuck!

Reaching forward, I cupped her face in my hands and looked down at her big, beautiful eyes.

"I don't need to be looking at you to see your beauty. It emanates from inside of you. Your goodness shines through like a fucking sun."

A smile bursts across her face as she nods and shifts nervously.

My instincts kicked in then and I knew without a doubt that something was bothering her. My arms crossed over my chest and I caged her in to the window, making sure she knew there was no escaping my question.

A better man wouldn't have done that.

A good man would be patient with her.

Would wait for her to tell him her secrets.

But I'm not a good man.

I'm rough around the edges.

I'm trying to be better, though.

And it was all for her.

"Tell me, baby."

Looking up from her feet with a slight shrug of her shoulders, she retreats from me.

"I have to finish these reports before the end of my shift."

Groaning internally, I nodded.

The sooner I could get her out of here and safely at home, the better off we would be. But I would be getting it out of her. One way, or another.

Following her across the lobby, I watched her slip behind the nurses desk and move the folders of papers around the desk, busying herself so she didn't have to look at me.

I leaned as close to her as I could and caught one of her hands in mine before she had the chance to move away.

"You gonna make me kiss it out of that pretty mouth of yours, Emberly? Cus' you know I will."

I watched the deep blush rise in her cheeks and I grinned at her.

I had an effect on her, too.

My thumb brushed over her palm and I felt the moment she calmed under my touch. I could see that she was hiding something from me, something that was weighing on her and I just wanted her to tell me so I could ease whatever worries inhabited her mind.

"What is it?"

Her eyes moved to mine and she nodded, putting the stack of files in front of her away and getting her purse from the bottom drawer of the desk before she took my hand.

"It's nothing, Hud. I promise."

I brushed my hand over her chin and leaned my head against hers as we waited for the elevator, not for one second believing that it was nothing. *She would tell me when she was ready.*

Turning her face into the crook of my neck, she deflected my question with a confession I hadn't been expecting.

"You look at me like no one else ever has before. You look at me like I'm-"

"Beautiful?" I interrupted her, shaking my head in disbelief at the words that fell from her full lips. Who had hurt this girl so badly that she didn't see how goddamn beautiful she was?

I didn't call her mine lightly. From the moment I saw her eating her lunch just outside of this hospital, I was hooked on her.

Hooked on her beauty. Hooked on her innocence.

I was just fucking hooked for her.

If I had to tell her every minute we spent together how gorgeous and perfect she was to me, I'd do it.

Because she was.

Her eyes snapped to mine at the word and a slow, shy smile spread over her face. As I pressed my mouth to the top of her head, I felt her melt into the touch.

"I really want to believe it when you say it."

As I led her into the elevator car and held her close, I whispered in her ear.

"I'll keep saying it until you do, Darlin'."

13

EMBERLY

"Stay in the car, Darlin'. I just want to check something," I heard his voice as the car engine turned off and I opened my eyes, blinking the sleep from them. On the way home I must have dozed off and Hudson had let me sleep the whole way home.

"Is everything okay?" I murmured, worried at the obvious concern in his steely, blue eyes. He nodded his head and rubbed a slow, soothing hand over my back, telling me it would be okay. But, I wasn't so sure.

"Okay." He kissed my cheek before letting himself out of the drivers side of his car and watching him wander into my garage, I gasped aloud when I saw what had him so worried. He'd turned on the overhead light on his way inside and it shone over my car, my beautiful little Mustang splattered with thick lines of red ink, but could have easily been blood, too. It was vandalized with words that left me shaking and suddenly afraid, as if at any moment the culprate would jump out at me. I took a few deep breaths, telling myself it was just some teenager playing a prank on me but my gut told me an opposite story.

It had been him. The man that stalked not only my best friend, Ashlee but me, too for the past month. If he had somehow gotten into my home and hacked the security code that locked my garage door, he could break in at any moment.

Even when I'm alone...

"Oh my god..." The cry left me on a sudden sob and fumbling with the door handle, I fled from the car as a need for air settled inside of my quaking chest. I had to get out of there. I had to breathe. And locked up in that hot car was suffocating me.

As I broke into a sprint in the opposite way of my house, I had one, repeating thought.

Run.

※

"Emberly! Fuck!" His deep and rough, angered voice trailed not very far behind me and biting at my lower lip in hopes of stemming the tears that continued to wet my cheeks, I ran faster.

Stupid!

God. I'd been so stupid to think that I could escape my past and find a man like Hudson; good, gentle, rough, sinful... If it was even possible to be a complete and utter contradiction, he was. He was all of those things and more. And when I was with him, I wanted it. I wanted all of him and more, more, more. But if seeing the letter from my father hadn't done a number on my resolve to move on from the dark, dark place my past had been, the message painted across my car did.

The letter... the texts... the vandalizing of my car...

They were all puzzle pieces that succeeded in tearing apart my belief that good things could last for me and even though Hudson was still here, he wouldn't want me after I told him my past, my secrets, my shame...

Even thinking about it created dreadful chills to skate down my neck and spine, reminding me of the danger that still touched my seemingly safe life. I'd left everything behind back home, not willing to take even an ounce of my past with me when I left for nursing school and later, my placement at the hospital. It wasn't much, but it was my life. It was a life where I was happy, content. I didn't have to look over my shoulder every second of the day, I didn't have to live in fear.

At least, that was what I thought.

Now? I was terrified, all over again.

"Hey, hey, it's okay, Darlin'. I'm here and I promise you, nothing will touch you as long as that's true." His voice was like liquid fire and the softest cotton, all at once. Hard with a determination he couldn't hide, even if he tried and laced with affection that I instantly wanted more of. Warm breath bathed the side of my neck while my fisted hands rested against his wide, hard chest, intent on pushing him away before it was too late for either of us. I didn't get to have this. My past wasn't going to let me go and he deserved so much more than the pieces I had left to give him.

Clenching my urgent fingers into the fine material of his shirt, I had to shake my head a few times before I was able to speak, unsure if my voice would hold.

"I don't- we can't do this anymore, Hud. We just can't." The words rushed out of me, the meaning behind them causing my chest to heave with anxiety and my heart to beat a frantic, hurried beat. The frown that marred his otherwise expression less face told me he didn't agree and with a shaky exhale, I did what I should have done in the beginning. I pushed him away.

"I'm sorry but I don't think you should protect me anymore." He rocked his head back and I watched his hair fall in front of his eyes as he shook his head at me, his frustration darkening his normally pale blue irises. I shook with the gravity of what I was doing, knowing it was one of those moments I would look back on and regret and also knowing that I couldn't change my mind.

This was for the best. If I let myself feel the crazy way he made me feel, I'd hurt him. Maybe not today. Maybe not tomorrow. But I would. Loving me would wreck him and the mere pieces I had of my heart wouldn't be enough to do his justice. I knew someday he would find a girl that could be what he needed. I just wasn't her. I couldn't be, right?

"I don't fucking protect you because of some detail, Em. I do it because I love you." He gritted out in a rough, aggravated whisper and silence met his declaration because in that moment, I found it hard to breathe; never mind speak coherently. He'd stolen my breath straight from my lungs. Was that even remotely possible? With him, I had a feeling it was.

It couldn't be true. He was my body guard. My protector. My lover...

As that revelation settled in my gut another one stopped my heartbeat, all together.

I loved him, too.

14

HUDSON

*S*he was as quiet as a mouse as she stood in front of me, her wet hair matted to her forehead from the downpour of rain that started not long after she ran out on me, never looking back until I'd forced her to face me as I'd chased her.

Never chased a woman in my fucking life but when she disappeared on me, there wasn't a second thought in my mind. She was all that mattered. I'd run to the ends of the world for her, if I had to. I was reminded of how my parents always told me that falling in love was the easiest part of a relationship. It was making that love last that was the true struggle and if you truly cared for and respected her, she'd never have a reason to leave.

I wasn't completely sure that was true, with Emberly. She was stubborn and jaded and so beautiful it sometimes physically hurt me to look at her. Her beauty shone brighter when she looked at me, with such love I was overwhelmed.

Did she know she looked at me that way?

Had she ever truly felt love in her life?

I doubted it and if that were true, it really didn't matter to me. I was here now and I didn't care how long I had to wait, I would make her see that a love like ours was possible. All she had to do was realize it.

"You can't, Hudson." Shaking her head, she tried once more to push me away, her dainty, little hands pressing against my chest as if she'd be able to budge me. Smiling wide, I dropped my head to rest against hers and claimed her mouth with mine in a hot, searing kiss I knew she'd feel down to her damn bones; one I hoped would get through that thick wall she kept around her big, beautiful heart. And when she moaned softly into my mouth and slid her fingers through my hair with a slight tug for more, I knew I had her.

Right. Fucking. Here.

"I don't know how to do this, Hud. I've never..." Her sweet voice trailed off as I slid my tongue down the pale column of her neck, earning another distracted moan from her lush lips. God, I loved those lips.

"Doesn't matter, baby. What matters is this..." Linking our hands together in a tight, seemingly unbreakable clinch, I raised them to my mouth where I kissed her fingertips and pressed our joined hands over my chest, where I knew she could feel my racing heart beat. I was finally getting all of her and I was a starved man, soaking up every ounce of my girl before she disappeared again.

"Us, Em. All that matters is us. Yeah?" Quickly nodding, she reached up and cupped my cheek in one of her small hands. She met my eyes with wide, understanding ones and that look of love? It shone in spades.

"I forgot something." She whispered, slowly rubbing her thumb over the hard line of my jaw as she spoke. Frowning, I arched an eyebrow at her and her warm, deep laugh met my ears before she caved and told me.

"I love you so much, Hudson. No matter what happens tomorrow, I'll love you."

Bliss. Grinning against her lips, I kissed her fucking breathless.

I laid Emberly on the bed as soon as I stepped inside her bedroom. Then I moved to the wall beside the door, flipped on the light, kicked the door shut at the same time. It had been a long month of watching her from afar.

Looking at her.

Watching her. Imagining all the ways I would take her.

Was this the moment I would take her?

Fuck, I hoped so.

"We don't have to do anything, Darlin'. I need you to know that. If all you want to do is sit here and watch some sappy ass movie that's what we'll do. But I gotta tell you," I paused to take a breath, then lowered to brush my mouth to her forehead, leaving it there as I finished what I was telling her.

I felt her hands come up to my sides, expecting her to push me back and away from her. To tell me I was wrong, that we were moving too fast, that she needed more time.

But she didn't do any of that. She dug her fingers into my shirt and slowly lifted it up.

"I. Fucking. Want. You." I growled the words into her ear and she melted against me, whispering my name, making me want her even more.

Not a minute later, my T-shirt fell to the floor and so did my leathers.

"Body, heart, soul- every fucking inch of you. Em, I just want you."

Her all too expressive eyes met mine then and she smiled shyly, nodding her head.

When her mouth pressed to my neck and her hands pressed to my chest, fingernails grazing over hot, over-heated skin, I groaned loudly.

Shit. I needed her naked. *Now.* I needed to take her and make her mine. *Mine.*

"Lay back."

She nodded and slowly pressed her head into the pink covered pillow.

Lust and fevered hunger raced through my veins as I moved to the end of the bed and begun unlacing her black converse sneakers. I felt her eyes watching me and I looked up, piercing her with what I hoped was a hungry look.

I was teetering between maddening lust and uncontrollable need for this damn girl and I hoped to God I'd have the capacity to be gentle with her tonight.

Her sneakers were slipped off her feet and I took my time drawing her lace stockings from them, too. I knelt between her parted legs and reached for the hem of her long, flowy skirt making sure to keep my eyes on her for any sign of uncertainty in those vibrant eyes of hers.

"You okay?"

Nodding excitedly, she gripped my hands that were grasping the soft fabric of her skirt, ready to rip it off of her the moment she told me to.

"I-" She stopped, her eyes closing and her chest moving rapidly as she tried to calm herself. As I waited, my thumbs rubbed gently over her hip bones.

She opened her violet eyes again and they captivated me with the trust in them.

"I want this so much," She whispered, her hands moving under mine to slip the hem of her skirt down her legs, her eyes holding mine intently.

"I want to be yours, Hudson."

The moment the words were out of her perfect mouth, I knew I was done for.

Fuck, she had no idea what those words did to me.

My control snapped.

15

EMBERLY

*M*y heart beat sped at a lightning speed as Hudson's cool, minty breath met my neck and he kissed a line down the skin there and to my shoulder. Moving the collar of my blouse away, he began to torture the skin there, moving on to my bare shoulder where he left playful nips and licks. My skin was pebbled in goosebumps and I all but hummed with pleasure beneath him.

"Have you ever been claimed, Darlin'?"

His words brushed along my warmed skin and I arched into his body in response.

I'd never had this crazy attraction to a man before, not only that I had never wanted it. Men were the reason my heart had been broken over and over again as I watched my father hurt my mother each night as a young girl.

Men were the reason I distrusted the world and almost everything it consisted of. I never thought I would be proven wrong. I never thought it was possible to meet a man like Hudson Lennox.

But here I was.

It scared me how deeply I wanted him, yearned for him, but I knew fighting it would be like fighting the inevitable.

My feelings for him were undeniable.

I had no hope of escaping our attraction and if I was honest with myself?

I didn't want to.

"No." I whispered, reaching down to push my hands in smooth locks of his hair. He groaned against my touch, pushed up my blouse to just under my breasts before diving in and kissing down my stomach, stopping at my hip bones. I blushed fiercely, shame rushing through my veins as I watched him lean back on his knees between my legs and just *look at me.*

Ugly.

Fat.

Unworthy.

My self hatred whispered inside my head, threatening to push away the joyful pleasure I had felt just moments ago.

"Breathe, Emberly. I can see that mind of yours going a mile a minute."

I tried to do as he said but fear of what he saw when he looked at me bore down on me like a tidal wave and I couldn't shake it.

"You're going to be mine but first I need to know what just happened that made you lock up like that."

I took a breath, finally looking down at him.

Expecting to see disinterest in his gaze, my mouth parted on a gasp when I witnessed the full on *hunger* he had for me in his eyes.

He wanted me.

I reached down and helped him remove my top from my body and then grasped his hands in mine as I told him.

"I don't want you to..."

"Reject *you?*"

His eyes dilated slightly as he heard what I was trying to say and before I knew what was happening, my mouth was crushed under his.

He kissed me roughly, like he couldn't help himself, like he needed this kiss to breathe and on a sigh I parted my mouth for his entry.

The first long, slow lick of his tongue over mine caused need to coil in my lower belly and to pool heavily between my legs.

I whispered his name against the kiss and felt him sigh as he pulled fractionally away.

"You are so fucking beautiful it takes my breath away when I look at you. When I saw you for the first time, as I'm sure you could tell, I wasn't expecting it. I was having a pretty shitty day. But meeting you made all of that fucked up shit disappear and that's what you do to me *every day*. I was hired to protect your best friend but in all honesty? I only stayed on her detail to be close to you."

Leaning forward onto his elbows, his body caged mine in and his hands, rough skinned and callused, whispered over my face.

"Do you believe me, Darlin'? That your perfect, to me? Because if I have to spend the entire night telling you that; I will."

Shaking my head at him, I smiled softly at his need to make me see what he already knew. I wished I could see myself the way he did and I was pretty sure by the time morning came, I would.

"I do. I believe you."

Relief sparkled in his eyes then, causing the pale blues in them to appear almost white.

Reaching down to grasp my waist, Hudson lowered his mouth to my collarbone where he teased the sensitive skin, making a moan to fall from my lips.

"Oh, god."

"You ready to be mine?"

Nodding, I pulled his face up from my chest and kissed him with all the desire and urgency that filled me in that moment. Nothing but giving myself to him would calm the affect he'd had on me and I knew, without a doubt, that I was ready to do just that.

This was the moment I let myself take a chance and I prayed he would take care of me.

"Please."

❀

Hudson's large, thick fingers slipped under the fabric of my laced panties and the action stopped my heart for a beat.

This was it.

My bra fell away from my body next and my eyes closed on a breathy sigh when his mouth lowered to my jaw, my neck, the sensitive spot behind my ear.

It was as if he knew all of my body's sweet spots and was honing in on them all at the same time.

It felt amazing.

The full, wet feel of his mouth venturing down the slope of my throat caused a moan to leave me because I knew where he was heading.

"Fuck, I could look at you all night and never tire from it."

His voice fell over my skin like sandpaper, rough and laced with sex.

A hot, hungered mouth caught the tip of one of my peaked nipples, causing toe curling need to unfurl beneath my skin, inside my belly, then finally settling where I needed him the most.

Suddenly, I was surrounded by him.

His *scent*- mint and spiced cologne.

His *hands*- large and demanding.

His mouth- licking and biting and kissing me senseless.

I was *lost*.

When his tongue traced down the apex of my thighs and his eyes, dark and filled with hunger, met mine, I gasped at the intensity I saw in them.

"Tell me your mine, Emberly."

I nodded, breathless.

"I'm yours, Hud."

His mouth dove straight for my center then, his sinful tongue tracing the outer folds of my pussy before it entered me.

"Oh god, right there, *Hudson!*"

I couldn't help but moan out his name, helpless to his ministrations on my sex, my entire body lighting up underneath him. Every thought of anything else slipped from my mind and there was just *him.*

Him, tending to me.

Him, kissing me.

Him, all but devouring me.

And it was impossible to deny that I wanted this.

I wanted him more than my next breath.

He leaned up on his elbows as he ate me, just like that.

The whiskers of his beard burned the smooth skin of my thighs and his teeth scraped tortuously over my flesh, enticing low moans from my lips as I neared the edge of oblivion.

My muscles began to tense as my orgasm neared, the tsunami of pleasure threatening to shoot me into sensations I was sure I had never experienced.

"Give it to me, Darlin'. *Come* for me."

At his roughly spoken words and one last sharp pull of my swollen clit, I did.

I screamed his name loudly as every synapse in my body fired all at once and I shuddered blissfully through the most intense orgasm I had ever felt.

Before the tremors that wracked my body let up, I felt Hudson cup me between my legs and a thrill of arousal sped through me.

"I don't want to hurt you so were going to take this slow."

I nodded meekly as one of his fingers slipped between my swollen folds, closely followed by a second. I felt utterly stretched as he pushed those two thick, callused fingers through my lips and toyed with my hyper sensitive folds before drawing them away. He repeated the action at least twice more before I heard the sound of his pants dropping to the floor. My eyes, wide and curious, flew down his hard, sculpted chest, the gathering of black hair that lined his stomach and happy trail. The sight of what lay in his hand then widened my eyes and created a deep ache in my stomach as I panted beneath him, every molecule in my body primed for his taking.

I didn't think I had ever needed something as much I needed him in that moment.

I had spent all of my life just getting by. I plastered on a smile and said the right things, did all of the things I was expected to do but I now realized I hadn't really been *living*. Knowing Hudson had been a shock to my system.

I knew people would say our relationship was fast.

Rushed.

Abnormal.

Intense.

All of those words would be true.

But I knew with a startling clarity as he parted my thighs even farther apart and knelt between them that I was safe with this man.

"Look at me, Emberly."

I did. The sky blues in his eyes were darkened with possessive need and I felt the same affliction tear through the jaded walls of my heart.

He graced me with a full on, no holds barred smile and I felt my lips tipping up in one of return before my breath stilled on a gasp. The large head of his cock rested against my lips, before he gently rubbed his hands up my bared thighs and I shivered in anticipation. The softened touch created tingles of calm to pebble my skin, allowing every muscle of my body to relax as Hudson readied to take me.

"I won't last like this, baby. I want to make this so good for you. I want this to be the best sex of your life."

A soft laugh bubbled up from my chest as he teased me, knowing that it would *in fact* be the best of my life.

It was my first time, after all.

A small part of my mind told me that making love with Hudson Lennox would be anything but gentle. Everything about him was the complete opposite of what I'd imagined my first time being.

I bit down on my lips as I toyed with the idea of how he would take me.

Would he take his time? Would he tease me?

I didn't have to wonder for much longer, though.

On a rock of his thick hips, Hudson pushed inside of me and I lost the ability to breathe for a few seconds as I felt the utter *fullness* of him inside me.

My core clenched with need and my stomach knotted as a sharp, shooting pain burst from between my legs and settled deep in my chest.

He caged me in like that, his large, muscular body all around me and his mouth one one of my pointed breasts, teasing with slow licks of his tongue.

"It feels... I didn't know it would feel like this." I whispered, almost to myself rather than the man loving my body.

I felt his fingers graze my cheek bone as he looked at me, a mixture of concern and hungered lust masking his normally stoic face.

"Like what?" He rubbed his lips up my neck and nipped my lips playfully before I parted them for his tongues entry. I soft moan left me as he took a taste of me, his hips locked against mine while my body struggled to adjust to his size.

"Like heaven."

Soon the pain between my legs lessened and my craving for him to move took my body over. I squirmed beneath his weight, pulling back from his wet kiss to beg him to move. But he must have known because before I could take another breath, he was pulling out of me, the slick head of him dragging over the bundle of swollen nerves inside my folds.

The absence of him inside of me made my walls contract and by the glint in Hudson's eyes, he'd noticed.

"You want me inside you, don't you, Darlin'?"

Nodding eagerly, his name was ripped from my mouth when he pushed deep once again, this time he didn't stop until he was all the way inside of me and not one inch of space was separating our bodies.

My body came alive with pleasure as he continued to drag himself out of my channel, pushing back in even harder, with more force than the last. His thrusts became quicker and my heart pounded a heavy rhythm as I soared to the brink of orgasm again, only this time I knew I wouldn't be the only one feeling pleasure. Hudson was right there on the brink with me.

"Hudson, I'm so close. I'm going to... c- come..."

My breaths came in fast, hiccuped sounds the higher my body flew.

"Fuck, you're so snug, so perfect for me. I knew it would be like this. So perfect, so right."

I arched up as Hudson's head lowered and his warm, wet lips caught one of my nipples between his teeth while he tortured the other between his thumbs and the sensations became too much for my body to handle.

"Hudson!" I screamed his name, a deep blush covering my face as I heard the cathartic sound being pulled from my throat. My walls spasmed as I came, my body going to pieces beneath him. With one full rock of his hips, I felt the rush of his orgasm coating my inner walls as he finally gave himself over to his own pleasure and I closed my eyes in the aftermath of what I knew would be *the best* sex I had ever had.

Hudson Lennox had ruined me and healed me and *loved* my body like nothing I had ever imagined. A blanket of sated calm settled over me.

"Fuck, Em, my Em." Hudson pushed his hands through my

hair that splayed over the pillow under my head, the touch gentle as he tipped my chin up and kissed me soft and sweetly. Bliss and sated need hummed slowly through my veins as I parted my mouth on a sigh, tasting the taste of peppermints and coffee on his lips.

"Hudson." I breathed as he drew away, a heart stopping smile spread over his face that I knew would make my knees go weak and my heart to tremble if I wasn't lost in him already. But, I was.

My fingers sunk into his hair and I smiled against his kiss.

"I knew It," I breathed, "I lost myself in you."

As he kissed me again, his smile widened and a twinkle of mischief sparked in his pale blue eyes, causing my belly to dip.

"Get used to it."

16

EMBERLY

A loud, sudden crash in the hallway jarred me awake from a deep, restful sleep and blinking the sleep from my eyes, I looked for Hudson in the space next to me, but came up empty.

Did he have to go in to work? It was Saturday morning and I was sure he'd taken the weekend off, as I had the weekend off from the hospital and often enough; where I was, so was he.

I slowly padded into the hallway, flicking the light-switch on the wall before finding the source of what woke me. A glass tumbler had been knocked off of the kitchen counter and I had a feeling as to how when I saw a bare chested Hudson standing in the dimly lit room, hands clenched tightly into fists at his sides. The muscles of his bared chest and shoulders clenched tautly, the power in his stance rolling off of him in waves. I shivered at the sight.

"Hud, baby, what's wrong?"

As if he'd only then noticed me hovering in the hallway, his steely, blue gaze snapped up to my face before they glazed over with a darkness I'd never seen before. My heart begun beating faster and my breaths became shallow, a familiar sense of dread filling my stomach.

Had he changed his mind about us after last night?

I watched as Hudson moved one of his hands from his side and grasped the cell phone I hadn't noticed laying on the kitchen island. Punk, glittery case, white frame...

Shit. It was mine.

"Want to explain this shit to me, Emberly?"

Hesitantly taking my iPhone from his hands, I glanced at the screen noticing the unknown number I'd come to memorize over the past two weeks since the overnight break in at the hospital.

Linda had said it was nothing, but I knew it had been a warning from whoever was stalking us. With each chilling message I found in my inbox, though, the more I realized that whoever was behind them wasn't looking for just Ashlee. He was after me, too.

Just Now, Unknown: We'll be together soon.

It read and I trembled as the words registered, fear permeating my chest and squeezing my heart in its grasp.

"I expect an answer." The rough, deep, voice came from Hudson and I momentarily stalled, biting my lips, not knowing what to say. He was so still, so quiet, so cold and I knew, beyond anything else- I'd done that to him. It was then I realized how unfair I had been to him. I hadn't trusted him enough to tell him, to confide in him. This man wasn't what I thought he was when we'd met. He was loyal, with a good heart that was honest to a fault.

How could I tell him that at the time the texts started, I wasn't sure if I could trust him? That I hadn't wanted to let this sick man, this stalker ruin what we had? I wasn't an *easy* person to love. I knew that.

I had enough insecurities to drive any man away, even the persistent, determined one standing in front of me, as large as a brick wall.

I wanted to trust in him about all of this but at the time, I just couldn't make that leap yet. I was scared to let him into my heart, knowing that it could very easily be broken. I opened my mouth to say something, to somehow ease his anger by finding out like this.

Before I could he was turning away from me, pulling his large, rough hands through his hair, his thick fingers gripping the smooth strands with what I knew now to be disappointment.

He wasn't angry that I'd received these messages and he didn't hate me.

I had so many opportunities to tell him the truth about... everything.

And yet... I didn't.

"What else are you fucking hiding from me?"

"Nothing! Hud... I'm sorry. I received the first message right before our first date, when you took me to the chinese restaurant. I was just admitting to myself that I wanted us and I thought that It would rock the boat. I didn't want that, Hudson. I wanted us to have time to just be together. Just you and me."

My chest heaved with a sob that crawled its way up my throat and I closed my eyes, willing my emotions in check. If this was the end for us...

"Look at me, Darlin'." His voice sounded much closer than before and I swore I could actually feel the heat emanating from his body, seeping into my skin.

"I'm sorry, Hud..."

"I *know* you are. I'm not angry with you."

My wide, wet eyes snapped open at his words and when I saw the affectionate warmth swimming in his beautiful blue gaze, I felt my entire body sag with the relief of it.

"When I saw you, I knew I shouldn't have gone there. I knew that if I let myself wish for something as pure as you, I would be done for. I know you've been let down before, baby and I can't take those memories away from you,"

He paused to let his course fingertips trail down my cheek, his hand gently holding my face as he shook his head, in a way

I'd come to recognize as bewilderment. He thought he didn't deserve me but he was so wrong.

It was me who wasn't deserving.

I had let my past and my worry of getting hurt in the future get between us and in doing so, I'd hurt this beautiful, crazy man. All he'd ever done was protect me and I'd kept pushing him away.

As he gave me a soft, reverent kiss on the top of my head, I swayed into the touch knowing that this was it. This was the moment I stopped pushing happiness from my otherwise void life. I was ready to let him in. If anyone was capable of carrying a woman like me, it was him.

My Hudson. I would *never* push him away, again.

"If you let me, I will make sure you are *never* hurt again, Emberly. But this is it, Darlin'. No more secrets. No more lies. No more walls. You're mine, got it?" I loved that even though his words were raw and his eyes were hard with determination, his voice was filled with the adoration I knew he felt for me, an affliction I felt in my own heavy, fastening heart.

"Yes." I pled in desperation, arching my neck in order to reach his mouth, my hands grappling for traction around his shoulders and I kissed him; pouring every ounce of regret and aching need into the connection of our lips.

"Em," No sooner had he uttered the cracked whisper that he had me lifted onto the cold, granite island and tugged my sleep shorts from beneath me, leaving them dangling loosely around my ankles as he nudged my thighs apart, making room for him between them. Feeling the callused fingers of his tanned, hands gliding up my legs, I clenched my core tightly, an oh so delightful ache in the place I longed for him to claim.

"I need you." Sparks flew beneath my skin as he dropped his head to my heated skin and licked a long, tortuous trail up my inner thigh leaving a delicious burn of his stubbled chin over my flesh. It was rough and sweet and it was Hudson. As I reached for his hair and tugged gently, I wanted so much more than he was giving me. There was not another word spoken before Hudson wrapped his hands around my hips and urged me to part my legs wider for him.

"More," he whispered and I obeyed, opening to him and moaning cathartically while he began kissing down my lower belly to my core. I ached for him so much.

"You are so fucking beautiful, Em, baby. I can't get enough," he murmured as his mouth came in contact with my opening. He rubbed up and down, teasing me and then finally, God, he settled in to taste me. Slow, long licks and soft nips to my flesh almost drove me to the point of a crushing climax, almost had me tumbling over into the abyss- but not quite.

Hudson hummed against my core, pressing two fingers inside me and rubbing in slow, deep circles. My skin lit up, my heart soared, and my sex clenched around him in an effort to make him go faster. I need-

"Aah - yes!" I called out suddenly as Hudson licked and pulled and devoured me in that wonderful way of his. I climbed higher and higher to ecstasy, so high that I knew this was going to be a high I'd never touched before.

"Please... Feels... Going to come, baby. Faster..." I moaned as the waves crashed through me, ripped me open and made me soar into orgasm.

"Let go, Darlin'. I've got you," Hudson whispered and when he sucked my clit hard and fast, - I fell.

"Oh, god!" I cried out, letting my eyes fall closed as a lay rapt in the pleasure he'd given me.

"Bed," he murmured into the hollow of my neck, before he scooped me into his arms and carried me towards the bedroom, weightless and *oh* so loved.

17

EMBERLY

"*How* do you feel?"

I blinked my eyes open against the soft light of my bedroom and I rolled gently over so my head rested against his shoulder. Looking up at him, I saw the gentility and possession in them, like the two sides of him were fighting each other within his eyes.

The soft- blue and bright, filled with playful mischief and humor.

The hard- a deeper shade of blue that was filled with hunger and an intensity that stole my breath away. I was coming to like both sides of Hudson and as I lifted up to kiss him, I felt his chuckle against my lips.

"Answer me, baby."

"Wanted." I murmured, my confession hung in the air between us heavily.

"Emberly." He groaned, pulling away from my mouth before taking my face into his grasp with a rough touch.

"You'll never feel anything less again. I'm going to *cherish* you"

Nodding, I leaned against the hand holding my face and somehow, found myself believing him.

I would let myself doubt this tomorrow, but for now I was content to believe in the moment, in this night with him.

"I know."

When he swept his mouth over mine again, I sighed into the kiss, but it ended way too quickly.

"Let me make you some dinner."

"Okay."

"Are you going to take me home now?"

I asked, my head resting against the back of the couch after a heaping meal of roast chicken and winter squash. Hudson stood against the large, wooden doorway of the living room and he smiled, slowly at first until that smile split across his face and the sight of it knocked my heart into over drive.

He had to know what that smile did to me. I thought to myself.

"No," He moved in front of me before lifting me by my hips until I was yet again, settled against his large, hard lined body.

"I want to spend the day with you."

Excitement bubbled in my chest as I nodded and with a gentle tug of his hands on my shoulders, he kissed me. The kiss wasn't like our last; soft and sweet after he'd made me come better than I ever had. Oh, no.

The kiss he gave me now was a claim. An owning. A passionate dance of lips and soft breath and his delectable tongue taking a long pull from my mouth before he drew back.

"I can't fucking think when I'm around you, Darlin'."

I blinked up into his heated gaze and felt the deep, scarlet blush rush to my face. My body hummed from the sensation of his kisses and his gentle touch at my hips, my waist, my belly. Awareness rushed into my veins to chase away the warmth his touch had given me when I felt his large, searching hands skim over the slight bubble in my mid section.

"I love your body." He whispered, his deep, rough toned

voice next to my ear helped ease my nervousness a moment before.

I knew he liked me and I loved that he did.

But my self awareness of my curves was something hard to ignore, even with his hands on me. The therapist I had been seeing for the past few years had helped me with those feelings of unworthiness.

But they still lay under the surface as I tried like hell to ignore them. I felt Hudson's fingers move to my chin and take hold before moving my face to the side and up to meet his stare.

There was hunger and softness laying in it and instantly, any other emotion within me vanished but the feeling of safety he brought me.

No one made me feel truly safe in my life, but somehow, he did.

"I love your eyes, so bright and full of life." He said on a slight growl and heat began to pool between my legs again. My want for him was taking over every molecule and cell, every inch of my heated skin and each breath I sucked through my lips. My mind wrapped around the word he had now said twice and cautious, almost undetectable hope begun to form inside of me.

I wrapped my arms around his strong, tautly muscled shoulders and he spoke in my ear, the rough whiskers of his beard rubbing against my face and neck.

"I love your kind heart. You care so much, maybe more than you should and it makes me want to be better, so that I can deserve you."

He edged away from me and I sagged, my knees feeling weak from the loss of our physical contact and his deep, rumbly voice.

"I will deserve you, Em."

Hudson cupped my chin again and pressed his face to mine until our foreheads were touching.

A soft breath left my lips as my mind cleared and I whispered,

"You already do, Hudson."

He smiled, one of those heart stopping smiles and sure enough, my heart beat halted for a few seconds as the intensity of his stare and the connection, electric and full of possibilities, hummed between us.

Taking my hands in his, he pulled me back into his chest and whispered in my ear.

"Come back to bed with me."

Nodding, I couldn't think of anything I wanted more than to do just that.

"Okay." I followed him up the stairs and couldn't help feasting my eyes on his round ass the entire way.

God, I wanted him.

I always would, I thought to myself.

The loud, sudden sound of his cell phone ringing fell between us and he turned to face me, his hand going to the front, left pocket of his pants to fish out the device.

"Fuck, I'm sorry. Do you mind if I take this?"

Shaking my head, I kissed his whiskered cheek before going into the bedroom ahead of him. I didn't want to intrude into his phone call, though I knew he wouldn't mind if I had. One thing I had learned about that man was that he was an open book. He was upfront and honest with me from the moment we met and that was something I admired.

I hoped I could give him that same respect when the time came to tell him of my past, my family, the real reason I had left my small town life and moved to the big city of Austin to work at the hospital.

I just didn't think I was ready to tell him yet.

Slipping past the door, I shed my jacket and shoes and hummed in appreciation as I got into the bed. My body sank into the soft mattress and my head rested on the plush memory foam pillow I loved so much as I waited for Hudson to join me.

I wondered what the phone call could be about at this hour of the night.

It could have been a call from the station or maybe his mother checking in on him. I hadn't even met the woman that raised him yet but I knew, just from the way he spoke of her that he adored her. She had raised a hell of a son, after all. My legs shifted on the bed and time seemed to go on and on as I waited there.

Sitting up from the pillows, I sighed.

What was taking him so long?

Was everything okay?

A loud ringing sound stopped my train of thought and I begrudgingly got out of the bed and padded on bare feet to where I left my jacket, I saw Hudson's sister, Harper was calling me. We had met up a few times for coffee or drinks at a local bar and hit it off instantly. While Hudson was brash and protective, his younger sister was fierce and kind hearted.

"Hey, girl. How was your date?"

She'd been on a date with her girlfriend, Bryn. They were the cutest couple and I loved seeing them together, smitten with one another.

I settled back into my spot on the bed as I spoke, excitement filling my belly to hear all the juicy details of her night.

"It got cut short, Em. I don't know how to tell you this."

My breath stilled in my throat at the sound of her choppy voice and instantly, I knew something wasn't right. I had expected her to be excited and happy, like she always was after being with Bryn.

But something must have happened because none of that was in her voice, now. She was upset.

A gnawing feeling sank low in my gut then and I knew, without a shadow of a doubt that something wasn't right.

"What happened, Harper?"

"There was an accident, Em. The doctors don't know if he will be okay. I know y-your with Hudson tonight but-"

"Who was in an accident? Are you okay?"

"It... it wasn't me. Tristan and Ashlee met us at the restaurant since we were both drinking and offered to drive us home. Tristan was taken to the hospital."

Oh god, no.

I shushed Harper as she cried over the phone, my shaking hands already pulling a clean pair of jeans up my legs, my heart in my throat.

Tristan was just as much a brother to her as Hudson and I knew how shaken she was by the news. I gasped as I realized just how hard it all would hit him.

"I'm coming to you, okay, Harper? I'll be there before you know it."

"You don't have to-"

"Yes, we do. I'll see you soon."

I hung up before she could hear the tears in voice, my fear so palpable it felt as if a fist was squeezing my heart in a vise grip.

This couldn't be happening. I thought to myself. I was pulling my jacket and boots back on when the door was pushed open and Hudson's footsteps rushed inside the room.

"I'm sorry, I have to go-"

My head whipped in his direction at his words and I saw his wide, pain filled blue eyes take in my appearance before his body was charging forward and into mine.

"Fuck, Darlin'. Don't cry. It's gonna be okay."

He swept me close by large, sure hands on my hip bones and I went eagerly into the embrace he gave me. My face landed on his chest and my hands clutched at his leather jacket. My hold on him was desperate and his was unwavering.

"Did Harper call you, too?" I whispered after my heart beat had returned to a some what safe level. I felt him shake his head and then his mouth pressed a kiss to my nape, calming me with the gentle touch of lips.

"My mom did. They are all at the hospital with Tristan. We've gotta go, now."

I nodded, inwardly trying to calm myself. As he rubbed my back and whispered in my ear that it would all be okay, I eventually felt calm enough to move away from the solace of his arms. The moment I did, Hudson took my hand in his and kissed the inside of my wrist.

"He's going to be alright, he's a fucking fighter, baby."

Nodding, I let him lead me out to the car.

My hand was captured in Hudson's much larger one when we parked outside of the hospital. Somehow, it felt different to me to be here. Though I spent half of my time in this very hospital, it didn't feel the same to me.

I felt Hudson tug on my hand that rested against the arm rest between us and my eyes lifted to his. Concern was etched across his face, that smile he'd given me not even an hour before no where to be found. I knew we were both filled with worry, but I still hated seeing it mar his handsome face.

"You ready?"

His deep voice calmed my erratic heart as I nodded. I had to be.

Our friends needed us.

The bright halls of the hospital were lined with patients and family members when we entered the emergency room where Hudson's mother had told him to meet her. That gnawing feeling in my stomach only grew the further we walked and I hoped fervently that Tristan was okay.

"Emberly! Thank god, you're here."

Ashlee stood by the window across the room and breaking away from Hudson's hold on my hand, I rushed toward her.

She was a mess. I never would have told her that out loud, but it was the first thought that flew through my mind as I wrapped my arms around her and felt her bury her face in my shoulder on a low sob.

"I'm so sorry, Ash. I came as soon as I could"

"I know." She whispered, moving away after a few minutes and wiping her face with the cotton sleeve of her sweat shirt.

"How is he?"

Hudson's voice was behind me, deep and tinged with worry and sadness.

I reached my hand for him and came up empty.

I looked back at him but he had his intense blue eyes trained on Ashlee as she struggled to maintain her composure.

God, I hated this for her.

"They placed him in a temporary coma to let his body heal. He was driving and some asshole hit us head on. We had no where to go, there was no way he could have seen the guy coming."

Another fat tear fell from her eyes and I pulled her in my arms again, gently rocking her in hopes of calming her down.

"He's a fighter. It will be okay."

She sniffs into my t-shirt and vigorously shakes her head.

My heart was squeezed in a vice grip as I held onto my best friend, knowing I couldn't make any of this better for her. If the worst happened...

Would she be okay?

Would Hudson?

To anyone else, it wouldn't seem like his loss would be as great.

Sure, they were partners.

Sure, they broke down doors and made arrests side by side.

But Tristan wasn't just his partner at the police station.

He wasn't just a guy he spent hours on end with or a man that he scarcely knew.

He was his best friend.

His brother, in almost every sense of the word.

They were thick as thieves and had a friendship built on mutual respect, trust and brotherhood.

If his injuries were too severe and his doctors weren't able to stitch him up, if the very worst of outcomes happened, it would shatter him.

"I love him, Em."

"I know, Ash. We all do."

Her cries muffled in my shoulder as she leaned into my body for support and I let her. I let her break down in this moment, because I knew she needed it. She needed to know that she could feel the pain of this news and be stronger for it when Tristan would need her, the most.

If he woke up.

"Emberly."

The sound of the heavy, rumbly voice that came from behind us had shivers of longing shoving my fears at bay and after kissing Ashlee's cheek and gently releasing her, I turned my head to meet his eyes; the eyes I knew held just as much worry and love as my own did.

"I need my woman, *now*."

Nodding, I turned my gaze back to Ashlee's, watching her regain her composure on the cusp of the emotions she must have been struggling with. She shook her head gently once and then leans forward to wrap her arms around my neck again. Feeling her shaking breaths against my hair had me holding her just as tightly as she held me and when she pulled away, I had to force back the sudden emotion clouding my eyes at the thought that the loving person she was would be lost if we lost him.

He had to be okay.

"He needs you, too, Em. My moms here and Tristan's sisters are on their way. I'll be fine."

"We'll only be a phone call away, okay?"

Sniffing back the sudden tears clogging my throat and slipping slowly down my reddened face, I squeezed her once more before letting her go.

I was pretty sure I didn't even breathe until his arms locked around me, the ferocious strength and safety I always found in them giving me solace I hadn't known I needed.

"He's going to be okay, right?"

His minted breath met the skin of my neck as he tightened his hold on me, even more.

"I fucking hope so, baby."

18

HUDSON

"$\mathcal{H}$e can hear you, honey. Talk to him."
      I looked up from my feet at the sound of my mothers voice and I nodded.

She'd arrived soon after Tristan was admitted, having gotten the call, she came right away. I didn't even have to ask, that was just the person she was.

Kind, loving, always supportive.

The fact that she was here for me meant I didn't have to do this alone.

Because she was my mom. She could see right through my strength and my nonchalance. Because she was my *mom*.

"I'm fucking scared, Ma. What if he doesn't wake up?"

Her hands landed on mine against my lap and I blinked quickly, refusing to show emotion right then. I would have plenty of time later on to worry about how his condition would effect us.

For now, I needed to be here for him.

How many times had he stayed by my side?

Through the thick and the thin.

That was our motto.

It was my turn to return the favor.

"Have faith, Hudson. You have to have faith that it will be alright. Maybe it won't happen today or even tomorrow. But eventually, he will wake up. And when he does, he'll need you."

I wound my arm around her shoulders and dragged her in close, saying without words how fucking grateful I was for her presence.

Her arms wrapped around my waist as we stayed like that, gaining strength from one another that I knew we'd need when the doctors finally told us the news we'd been waiting on for hours now.

"Thank you." I pressed the words through my clogged up throat, trying to push through the rawness of emotion slowing my heartbeat and quickening my breath.

I couldn't lose him.

He was so young, so stubborn, so good.

And he had Ashlee.

He wouldn't leave her, *right?*

"I'm so sorry, my boy. I know how much you care for him."

Nodding, I kissed her hair, savoring the calm before the storm I knew was just on the horizon.

I just hoped Tristan's life wouldn't be a casualty.

"Where's this girl you've been telling me about?"

Her question had bright, warm light rushing through my body, the cold fear and stilted worry in my chest weakening as my need for my girl overshadowed those feelings.

"She went to get us some dinner in the cafeteria downstairs. Should've been back by now."

Felt her gentle fingers on my chin as I looked toward the slightly ajar door of the hospital room, my gut suddenly tight with a different sort of worry. *Worry for my girl.*

"I'm sure she'll be back soon."

"You gonna meet her when she does?"

I asked, instead of doing what I was inclined to do, which was set off in search for her. There was something wrong, I could fucking feel it. But this was my mom. I didn't want to leave her here, alone.

I felt her nod and it had a smile; one I hadn't felt on my face in the hours since getting that call, spreading.

It may have been a simple thing, my mother meeting the woman I loved, but it was something to look forward to and in the wake of the darkness our world was shadowed with, I held tightly to it.

Time seemed to slow while we sat there and prayed as we waited for his doctors and though it was the worst circumstances, I was glad my mom would finally to meet my girl.

It was about time.

I let an entire thirty minutes go by before the instinctual worry in my gut couldn't be ignored, any longer. It was this feeling, one I couldn't explain.

It wasn't longing or sadness or grief. It wasn't the fact that my arms seemed heavier to carry without my girl between them. It wasn't the deeply ingrained instinct in me to be near her, because I always had that feeling with me.

No, it was this crushing weight on my chest that told me she needed me right now. And I would be a fucking fool to ignore it.

"I'm going to go find her, Mom. Will you be okay here for a while?"

Bright, blue eyes looked up at me as she sat beside me, her small, dainty fingers resting against one of Tristan's hands; the one that wasn't all twisted up with wires.

"Of course I will."

I bent to press a lingering kiss at the top of her head before responding to her.

"Be back soon. I have my cell on me if anything changes."

I stilled as I felt her warm hands come up to cradle my face, the way she has always done when she felt words were inadequate.

"I'm so proud of you, Hudson. The man you have become has surpassed my hopes, in bounds. I always wanted you to grow up to be a strong, good man with values and the ability to love and care for those around you, but I never pictured it, until now. You've made your father and I very proud."

Blinking away the moisture that clouded my eyes at her admission, I nodded within her grasp. Dropping my head to the top of hers, I kissed her there, knowing words wouldn't suffice.

"Love you, Mom."

"I love you, my boy. Now go."

After another hug, I let her go, striding out of the room as quickly as possible because what I really wanted to do was run. The dread inside of me intensified with each step I took toward the bank of elevators behind the nurses station and I cursed the fact that I'd let her leave without me, in the first place.

I was so consumed in my best friends well being that I'd barely looked in her direction all afternoon, having her presence by my side was enough.

But Emberly deserved better than that. I promised her that she would never be hurt again. *If she had gotten hurt because of my own selfishness, I would never forgive myself.*

Goddamn it, I was supposed to *protect* her.

Both physically from the sick fuck that had been trailing our every move for months now and from anything else that could hurt her.

Because losing that girl was not an option.

I loved her, too much. I dropped my head as the elevator doors closed and muttered a foul curse at that thought.

I didn't just want her. I was fucking in love with her.

And I knew I had to tread lightly because she would run. She'd been put down by someone in her past, I knew that much. She'd been mentally abused for years, I just didn't know who had done it. Her anxiety had told me that, because she hadn't.

My Em tried to put on this front to everybody around her, so that they wouldn't see what I did.

Someone had tainted her image of herself, to the point where she couldn't see beauty if it hit her upside the head.

But I saw it. And one day, I would make her see it, too.

"Excuse me?" I stopped at the nurses desk and asked the brunette behind the counter for help, knowing walking around in circles wasn't getting me to her any faster.

"Hi, can I help you with something?"

"Yeah." I took a breath, realizing I'd been holding mine since walking out of Tristan's hospital room, the ache to get to Em overshadowing my need for air.

Sounded corny as fuck, but she was my air.

She was everything to me.

"I'm looking for my girlfriend. She's about five foot, two, shoulder length blonde hair? She would have been heading to the cafeteria about forty minutes ago, but she never came back to the room."

A sliver of hope curls its way into my veins when the girl's eyes light up and she nods.

"Yes! She headed into the bathroom a while ago, I didn't see her come back. She left her purse with me, so I would have seen her come back to retrieve it."

Fuck!

"You're sure it was her?"

"Yes, sir." I didn't waste another second asking her questions and took off toward the closed bathroom door, the instinct to *find* her driving my long strides and intent focus.

Adrenaline pumped through my veins when I pushed the door open, the bright, florescent lighting in the bathroom allowing me to scan the area quickly but I didn't see anything amiss. Not until I saw a shoe laying on the ground in front of one of the sinks that lined the wall. My eyes took in every detail of it and there was no doubt in my mind.

It was hers.

"Baby?"

My voice was hoarse and rough, hard edged from the fear that filled my chest and occupied my every thought.

Emberly.

"H...Hud?"

The voice was so small, I wouldn't have heard if it wasn't for my intense focus on hearing it or my familiarity with the sound her voice made.

My chest constricted in pain at the sound, the pained whimpers that followed worsening the affliction until I couldn't feel anything but the agony of her soft cries.

"Open the door, Darlin. I'm right here. I'll always be here."

"I...I'm scared. Is he still here?" Bewilderment permeated my worried thoughts at her words and I scanned the area of the bathroom once more, only then seeing the smattering of dirt on the otherwise clean, tiled floors and the spots of red on the edge of one of the sinks, as if...

I caused this.

I was distracted and worried in light of the news of Tristan's accident and because of that, I'd taken my eyes off of what should have been my only priority.

Keeping my woman safe.

I knelt down by the locked bathroom stall door and outstretched my shaking hands underneath, desperation to calm her fueling me. And then I held my breath, because I was powerless.

Powerless, because I'd failed her. My hands laying bare on a bathroom floor, in hopes that she would let me help her.

I was asking her to trust me, knowing damn well that I was undeserving of it. And I hated myself, because her being hurt was the last thing I would have ever chosen. I was going to ruin the man that dared to touch a hair on her head.

My girl.

My fucking world.

I didn't know how much she meant to me until now. Because

if she chose not to trust me, again? If she yelled and screamed and hated me after this, I would never recover from it. There would be no *moving on*. No *getting over her*.

I'd be ruined.

Forever.

But then I felt the unmistakable sensation of her fingers locking with mine, the soft pads of her thumbs gliding over the skin of my wrists and her hands, so much smaller than mine, squeezing three times as if to say *I trust you*.

I felt her stand up, one of her clammy hands loosening around mine and releasing its hold, only to go to the metal lock on the inside of the door to unlock it.

She was trusting me.

I didn't know how she could trust me after I'd inadvertently put her in danger, but I was grateful for it.

I needed her way too much to even think about letting her go. The second I saw her, rage like nothing ever before coursed my veins, fueled my anger and consumed my mind.

He was fucking dead.

Yet, I schooled my expression, knowing now, more than ever, she needed the reassurance that I didn't see the bruises or the imaginary flaws she saw within herself. My feelings for her hadn't changed because of this and in fact, they were stronger; I knew what it felt like to face losing her, now.

"Who?"

I spoke roughly into the nape of her neck, my arms tightly bound around her waist, my head buried in her hair and my mind a fucking mess.

How anyone could lay a hand on this girl, I would never know.

But they would pay for it.

In spades.

"Brad."

One word and I knew who he was.

Bradley Sullivan was the last collar I'd done before being

assigned to Ashlee's detail. He was a sick son of a bitch and I knew from the moment I met him of what he was. He'd broken into the home of a family living in Wicker Park and tied up the mother and father while he brutally murdered their three children. He'd made them watch as he fired at each child's head before turning the gun to the father and ordering his wife to open the safe where they kept all of their savings and expensive jewelry.

After taking every last shred of wealth they had, he shot the man and kept the woman for three days before depositing her into the river.

I was damn glad to be able to put him away for his crimes after hearing the brutality he'd doled out to a family that had done nothing but give to the city of Austin and anyone that was in need.

When he'd appealed the ruling three months later and was released, I didn't think anything of it.

Because men like him were almost always repeat offenders.

It was only a matter of time, or so I'd thought.

"I'm so fucking sorry, baby."

Her blonde head came up from its place on my chest and wide, sad eyes looked at me with so much trust I was *lost*.

"It wasn't your fault, Hudson."

I knocked my head back against the tiled wall and held her as close as I could get her. I pressed my mouth to her hair as I whispered.

"Yeah, Em, it is."

19

EMBERLY

"*You* should eat, Hud."

His eyes were stripped of emotion as he nodded from his place next to Tristan's hospital bed.

I knotted my fingers together in my lap as I looked at him, the tightly wound ball of worry in my stomach grew the longer we waited. Tristan was his best friend and before we met, he was the one that Hudson relied on, trusted in, confided his deepest thoughts to. He *had* to make it through this. He *had* to be okay. And not just for Hudson. For his parents that were waiting in the hallway just outside of his room. For Ashlee, who loved him more than anything in the world. If we lost him, *we lost each other.*

God, I'd already lost too many people in my life. I didn't want to lose him, too.

"Hudson, baby, please. I need you to eat something."

My softly spoken endearment seemed to snap him out of whatever thoughts he was trapped in, because he finally looked at me. His crystal blue eyes looked into mine and a small, sad smile lifted the corners of his mouth.

"I'm sorry, Darlin'. Come here."

Loosening my grip on the wall I'd been leaning against, I

137

moved to him, my steps taking me the small distance between us. I stopped a foot away, my knees brushing his. My hands landed on his shoulders, fingers skimming over the fabric of his Austin P.D. t-shirt before moving to wrap around the back of his neck, tipping his head up until his haunted eyes met mine, again.

"I know how worried you must be. I am, too. We all love him."

Hudson's mouth met my collar bone as his strong, harboring arms finally wrapped my waist, holding me just as he always did; gently but fiercely, as if they would protect me from anything that threatened to harm me. I knew that they would.

It didn't matter what we faced or how many times I worried that he would walk away from me when he learned the truth about my past, the moment his arms surrounded me, I was safe.

Protected.

Loved.

Hudson never had to say the words, either.

Every touch, every kiss, every word he said to me told me of his feelings for me.

Did I give him the same thing?

Did he know how much I needed him in my life?

Did he know how much it meant to me?

To have him?

I wasn't sure if he truly did.

But I'd prove it to him.

I felt warm wetness slide down my chest and felt my heart stop in response.

"Hudson?"

He didn't look up at me as he wound a large, strong arm around my shoulders and buried his face in the nape of my neck, dampening strands of my hair as he let out a gut wrenching sound; a sound that was half an agonized whimper of his heart and a painful call from his soul. And I couldn't stop the sounds from slipping from his perfect lips, because I felt it, too.

The soul crushing fear that lingered in the air around us, the coldness that speared his heart as he watched Tristan sleep, not knowing if he would ever wake up.

Would he?

And so, I held onto him. Just as tightly as he always held me, I rocked us back and forth in a gentle, swaying motion that I hoped calmed him because I needed to fix this somehow, for him. I never thought about what it would be like, to be on the other side of my job as a nurse. Of course I felt the pain and loss that came from losing the lives of my patients, but to feel it like this? I'd never felt this.

"Hudson," I whispered, my heart suddenly racing within my chest and I tried desperately to calm it, because from where his ear was pressed against my chest, he'd hear it.

And the last thing he needed was to worry about me.

Not then. Not when his own heart was in danger of shattering to pieces as he faced losing a man he'd called his brother for the last three years he'd served alongside him for the department.

I knew I couldn't fix this for him, no matter how much I wanted to.

But I could give him the only part of us that I'd been keeping at bay for the weeks we'd been toeing the waters between us, finding our rhythm as my fears pushed him away and his protective nature allowed me the safety I needed so badly.

He'd become my home.

My safe place to rest my head at night, my shield; both of my physical safety and of my delicate, fragmented heart.

I knew I should have said it before today, but my fear of being rejected had kept me quiet, because if I told him how I felt and he didn't feel the same?

I wasn't sure I could withstand that.

"You're not alone anymore, Hud. I need you to know that. The day we met, I knew it. You were different than any other man I'd met. You were a good man. I could trust my heart with you, trust that you would never hurt me intentionally. And then my fears got the best of me and I got scared. I thought keeping my feelings inside would mean I wouldn't have to face being hurt if you didn't feel the same way. But, baby, that's the thing about love that I'm learning. It's a risk. A risk that you'll hurt me. A risk that you'll reject me. But it's a worthy risk, to me. Because to have all of you, every piece, every inch, everything? It's the ultimate prize."

I closed my eyes, then, because my heart was so full of love for him I was sure it would burst. I felt rather than heard him move away from me and as my hands dropped to my sides, so did any hope for us. Because if Hudson couldn't accept me for who I was and love me in spite of it? We'd be over.

I would have to let him go.

"Shit, Darlin', look at me. Right now."

It was both a plea and a command, the harsh bite of the words coupled with the desperation in his voice making it impossible to brush off.

I held my breath when I found Hudson's eyes with mine but my worry for what I'd see there diminished the second a large, no holds barred smile graced his face.

"About time." It was all he said before his hands took my face in a strong, possessive hold and dropped his head beside mine, the lips my dreams were made of crushing me under their intensity. And I melted.

As I always had.

My breathing escalated to short, ragged pants as he ravaged me with his mouth, merciless and hungry for a taste of me. I was grabbing at his shoulders and grasping the collar of his shirt in frantic fingers, the realization of what it all meant hitting my chest and quickening my heart beat all at once.

He loved me. Suddenly, I didn't need the words he would say or the sentiment of love I'd yearned for in my dreams. Because the emotion in which Hudson kissed me told me what I needed to know.

"Em," He breathed against my forehead as we parted, our ragged breathing and the slow beeping of the machines around us the only sounds in the room.

"I know." I whispered, placing my hands on his chest, feeling the slow, but sure beats of his heart through the fabric that separated his skin from mine.

The smile he'd worn before our kiss returned to his beautiful features and I smiled, too, because it finally felt like I'd given him some of what he'd been gifting me every time we were together.

Love.

"I'll go get us something to eat. What do you feel like?"

Kissing me softly, but reverently, I felt him shrug his shoulders against my hold.

"Whatever gets you back to me sooner."

The hairs on the very back of my neck stood on end unexpectedly as I turned the lock in the small bathroom stall, the water I'd had earlier in the day pressing on my bladder even as a shiver of unease slid down my spine.

Someone's watching me.

The thought wasn't a new one but for the first time, it was inescapable.

The tremors in my hands begun as I folded them in front of me, legs shaky while I held my breath, listening for a sound. *Any* sound that would tell me I hadn't gone crazy.

Cold chills covered the surface of my skin and a feeling of dread I'd never felt before coiled in the pit of my stomach and then I heard a voice.

"Come out, come out. Wherever you are..."

No, no, no!

Not now.

Not him.

It couldn't be...

"You can't hide forever, *sweetheart.*"

The voice was oddly familiar, with a husk that told of old age and a slant of Irish descent. But it was the roughly worded endearment that had me clutching the metal handle of the stall with a desperate hold, the memories of darkness and forgotten shadows engulfing me in bone chilling shivers that wouldn't cease.

Brad?

The abrupt and terrifying sound of the stall door crashing open, the force of the action breaking through the metal of the lock and the last shred of protection from the stranger on the other side was gone. A large, darkly skinned hand reached out and took a hold of my hair and the quake of my body intensified as the realization that he's found me registers in my mind.

But he's not a stranger, is he?

He's the shadow you've been running from.

He's the man who almost took your innocence.

He's the man who almost broke you.

"B-Brad?"

His clutch on my hair has a cry of pain falling from my lips, the tearing agony of his fingernails in my scalp keeping me from staying quiet.

"Yeah, *Sweetheart.* That's me."

Brad Sullivan was my fathers most trusted adviser in his business and he was a constant in my life from the age of ten years old. As I grew up, he started taking an interest in me and at first, I thought he was nice. My dad always said he was like a brother to him and that should have been my first clue. Because any man that could befriend my father had to be bad news.

God knew my father was.

When I was sixteen years old, Brad cornered me in my fathers office one of the few summers I worked for his law firm.

My father often said I had to pay him back for all of my failures in his eyes.

I was always inadequate, no matter how hard I'd tried to make the man proud.

"You've grown up, Em. I think it's time you and I get to know each other a bit better."

"Brad- no... I-"

"Shut up, Bitch."

His hand was up my skirt before I knew it but when one of his large hands grabbed a breast, something from deep inside of me broke free from the chains my fathers world had on me. And I fought back.

My knee collided with his groin and the second he released me, I ran.

I'd ran the whole way home with blood dripping down my neck from where he'd bitten me when he'd kissed me and I went straight into the shower, intent on scrubbing away the grime his touch had left on every inch of my skin

I didn't stop until it was raw and red from the loofah and even that wasn't enough. When I heard the front door slam shut with a loud, deathly sound I knew my dad had likely found out what had happened. I didn't have any hopes of him believing me, because he wasn't that kind of parent.

He would say it was all my fault.

But it wasn't.

"Don't... don't you dare touch me."

He kept approaching me, though. My skin crawled with fearful goosebumps and my heart was racing in its effort to keep up with my rapid breathing but I had no hope of calming. Because if he got any closer, I wouldn't be able to fend him off.

Not this time.

Not him.

The man had gotten bigger, I could see the definition of his arms and chest, the angry tick of his neck telling me he wasn't having any success in keeping his fury at bay.

That terrified me even more.

"Funny, you don't get it, do you? Let me clarify a few things, for you."

The sensation of his fist hitting my cheek brought on the most intense pain I'd ever felt and I was on the ground beneath him before I knew what had happened.

"I. Own. You."

The words were spoken with such anger, such possession, I begun to shake with the meaning I knew they held.

He'd been watching me, this whole time.

After the near miss in my fathers office, I'd gone to stay with my grandmother. Unlike my father, she was a good soul.

Kind.

Smart.

Sassy.

She didn't take shit from anyone, least of all him.

But her health was deteriorating and by the time I graduated nursing school, she was gone.

I felt her loss heavily, because she'd been the only person in my life, besides my mother, to show me true love.

She'd loved me.

She'd wanted the best for me.

But she'd been taken from me.

The pieces of what had transpired between then and now begun to make sense as I laid there, barely breathing while his cold, emotionless voice told me of all the ways he would make me pay for denying him of me for so long.

The agony of the kicks to my stomach ceased as he knelt down at my side and ripped the top of dress open, his horrid laughter in my ear a taunt if I'd ever heard one.

He was demented in his obsession of me and all I could think of was *Hudson*. He would find me before it was too late.

He would always protect me.

He'd made me that promise.

His hand was back in my hair as his spit landed on my face and I clenched my eyes shut, willing it all to be a nightmare.

Because that's what it felt like.

"This isn't over."

And then he was gone.

Everything *hurt*.

Every muscle, everywhere.

All I felt was the physical pain he'd given me but the memory of what had almost happened by his hands years ago was the thing that hurt the most.

Dragging myself from the floor, I struggled to my knees and crawled across the tiled floor to the still open stall door, with the last of the strength, I shut myself behind the door and engaged the lock, just in case he decided to come back to finish the job.

Clutching my knees to my chest, I dropped my head to my lap and whispered a prayer.

Hudson.

Please find me.

My thoughts stayed with him until my eyes drifted shut, the pain giving way as the harsh weight of exhaustion took me over.

"Em?"

Hudson.

I didn't know if I should believe it, but it was his voice.

Right?

"H...hud?"

It was my fears that kept me back.

Didn't they always?

"Open the door, Darlin. I'm right here. I'll always be here."

"I...I'm scared. Is he still here?"

His hands appeared beneath the stall door and I knew it was him.

My man.

My protector.

My home.

"Hudson." I whispered on a broken cry, fresh, hot tears spilling over my cheeks as I realized what I should have known all along.

I could trust him.

As my hands met his much larger ones, the hands that had given me so much care, so much solace, my heart begun to calm its pace.

And it was a painful and a beautiful reminder.

He was my home.

It was with that hope in my heart that I stood on still shaking legs and slid my fingers to the lock of the door, using the last bit of my strength to loosen it from its cradle and then it was his eyes, skimming the damage.

His hands, tightening in mine.

His love, shining in his blue irises.

And the strength I'd thought *he* stripped from me was restored.

"Who?" His voice was rough, broken, agonized.

I'd done that to him.

"B...Brad."

I saw it, the recognition, the fury filling his usually expressive eyes and the proverbial shutters fall as they blocked me from witnessing it all.

How did he know Brad?

Tears soaked his t-shirt, my head dropping to his chest, the gravity of what had happened making me weak and desperate for the solace I knew I'd found in his arms. I heard his foul curse before he wound a large, possessive arm around my waist, pulling me too gently to his chest, where I belonged.

Where I'd always belong.

"I'm so fucking sorry, baby."

His face was in my hair and I felt it, for the second time that day.

He was crying for me.

"Hudson." I whispered, but he wouldn't budge from his hold on me.

As if our bodies were incapable of parting.

As if we were two halves of a whole and without me, he'd been nothing.

I drew gently from his grasp and grabbed his face in urgent fingers, needing his eyes on me when I assured him of this.

"It's *not* your fault, Hudson."

He didn't believe me.

I felt it.

I saw the evidence in his gaze.

But he would.

Someday.

So I did what I knew he needed the very most.

I let him hold me.

And it was enough.

2 0

HUDSON

*F*ear like nothing I had ever experienced overcame me the second I found my beautiful girl in that bathroom stall.

Her eyes, dark and haunted by shadows I knew plagued her spirit and pained her heart. The bruises he'd left on her otherwise perfect skin incited the most intense fury I'd ever felt and I knew precisely what I would do with it.

Destroy. Because this woman was everything to me.

My air. My breath. My life.

It was my job to protect her from ever being hurt, again and the second I took my eyes off of her, I failed her. The arm I had secured around her still shaking body tightened at the realization and I muttered a foul curse under my breath. She deserved so much better than me.

My eyes roamed her upturned face while she slept and I knew one thing for certain. I could never let go of her. Maybe before her attack, I could have forced myself to let her go but that wasn't an option anymore.

It never would be, again.

This girl right here was the missing part my heart had been missing. She was the woman I'd always hoped to find. The kind of woman that would stick by my side, through thick and through thin. The woman that I would someday marry.

Yeah, that shit was happening. *Soon.*

Almost losing her had opened my fucking eyes. I was in *love* with her.

Despite the walls she put up around her heart and the secrets I knew she kept locked away deep inside of her she'd yet to tell me. It was all a way for her to protect herself. And I got that.

Emberly hadn't had a good life thus far. The darkness I sometimes saw in her eyes were proof of that. That ended now.

Smoothing her matted hair away from her face, I dropped my head gently to hers, placing a kiss to the top of her head as I realized what I'd been fighting against since the second I laid my eyes on her. *I loved her.*

Her hands wrapped around my neck as I moved to pull away and I instantly knew she'd fallen into another nightmare. The night terrors that plagued her dreams most of the night were wreaking havoc on her psych and I didn't have to see her eyes to know that the darkness of her past was back at the forefront of her mind. I wanted to punch the nearest wall, yell and scream, anything to take away the agony my girl was engulfed in, but I knew none of those things would bring her solace.

When I touched her, like this, it helped. Her small, thin fingers clung to my neck as if I was her lifeline and fuck, I wanted to be.

I wanted to be the anchor that kept her grounded and the home she needed when life got rough. I wanted to protect her with my life, just like I had for the citizens of the city of Austin in my service to the police department. Because *that* was me.

It had been ingrained in me from a very young age to shield the ones I loved from anything that threatened to do them harm.

Emberly was my only priority, now and protecting her was all that mattered. Somehow, I'd find a way to shield her from all of this.

I had to find a way.

"Fuck," I cursed when I heard the shrill ring of my phone interrupt the quiet calm of my bedroom and I hastily pulled the large comforter her more tightly around her body and slipped out of the bed to retrieve the phone.

Finding it on the edge of one of my bureaus, I pressed *accept call* and carefully shut the bedroom door behind me before padding into the large, open concept kitchen for a glass of water.

"Officer Lennox."

"It's Sergeant Lewis. How's my daughters security coming along?"

All the blood drained from my face at the voice and I inwardly cringed.

I didn't even spare a glance at the screen before answering the phone and then I'd wished I did. Because I really didn't feel like having this conversation.

"She's perfectly safe, Sir. The threat isn't hers, it's my girlfriend."

A long, pregnant pause met my ear and then what sounded like a sigh of relief coming from my sergeant.

"Are you sure?"

"Yes. I've guarded her for two months now and as far as I can tell, she isn't being followed. The stalker didn't have his sights on Ashlee."

"Alright. You said something about your girlfriend? I wasn't aware that you were dating."

Because it's none of your business. Didn't dare say that, though.

"Her name is Emberly. She's a close friend of your daughter, sir."

"I see. What happened?"

I took a deep breath before saying the words, because they felt foul on my tongue, but I had to tell him in order to do my job. Except now, I had two jobs.

One was as a police officer under his command.

And the other? Was to protect my girl.

"She was attacked in the hospital tonight. I think whoever did it was the one stalking Ashlee for these past few months."

"Shit, I'm very sorry to hear that, Lennox. If you need anything-"

"I need a few days off, Sergeant."

I hadn't told him about Brad Sullivan and didn't plan to.

This shit had gone on long enough and I knew the second he knew of my history with the suspect, he'd pull me off. Granted, he couldn't stop me from staying close to my woman, but he could force me to take another assignment.

I didn't have time for that. I had to find him and deal with him, myself.

It was the only way.

"Of course. If it was Sarah, I'd be doing the same thing."

He muttered, his voice taking on a lighter tone as he referenced to his wife.

"Thank you, Sir. If I have any updates on Ashlee's safety, I'll let you know."

The line clicked off a minute later and I lowered my phone to the kitchen counter I'd been leaning against. Dropping my face into my hands, elbows braced on the island, I struggled to get a hold of myself.

I was coming apart at the seams and I needed to get it the fuck together.

Em needed me.

"Hudson!"

My head whipped to the side the instant my ears picked up on the sound, the mixture of despaired sadness and confused awareness in her voice calling straight to my soul. I was running toward the sound, acting on pure and uncontrollable instinct and I didn't stop until I stood in the doorway of my bedroom. After having a doctor check her bruises and the large cut on her cheek from where the fucker had slammed her head into the bathroom sink, I'd taken my girl home with me because this was the safest place for her. Her apartment had little to no security and the lock on her front door was faulty at best.

That shit wasn't good enough to keep her safe.

Her wide eyes landed on me and the stark fear in them damn near brings me to my knees. Then she blinks once and the thick tears that fall over her beautiful, battered face had my heart splintering to pieces.

"Shit, *baby*, I'm here. I'm right here."

Lifting her into my arms, I carried her into the half bath attached to the room and gently set her on the lip of the large, oval tub.

Her face was buried in my neck, her blonde hair matted against my skin and her tears soaking my shirt, causing another fraction of my chest to seize with every horrid drop that fell.

What I would fucking give to take them away.

Her body begun to shake violently and all I could do was tighten my grasp on her, intent to never let her go if I had to. The words that left her full lips had me gasping for air, because this level of fury never touched me until now.

I'm not going to lie and say that I'm a good man.

I'm not.

I've killed people.

I've sinned.

I've done my fair share of horrible things.

But none of that matters now, because the second she's strong enough to be without me, I'm going after the motherfucker that hurt her.

And I won't stop until he feels the pain he'd so easily inflicted on her.

"I can still feel his hands on me, Hud. I can't..."

Her voice broke as a ragged sob, loud and filled with torment shook her small body and penetrates my heart which for so long, I'd thought was devoid of emotion. Being a cop, you have to steel yourself for the worst of situations.

You could never let emotion cloud your judgment and

because of that, I'd learned early on to blacken my heart from those around me.

I didn't have a chance of doing that with Em.

She's mine.

"The only man that will have his hands on you from now on is me, Emberly. Just me."

Her head peeled from my throat as she nodded slowly and her hands made contact with my jaw before she lets her eyes meet mine, again.

They aren't filled with sadness or pain, though.

They're filled with love.

And that's mine, too.

"I...I love you."

Something deeply rooted inside of me shattered at her soft confession and I couldn't hold down the overwhelming press of emotion anymore. Dropping my face into the nape of her neck, I banded my hands across her hips, needing her to anchor me as I broke for the second time in the past twenty-four hours.

The first time was for Tristan, my brother-in-arms. But this time, it's all her. *I can't fucking lose this.*

"I don't know what I would have done if you weren't okay when I found you. I'm a fucking mess because losing you is not something I'd survive. You own me, Darlin. Heart. Body. Soul. Everything."

"I love you, so much."

Those words healed the broken in me and I nodded against the top of her head, not knowing what I would have done if I'd have lost this.

"*Em.* I love you with every thing I'm made of. You have my heart. And I don't want it back, baby."

The words are straight from my heart, the heart I gave to her the second her gorgeous eyes met mine outside of the hospital, a little over two months ago.

The day my entire world changed.

The day I begun living, again.

She doesn't say another word before she drops her face into my chest and grips the fabric with desperate fingers, holding on for dear life- just as I was holding on to her.

But when she whispers in my ear, I felt it in my soul.

"Don't let go."

The sudden empty space against my side forced me into consciousness what had to be hours later. By the time my girl was able to fall asleep again, it was barely dawn. And I was exhausted, to say the least. Somehow, I must have fallen asleep because the bright, early morning sun that peers into my bedroom tells me that much.

My hand automatically searched for the warmth of hers, my body's natural inclination to seek hers driving me. But when I felt the chilled fabric of my sheets instead, awareness of her absence has me rushing off of the bed in an instant.

"Baby!"

The thick, blue comforter was thrown somewhere on the floor as I stumbled to my feet, eyes assessing the room before landing on the slightly open door of the bathroom. My thundering heart beat calmed when I heard the familiar sound of the shower running from inside the room. I'm reminded that we'd never showered last night- my beautiful girl had been physically and emotionally drained and sleep was what she needed more than anything else.

I grabbed a towel from the warmer near the bathroom door before moving toward the clear shower stall where I'd find her. It's the soft sound coming from her direction that had my heart stopping in my chest, my pulse thrumming in dread and the renewed fury I'd felt after her attack coming back twice as powerfully.

What the fuck?

The first thing I noticed was the thick bruising on her

normally pale, slender shoulders. They'd begun to yellow but the outline of a mans fist was evident. If I hadn't already hated her attacker with everything inside of me, I would have after seeing her like this.

Darlin', I'm sorry.

"Em?"

She spun around as quickly as her injuries allow and I fucking hate seeing the broken look in her eyes when she did. That wasn't what had me gasping in a strangled breath and stumbling back a step. It was her eyes and the hopelessness emanating from their depths.My eyes moved from her face and to the rest of her and the blistered, red skin of her arms, legs and stomach has me grabbing onto the wall beside me in a futile effort to remain standing.

Steam filled the room from the hot water she let plummet her body and her ragged breathing told me how much pain she was in. But then her lavender eyes dropped from mine and she begun to scrub vigorously at her skin again and I fucking snapped. It took me two strides to get to her and even that distance was too far for me to fathom.

"Baby. I need you to fucking listen to me, right now. Got it?"

My grasp on her face was too rough, too urgent but I didn't know how to ebb my desperation for her.

Her eyes, dull and lifeless when she looked up at me and for the first time since meeting her, I was afraid she'd deny me. Because the warmth wasn't there when I looked at her. She could so easily rip herself out of my grasp and blame me for all of this and fuck, she would be right.

But if that happened, if I *lost* her? I would be nothing.

Stepping closer into my space, she nodded her head just slightly, small, trembling hands curling around mine as they held her face and its like I could breathe again.

Made sense doesn't it?

She's my fucking air.

"You aren't dirty, baby. You don't need this, you don't need to do this. You're safe now, Em and I don't care what I have to do, how many laws I have to break, I will keep you that way."

I looked down into her eyes, not knowing how to fix it all. The motherfucker had made his way into her mind and fucked with her in ways I didn't know how to reverse. *How the hell was I supposed to fix her if I didn't know what I was up against?*

Ever since I first saw her, I could see everything she was thinking; feeling in these eyes. But right then, I couldn't see a damn thing. All I saw was her sadness, her pain, her fucking fear.

And I hated it all. So I did what I knew would get through to her.

Lifting my shirt from the collar, I ripped it off of my chest and threw it onto the tiled floor before binding one arm around her waist while reaching for one of her still shaking hands with the other.

My fingers easily slipped through hers as I pressed the palm of her hand against my chest for her to feel the frantic beat of my heart against her fingers.

I knew the very moment she felt it, because she gasped before letting her head fall to my chest, next to where I'd placed our joined hands and I heard her low sobs muffled against my skin. It was breaking me to see her like this, my normally strong willed, courageous girl stripped away from her in the wake of the darkness our world was now covered in.

"I'm your shield, Em. I'm your armor against any threat, any fear, any heartache. As long as you have me, you'll have a place to land."

"Hudson-"

"Shh, I know." My hand goes to her cheek, where I graze my fingertips over her skin before lowering my mouth to hers in a gentle pass of lips that is more of a whisper than a kiss.

It's an apology.

It's a prayer.

It's a breathing of our mouths and a singing of our hearts and I relished every second of it.

"I want to tell you everything, Hud. Everything I've kept locked away. I need you to know."

Nodding, my mouth whispers over her forehead next.

"I'll listen, Darlin'. When you're ready."

"I am."

21

HUDSON

$\mathcal{T}$he mild grasp Emberly had on my shoulders intensifies as I moved my hands under her lush ass and lifted her up my body, the sensation of warmth her sweet curves emanate causing my dick to stir to life in my boxers.

Fuck.

Pausing my steps toward the bedroom in order to take a few deep breaths, I shook my head because that shit isn't needed right now.

Right now, I need to get my girl to confide in me and sex can come later.

God knows I need her body under mine, again.

Soon. I silently promised myself.

"Hudson, I-"

"You don't have to tell me, Darlin'. I need you to know that. I can see that whatever it is in your past is dark and most likely hard for you to relive and Em, I don't want you to hurt, not if I can avoid it."

I swear I could feel her smile against my cheek as she nodded once.

"I know that, Hud. But I have to relive it. I want you to know me, *all* of me- like I know you, now."

158

My hand goes to the back of her head where I took the time to stroke her hair before muttering a curse.

Seems I do that a lot lately.

"Emberly."

Meant to say more than just her name, but I found words hard to form in the chaos within my mind.

So I hold her a bit tighter while I slowly lower her to the edge of my mattress and begrudgingly release her.

"It's okay."

Her softly spoken words are both a reassurance and a comfort and I soak them in before lowering myself to the bed beside her and grabbing one of her hands in mine.

Interlocking our fingers, I realized something I hadn't noticed in all the times before.

We were a perfect fit.

The thought was sappy as shit and I'd never admit to it. Nonetheless, I was grateful for it.

"I just need you to listen, okay? If I don't say this now-" I rushed my mouth over hers, the sound of her mounting anxiety burning my ears, awakening my rage all over again.

"Not going anywhere, Darlin'. Tell me what you need to but know this."

My hands cupped her pale, tear stained cheeks and the roughness of my flesh against hers draws my attention before I looked into her soulful, colorful eyes and just like every other time we're close, I get lost in them.

"I'm in love with you, Emberly. Madly. Whatever shadows are in your past won't change the way I feel about you. Nothing will."

Her eyes gave nothing away as I said the words but the minute they registered, they closed tightly and her body softens in my hold before she peered at me, again.

"I love you, Hudson. More than you know."

Didn't have words to express how fucking wrong she was, since in everything she did, I felt the way she loved me.

Every time she made breakfast for me in the early hours of the morning, even on the mornings where she had to work early and could have used the extra sleep.

The way she watched me when we were together, as if she couldn't take her eyes off of me from fear that I'd disappear. Whether simple or complex, her ways of showing me her feelings for me were a knockout punch to my chest and it was crazy that she wasn't aware of any of it.

I wasn't stupid; whatever she'd been avoiding telling me all of this time was big. Huge. Because otherwise, she'd have told me before today. She was the most open and honest person I'd ever met, even with her guard up. If she hid something from me, it was because she was afraid to lose this.

Felt the same way. Difference was that I knew it'd be okay in the end.

Walking away from her wasn't an option.

"I think I always knew my dad wasn't right. Not like fathers should be. Warm, loving, *good*. That wasn't my dad. Or maybe at one time it was, before everything went wrong. When I was five years old, he lost his job at a cushy law firm he was a partner in. He'd had a contract with them, but it defaulted when the firm went under.

Since my mama hadn't worked since giving birth to me, there wasn't any money coming in. Soon after that, he started drinking."

The sensation of her hands loosening between mine put my entire body on high alert and while bracing a hand on her hip, I pulled her closer to my chest and pressed my mouth to her forehead in what I hoped was a reassurance that she was safe, here with me. *Always.*

I couldn't imagine the heartache this woman had felt in her young life but none of it mattered now because I was here. She was *mine*, now and it didn't matter how many voices in her head told her she wasn't worthy of this. I'd be beside her to quiet every one of them.

"I got you. Take your time."

"It's okay. It's just hard to think about it, I've avoided it for so long, now. Thought it was easier that way."

I nod, but don't take my lips from her skin as I speak.

"Sometimes it is. But keeping all of this inside is a big burden to carry. You have me, now. You don't need to carry it alone, anymore."

"I know that," Her hands come up to my neck where she laced thin fingers through my my hair, a soft touch that speaks volumes.

Like I said, little things.

"I didn't think I'd have this, Hudson. A relationship didn't seem plausible, with my past. I knew whoever I chose to love would have strong soldiers, able to handle anything and everything thrown their way. I know I've kept you at arms length at times and I haven't always been easy to love-"

"Loving you is like breathing to me, Em. It's fucking easy. And even if it wasn't? Even if I had to fight everyday to get inside your heart? I would gladly fight with you. Because that's the thing about love. It's unconditional. I don't love you because of how you look or if your thin. I don't want you because you fit a type, because you don't. And that's why I fell for you, so fast, so hard. You have the biggest heart of anybody I have ever met and it's beautiful. It's beautiful the way you care for those around you and love so deeply. The way you make others feel is what drew me in. You have this way of lighting up the room you walk into and you never have to say a word. Darlin', you're perfect for me and I don't care whether it's easy."

My voice was rough and unsteady and so was my touch as I caught her blushing face in ardent hands and leaned my forehead against hers as I uttered the rest.

"You are worth the fight."

Her mouth was on mine not a second later and despite the crushing weight on my chest and the uneasiness of worry that settled in my gut at the very thought of having this conversation,

I found myself breaking the brushing of our mouths with a stunned smile.

"Tell me."

Two whispered words but I knew she heard them because she again settled herself into my side and nodded.

"I hated the night time the most. I would lay in my bed and listen to it all happen but I never got out of my bed, I never... *protected* her. If I could change anything in my life, it would be that."

"Em-"

My chest felt like fucking led as I heard her words, the breaks in her voice and the subtle tremble of her full, bottom lip but her hand pressing to my chest stopped me from interrupting her. I wanted to tell her that I didn't need to know. That she didn't have to share this part of herself with me.

That would be a lie.

But if saying it meant she wouldn't have to relive it all, it'd be worth it.

A white lie.

Isn't that what they call it?

"He'd blame it on the house being a mess, call her lazy and ungrateful. He didn't just beat her, he beat her heart down. Her soul. I remember hearing the horrible, awful things he said to her, late at night when he thought I was asleep tucked in my bed and I wanted to run downstairs and scream at my mom to fight back. To be strong. To protect herself. Imagining her sitting there, just taking his nasty words was even worse than when his belt came off. Her cries as he hit her. Her begging him to stop, the desperate pleas that went unanswered. I hated him for so long, I don't know if I ever stopped."

I was sure I read somewhere that when someone talks about their demons, their past, the last thing you should do is touch them. It could cause the person to lash out, to get spooked or shut down emotionally.

The thought was fleeting that I should have kept my distance and let her say the rest before pulling her close.

That didn't stop me from reaching between us to take hold of her beautiful yet saddened face, hands shaking, the roar of rage that begun building up inside of me in that hospital bathroom stall becoming a living, breathing thing, an instinctual determination clouding my brain and erasing everything but one simple truth.

I would protect her with my life.

Her haunted gaze dropped from mine and her eyes closed as I pulled her small, body impossibly closer, until her face was pressed to my neck and her knees hooked over my waist, not even a breath between us.

Even that was too much for me to handle.

"I'm so fucking sorry, Em. Breathe now, it's okay, baby. It's okay, now. You're okay."

The feeling of her shuttering breath on my throat had my anger growing and it's not only for Brad.

Fuck, no. It's for her father, for being the monster that he was and I'm sure he still is. People like that don't change.

Seen enough bad men in my line of work to know that. She'd been just a child. A little girl. She didn't deserve his hate.

No one deserved *that*.

When I felt her hands, frantic, pulling at the fabric of my shirt, her fingernails scratching at the collar, it took me a solid minute to realize what she needed.

Her body had gone ice cold.

She needed to get warm.

Shit!

Adrenaline flooded me as I quickly reached a hand behind my neck and gently pried her free from my chest just long enough to slip the shirt over my head before gently pulling her body back into my arms, easing her down onto the bed with me where she nestled her head on my chest, the shivers racking her body lessening the tighter I held her.

"How old were you when it started?"

I murmured the question into her ear, not wanting to push her for more information than she was ready to divulge and was thankful when she tipped her face towards mine and met my stare.

"Probably six? I remember it was after I begun school. My mom used to walk me to the bus stop in the mornings. But after it started, she didn't do that anymore."

"Because she couldn't leave the house."

She hadn't said the words, but I read between the lines.

Her father had hurt her mother so badly that she couldn't make the small walk to the bus stop with her daughter. Never laid my eyes on the man but hell, I hated him, too.

"Did he hurt you, Darlin'?"

My Em didn't look at me when she answered but her nod told me all I needed to know.

"I stood up to him. It was stupid and naive to think I could stand up to him, make him see reason, but I needed to try. For my moms sake. He would hit me with his belt or slap me around. Eventually, I stopped fighting back."

Her words were so shallow, so weakened by the darkness that smothered her and I was a helpless man, because I didn't know how to fix it.

This beautiful, kind, amazing woman deserved the fucking world.

She deserved so much more than the pain and abuse she'd had to endure and for so long, she'd endured it alone.

Taking one of her hands fiercely in mine, I tipped my mouth over her pale fingertips in a silent acknowledgment that she wasn't alone, anymore.

She would never walk alone, again.

"It wasn't so bad after mama passed. He hated being in the same room as me so I barely saw him after her service. I thought he was feeling guilty, I thought it would get better after that." She huffed a heavy breath, her beautifully anguished irises sparking with anger and resentment before they dulled into a pain I'd seen so many times before in that haunted eyes of hers. The colors of her violet eyes dimmed under the weight of the darkness she was being forced to relive and I just held her small body tighter, hoping that my presence would ease it all.

"When I was sixteen, my dad told me I needed to repay him for all of the trouble I'd given him and my mother. He didn't give me a choice so I went to his office that summer and assisted him in any way I could. I was so stupid, Hud. I thought he'd finally be proud of me for working hard that summer, showing him I was more than the disappointment he'd always had for me."

Fuck.

"Emberly, look at me." I urged her, urgency to take away the sadness in her voice crawling through my veins.

It took her a few minutes but when she did lift her head from my chest and those eyes of hers met mine, the emotion in them broke me.

A lesser woman would have been broken by the hardships she had faced but not my woman, not Em. She was so fucking strong and the worst part of this was, she didn't even *know it.*

She had no idea of what she was capable of and that, to me, was a crime.

Because she deserved to know that she wasn't the weak, broken girl she believed herself to be. Her father may have spent years of her life engrossed in his hatred for the world, placing the weight of the world on her young shoulders instead of being a decent human being and being the father she'd needed so badly.

She had me, now.

"You weren't stupid, baby. You were just a child needing her fathers love and that shit is normal. The rest is on him, alright?"

Emberly looked up at me with wide, haunted eyes for countless seconds before she nodded slowly, understanding washing over her face. I watched, rapt, as the softness of her elegant features returned and a sudden, overwhelming warmth covered the shadows I saw in her eyes only a moment before. Her hands covered mine on either side of her face sending sparks of awareness across my skin and I looked down at her, shaking my head in renewed astonishment that she was actually mine.

All mine.

Didn't seem possible to me, but that didn't mean I would let her go.

I'd done that once and it almost got her killed.

It only took a few meager minutes of me taking my eyes off of her and Em had been hurt, right under my nose.

I could have lost her yesterday.

I could have lost her and that shit didn't sit well with me.

I wasn't about to take my eyes off of her anytime soon.

That was for damn sure.

"There's more." She whispered and instantly the muscles in my upper body locked up tight, as if I was readying for the fight of my life.

There was more than her abusive father and her horrible childhood?

How much more had this girl gone through before I found her?

Shit.

"There was this man that worked with my father. He was one of the lawyers on his team in a big case he was working on the last summer I worked for him. He was... he scared me. He would corner me wherever I was, whether I was in the supply closet, my fathers office, the lunch room... it didn't matter where I was, he'd find me. He tried to force himself on me, he would t-touch me, I swear I tried to fight him off every time. But eventually I just let it happen. It didn't matter what I wanted anyways, no one cared back then. I was just the boss's daughter. I was fair game to him, I guess."

The broken tone of her voice had my chest clenching in a mixture of abrupt pain and wild, untamed anger- an extreme of emotions I'd never experienced before. Fisting my hands at my sides, I let my beautiful girl continue knowing that if I stopped her, she would keep the pain inside of her longer than she already had and I couldn't let that happen. She needed to let it all go and I would take care of it.

I'd go to the ends of the earth to free her from her darkness.

I would have done any-fucking-thing for this girl and she needed to know that. As she went on to tell me about the sick fuck that dared to put his hands on her, unease crawled its way up my throat and left a bitter taste in my mouth. My mind was spinning with the new information and I was constantly shifting between staying present, here, with her and making a connection to the danger she was in after the attack and the loom of the unknown stalker we'd thought was the source of the threats that started all of this.

Her wide, assessing gaze moved from mine to my chest where she linked her fingers through the gold chained cross I always wore around my neck. It was one of the only items I had left of my grandfather and it was a reminder.

A reminder to protect those I loved above all else.

It was a reminder of the reason I'd decided to become a cop in the first place.

Protect and serve.

"I...I didn't know it was him. I don't know how he found me..."

"What are you talking about?" Kissing the side of her head, I gently ran my thumb over the crease under each of her eyes, collecting her tears and kissing each one of them away, my only way of healing her pain and taking away the darkness in her eyes. When she smiled at me, a soft, barely there one, I soaked it up like it would be the last time. Her smiles were everything to me. "It's Brad. All along, it was Brad." The words didn't make sense at first. If what she was telling me was right, it was way more than a mans jealousy or a rivalry between criminal and cop. It was more than that. Brad's part in all of this had to be much larger than any of us had thought. He was the one targeting Emberly. He was the one I should have been looking for all along. I was just too blinded by the aura of a stalker to see it until right now. Fuck!

What if it all had been a lie?

What if Brad had gone after her after I'd taken an interest in her?

What if it was all my fault?

Did I cause this?

The what ifs continued to plague my thoughts as I felt Em's petite body shift in my arms and felt the warm sensation of her small hands on my jaw, whispering touches of her fingertips on my skin pulled me from my self loathing thoughts and toward her.

"You still here with me?"

"Yeah, Darlin'. I'm always here."

"I didn't know it was him, Hudson. If I had..." I dropped my head to hers and silenced her with a chaste kiss, dragging my lips over hers in what I hoped was a reassurance of what we had, of what I felt for her. When her hands came up to my neck and her slim fingers dove to the back of my head, I knew she felt it.

I love you.

I embedded the words into every hungered sweep of my tongue between her pillow soft lips and sung them between the breaths I couldn't catch when we kissed. And just as every other time before, breath wasn't a necessity because kissing her was all I could focus on. You make me breathless. I would have said it if she hadn't stolen my breath with her perfect fucking mouth so I did the next best thing.

I kissed her again.

"Hudson?"

Her voice was so quiet I barely heard her. I pulled away from her lush, perfect lips and used my thumb and forefinger to tip her chin up until her saddened eyes met mine.

"Make me forget."

How the fuck could I say no to that?

22

EMBERLY

he backs of my knees met the end of the bed and I fall back, gasping for breath against the ardent mouth that's captured mine in a searing, burning kiss. The kind of kiss dreams are made of. It reminds me of our first kiss, the requisite lust and famished devotion making my knees weaken from beneath me and my heart raced so rapidly that it felt as if my chest would collapse from the force of it.

Taking hold of the warm, taut skin of his hard, muscled back, I held on tightly, not wanting to be anywhere but right here, right then.

Our first kiss was blazing, surprising, earth shattering. But, this one was a reclaiming, a reaffirmation of a connection that's hummed between us from the beginning. The strength of it used to scare me, terrify me, actually.

How could something so sudden and so powerful last?

I wasn't sure it could. Even if it was fleeting and would be gone someday, I needed to take hold of it.

It was everything.

"Do you know, Emberly?"

His rough, gritty voice was next to my ear, warm, mint laced breath wafting over my face and I hummed, anticipation curling in my stomach and attraction pebbling over my heated skin like the first sparks before an explosion.

Moving my eyes from the mass of tanned skin that stretched over Hudson's chest, I looked up, not surprised when I found that the intensity of his gaze was already trained on me. He took his time placing a series of blistering, open mouthed kisses along the slope of my throat toward the sweet spot behind my ear. A harsh moan fell from my parted lips when he nipped into the sensitized skin and I tightened my hold on his shoulders, lost in him, already.

"Do I know what?"

"Do you know how much I love you, Darlin'? Shit, *this* I've never had this. Never wanted it. Never needed it. Had my badge and shield, my family, a few close friends. What else would I need?" He shook his head at himself, as if he was crazy for saying the words but I heard the truth in them. He may not have been alone in the traditional sense of the word, but he hadn't let love into his heart. Hudson was so many things and I was learning more about him every day.

He believed that love and marriage would come later in life and that in order to succeed as a police officer, he had to push everything else in his life aside.

But this man, this strong, protective, sensitive and astonishing man, deserved *love*.

Happiness.

Joy.

Fulfillment.

I hated to think of the man he would have been before we'd met.

Jaded.

Alone.

Throwing himself into his work day after day instead of stopping to truly live in the moment, like he was now.

His nose skimmed up the length of my neck, causing a shiver

to rise up my spine, the heady awareness my body hummed with taking me over.

"Wasn't expecting you. Didn't know you were in store. Didn't know how not to claim you. Look at you, how could I not?"

Suddenly, his mouth was crushing mine, my name a grunt of approval when our tongues met and his taste engulfed my senses. I felt him grab for the bottom of my shirt, wasting no time in tearing the fabric over my head. I gasped in a shuddering, much needed breath of air before the rush of his rough, callused hands heated my skin and I was dizzy.

His touch.

The fervor in which he kissed me.

It was both overwhelming and unsatisfying and I reached for the buckle of his low slung jeans, needing so much more.

"I need you, Hud."

My words were hushed, just a mere whisper over the pounding of my heartbeat in my chest and the heat in my core telling me where I wanted his touch, the most.

He didn't say anything.

He didn't need to.

His blue, so blue, eyes said all I wanted to hear.

He loved me.

I wanted to say something, to tell him the gravity of my feelings but suddenly words didn't seem like enough. They were inadequate compared to the emotion that welled up inside of me, the stinging, joyful tears spilling over when strong, sure hands took hold of my curved hips, fingers pressing into my skin before the round, head of his cock was at my entrance. Precum was already seeping from the bulbous head as it pressed between my swollen folds, teasing me for long, torturous seconds before I was shown some mercy when Hudson groaned, thrusting inside of me with one, harsh movement and I was claimed, all over again.

He begun a slow, steady rhythm and it was just what I needed.

I blinked up at him, not knowing how to express the feelings that pulled through my chest and tugged at my heavy, heart.

It was beyond love. Beyond need. Beyond longing.

It was this desperate craving to cement our connection in the realest of ways because if the last twenty forty eight hours taught me anything, it was that life was way too short to waste time being scared.

I'd let my fear of being hurt stop me from giving in to us for too long.

When Hudson swiveled his hips and dragged the large head of his cock along the swollen bundle of nerves of my labia, I instantly bore down on his length, clamping my walls around him to keep him doing just that. And he chuckled in my ear, that irresistible smile bursting over his hard edged features, making him look boyish, carefree.

I let my gaze linger over his face, needing to memorize every expression that passed in his eyes because it could all be gone in a second.

Tristan's accident was teaching me that.

It had opened my eyes to what I'd been doing, pushing my feelings for Hudson away anytime we got close.

I was done with that.

I loved him.

But right now, I needed him.

More than air.

It was crazy and it was powerful and it was perfect.

"Oh my god, *baby.*" I cried out, panting for breath when he hit a spot inside of me I hadn't known existed. The sparks of pleasure that soared through my body had me quivering, the cusp of the point of no return only a touch away. I tightly, clinched my legs over his lean waist, gasping in surprise when in a swift move, he flipped us over. Suddenly I was on top of him, my weakened knees holding me up as the evidence of my arousal leaked down my thighs and I blushed deeply, closing my eyes as he groaned a harsh breath, rocking up into me, hitting a nerve inside of me that had me trembling all over.

"Fuck, you like that, don't you?"

I couldn't answer when dots of white light sparked beneath my eyelids, only nodding my head in affirmation of his hoarsely spoken question.

"You're so sexy, baby. You have no idea... Shit..."

The rough pads of his thumbs barely skimmed the taut points of my nipples and it was like he'd lit a grenade between us. I couldn't hold on anymore.

"Hudson!"

"That's it, Darlin'. Milk my fuckin' cock."

His words were the last thing I heard as I melted into the ocean of rushing, catalytic pleasure that smothered my body. Making rational thought or words of endearment irrelevant, only the joining of our bodies and the foul curse that fell from Hudson's full mouth as he found his release shortly after me held my attention. The second I fell back to earth, his strong arms were around my waist, keeping me close to his chest, where I belonged.

Where I'd always belong.

"Love you."

The words were uttered as exhaustion heavied my eyes and I didn't have to open them to know my man was smiling against my hair, his lips pressing to my ear as he muttered,

"You're everything, Darlin'."

23

EMBERLY

"Good morning, darlin'."

A deep, amused voice roused me from sleep and blinking open my eyes, I grinned. Hudson was standing beside the bed, his bare chest showing off a mass of taut, tanned skin and the defined muscles that rolled beneath the surface. I stretched my arms over my head, the sensation of the sheets against my chilled skin heavenly. As I sat up, he leaned in close, mouth pressing firmly to the top of my head, the loving gesture spreading warmth through my chest.

"How long have you been awake?"

Setting the two coffee cups in his hands on the nearby table, I felt his hands settle around my waist and on a gentle tug, I was pulled back to his chest, the warmth that radiated from his body seeping into my skin.

"Not long. Didn't have the heart to wake you."

His thumb nudged my chin up, my eyes meeting his and the adoration I found in them stole the words I'd been about to say away.

"You're sweet."

A predatory look passed over his features before he chuckled softly, moving his thumb in circles over my cheek.

"We've talked about this, babe. I'm not-"

"Yes, you are, Hudson. You're so much more than you let others see. But, I do."

His blue hued eyes narrowed just enough for me to know he heard me, heard the meaning behind my words and then he just shook his head, muttering a curse that didn't phase me.

My man was sweary. Many would say he was rough around the edges, crass.

But I saw the man behind all of that.

I saw *Him.*

"Fucking lucky to have you, Emberly."

"Yeah, you are."

A hearty laugh met my cheek as he shook his head at me, again.

"Come and shower with me before I go."

I was nodding before he'd gotten all of the words out but when their meaning registered, I stopped short , faintly hearing the sound of the water coming on in the bathroom.

Stepping inside the door way, Hudson's gaze came to mine and I saw the determined rage darkening them, the expression one I hadn't noticed moments before.

"Where are you going?"

"Em-"

Oh, no, no, no.

He begun to advance on me, his hands tightly clenched at his sides and I saw it, his control slipping from him. Taking a step back, I just needed to get my thoughts straight before his touch made me forget the palpable fear that spread through my veins like acid.

If he went after Brad, he could be hurt.

I couldn't let that happen.

We were finally letting one another in and I knew we'd be happy.

If Brad took that away...

My eyes stung as my emotions welled up inside of me and as

they spilled over, Hudson's eyes softened, the pain I was feeling reflecting back at me.

"Just let it go, Hudson. I'm sure he'll leave me alone, now..."

My voice trailed off when his eyes darkened, the warmth seeping out of their depths as he stalked to me. His steps, loud and determined, hands grabbing mine with a rough, powerful hold, similar to the way he'd taken hold of my heart that beat frantically within my chest, each thundering beat only adding to the knot of anxious worry in the pit of my stomach.

I closed my eyes tightly, feeling his thick fingers pressed to either side of my face, the pressing touch urging me to look at him, but I resisted.

Looking at him meant seeing the hurt he felt at the thought of leaving my side. The love I always saw in his face when he looked at me. The devastating, anger that emanated from his massive body and blackened his normally expressive eyes.

"*Really*? You're fucking sure the egotistical maniac that attacked you, *hurt* you is going to let it go? The monster of a man that went into an innocent families home and terrorized and murdered four people in cold blood? You really think he's just going to walk away from all of this?"

All the blood drained from my face at his words and I was grateful for the fortifying strength of his hands capturing mine because without them, I was sure I would have fallen to the floor. He had told me of his history with Brad, but not the extent of it.

I hastily shook my head, the image of blood and pain and wreckage Brad had done by his hands enraging me to the point where I shook from the force of the emotion swarming through me. I knew he needed to pay for all of it, every ounce of despair he'd caused to those around him. And I hated it, because I was powerless.

I couldn't protect myself when he'd come after me, he was just too strong.

But Hudson could, I knew that.

I slipped my hands from his much larger ones, opening my eyes, instantly looking deep into his gaze, through the sadness and the fury and the darkness.

To the man that I loved more than I thought possible.

I ignored my own anger, my own hatred for the man he was about to hunt down because to me, it just didn't matter. We were what mattered.

Him.

Me.

Us. And the connection we had was stronger than all of this, I felt it in my heart.

"Hud-" His head dropped to mine and I sucked in a grateful breath of air, needing his scent in my lungs to strengthen myself for whatever came next.

"*No*, baby. He doesn't get a free pass because you're scared."

I gasped audibly at his answer, pushing at his chest with closed fists, my anger for my attacker morphing into utter, disbelief at the man in front of me.

"Don't say that. God, don't say it like I'm protecting him. I'm not!"

"Then what is it?" I shook, emotions overwhelming me as I stood there, feeling as if the ground was slipping from beneath me and I was losing my footing.

How could I tell him how panicked I was of what would happen if he found him? I felt one of his thick, callused fingers on my jaw, urging me to look at him but I couldn't. I trained my eyes on the tiled floor of his kitchen, memorizing the pattern of it instead of facing him.

The idea of Hudson being hurt or worse for the sake of protecting me was like the sharpest blade, planted in my heart.

I couldn't take it if the worst happened and I lost...

"Need to see you, Em."

When I did, I saw the love, the warmth, the urgent need and possession, all reflected in his now blue eyes. God, I loved his eyes.

Someone once told me that the eyes were the window to the soul. I never thought much of it, until I saw him. I could always read his emotions, right there, in his eyes.

It was one of the many, many things I loved about the man and I blinked against the build of tears in my own eyes as I realized I wanted to keep learning about him, loving him more and more each day. Endless, that was how I felt for him.

Would it go on, if I lost him?

Yes.

I knew the answer the second the thought crossed my mind and I didn't want to face that.

I wanted to spend my life loving Hudson Lennox. If he chased after my demons, I might not get that chance.

"Every single person I've loved in my life, I've lost them. My mom... everyone."

I uttered the words, hearing the break in my voice as I spoke but I pressed on, because I needed him to hear me.

"I can't...please, Hud. I can't lose you, too."

I caved, then, letting my face drop to his chest where I inhaled his musky scent, chills racing up my spine at the knowledge that it may be the last time.

The room went quiet for only a matter of seconds before I heard him curse, moving his hands from his sides and up my bare back, leaving shivers of longing in their wake. All I could do was hold onto him as he lifted me off of my feet, carrying me back to the bed, where he gently, oh so gently, laid me down before getting in behind me. The soft kiss of his lips on the shell of my ear was a wordless apology and I cuddled closer, needing the warmth of his embrace more than anything else.

"I know how scared you are, Darlin'. I'm not going out there blind. Tristan may not be with me..." His deep baritone dropped off, as if he'd only just remembered his best friend and the accident that left him unconscious and in critical condition.

"But, I have my men. I have officers I would trust with my life, have trusted with my life. I won't be going in there alone."

Turning in his arms, I gently took his face in my hands, imploring him with my eyes not to go. Why did it have to be him? Why did he have to put his life on the line instead of the many other capable police officers in his department?

It wasn't fair.

"It doesn't have to be you."

He grabbed my hands, not moving his gaze from mine for a second.

The emotions in them were clear as day and I knew what he was about to say before he uttered the words.

"It has to be me."

24

HUDSON

$\mathcal{I}$ lied to her.

There was no backup. No plan B. No rationality to what I was about to do.

Would do it, anyway. This was for my Emberly.

For the young, innocent baby girl she'd been, only wanting love and acceptance from a father that took and took and took, from her.

A monster.

Similar to the one I was hunting down, like the vile, despicable animal he was.

Murderer, rapist, pedophile.

But those crimes weren't what had gotten him in my wrath.

A low chuckle escaped me as I imagined all of the ways he'd suffer for ever touching her.

Hurting her.

Bruising her beautiful, flawless skin.

Tainting her loving, kind soul.

Cracking her insecurities open, again just after I'd succeeded in putting them to rest.

That was his doing.

And he would pay for it, *with his life.*

I pulled the keys of my truck from the ignition and tugged the hood of my sweatshirt over my head before stepping out of the cab and taking the front steps of the ranch styled house in front of me. Grabbing the handle of the front door, I pushed it open expecting it to be locked and ready to break it down if I had to. Except, it wasn't.

It wasn't hard to find Brad Sullivan's main residence with a little digging and though it was doubtful he'd make it that easy for me to find him, it was the first step in my search.

Flipping the light switch by the front entrance of the house, my eyes scanned the room, noticing the bare walls and scarcely furnished living room. I moved toward the kitchen, noticing a small lamp illuminating the room. If no one had been here in a while, why would he leave a light on?

It didn't make a lick of sense until I cleared the threshold of the kitchen and noticed a notepad and disposable cell phone sitting on a nearby table.

A shudder raced up the length of my spine as I froze where I stood, the fury I'd had for my target morphing into dread that chilled me down to my bones.

What the fuck?

I paused to tuck my gun into the back of my jeans before I tore the note from the pad of paper and read the message left for me.

You're smarter than I thought, Lennox.
I knew you would be looking for me soon enough.
Took you long enough.
Take the phone.
I'll call you about a meeting place and time shortly.
We have a few things to talk about.
Bx

My hands tightened into fists at my sides as I read it, my body vibrating with the need to find the fucker and finish this.

I'd dedicated the last five years of my life to upholding the law and protecting the citizens of Austin.

Never straying from the oath I'd taken to protect, serve and put away the bad guys.

If you asked me then, if I would break that oath I would have said no.

Hell, no.

But, I had run out of fucking options.

It was my job to protect my woman from anything that could harm her.

He had hurt her.

I could have called the police and let them investigate the case.

I could have done the *right* thing.

I could have done a whole lot different than the choices I made.

Couldn't risk her safety.

That was all that mattered now.

So, when the loud, ring of the flip phone in my hand filled the air, I didn't hesitate in answering it.

"Where?"

"It's good to hear from you, too, Officer."

My blood boiled beneath my skin.

"Don't push me, Brad. You wanted to meet me because you knew that if I found you on my own, you'd be a dead man. So tell me where."

The sarcastic hiss that sounded on the other side of the line only heightened the anger inside of me and I felt my control slipping away from my grasp.

"Okay, okay. *Testy!* I will be at the abandoned warehouse on Lakewood drive in ten minutes. I'll expect to see you there. And don't be stupid, I'll know if you bring backup."

I was out of the house and next to my car by the time he

finished his taunt and I seethed on the inside, my fingers itching to wrap around his neck, feel the spineless, sorry excuse of a man take his last breath.

"Got it."

Throwing the phone on the passenger side of my truck, I started it up, peeling out of the driveway as I headed toward the other side of the city, to finally put an end to Brad Sullivan.

Everything I was made of rebelled against the action as I drew my gun out of the waist of my jeans and trained it in front of me, slowly approaching the run down building I'd been lured to. This wasn't me.

I wasn't a killer.

All of my life, I'd wanted to protect those around me.

I wanted to help people and make a difference in this fucked up world.

Never would have expected to have to strip my badge and shield in order to do just that.

Protect her.

A dull, ticking sound from behind me raised the hair on the back of my neck, my body instantly on alert when the heavy door I'd come through heavily, shut behind me and I heard a lock engage.

What the...

"Ah! I'm happy to see you made it. I was worried you wouldn't show up. Coffee?"

My eyes narrowed on the man that stood just inside the large, bare room, only a singular desk and chair inhabiting the space. He was the picture of calm, his knowing smile and dark, raised brow telling me he was enjoying taunting me, luring me here to the place of his choosing, leaving me vulnerable in a way I didn't fucking like.

"I'll pass, Brad. Did you think you could trick me? Because

all of this, this stupid game, doesn't fucking phase me. You're a dead man walking. And trust me, I will enjoy ending you."

His sneer widened as I approached him, my steps slow, calculating, deadly.

"Uh, oh, not so fast, Officer. Well, you don't have backup do you? You've gone rogue, hunting me down to avenge your sweet Emberly. Not for long, though. She'll be mine, soon enough."

I was on him before the last word slipped from his vile mouth, my clenched fists lifting him from the ground while I used an arm over his windpipe to silence his response, not wanting to hear one more thing from the sorry excuse of a man.

"Don't fucking say her name. You want to live? Tell me why you came after her. Why mess with what's mine? You had to know it wouldn't end well. Had to know I protect what's mine, always will."

A barely audible cackle burst from him and letting up on his throat just barely, I waited for him to start talking.

No matter what was said, I was going to end him.

Slowly.

"Do you hear that?"

My focus shifted when I heard it again.

Tick. Tick. Tick.

Fuck!

"What the fuck?"

My first instinct was to release him and find whatever device he'd placed in the warehouse, I was guessing it had to be close since I heard the tick of a timer when I'd come inside.

The door.

He more than likely hooked it up to the heavy, metal door I'd come through and had the timer engage as soon as it opened. Which meant that opening it again would set off the detonation.

He'd tricked me.

"Did you think I would make this easy for you? That door has a bomb traced to its hinges. That means only one of us can get out of here alive. Through the window. So, you have two options. Kill me, or say goodbye to your precious Emberly."

I gripped his arm in the next second, twisting it behind his elbow until he writhed in pain like the weak man he really was. Maintaining my hold on his throat with the other, making it barely possible for him to breathe as I gritted the warning, low and venomous.

"Don't. Fucking. Say. Her. Name."

Releasing my hands from his throat, I barely registered him stumbling against the wall behind him, his dry heaving background noise to the thundering in my head. I roared with agitation and fury, damn near ripping my hair from my scalp as I begun pacing the room, mind scrambling at the sudden realization of how naive I'd been.

Walking directly into the trap he'd set up for me.

Tricked by his easily laid out plans.

I was a *cop*.

Should have seen this coming.

Blinded by rage and painful remorse for my beautiful girl, I was putty in his hands.

Taking a deep breath, I waited until my composure returned, letting the mask of indifference slip over my face before I turned back to Brad, knowing I had to allow him to believe he'd won this round; no matter how much it grated on me.

"What do you want?"

Gone was the sneer of his humored malice and all that was left across his face was fury, same as mine except his, wasn't justified.

"You thought you could take her from me? She was *mine* first."

A scoff met my ears as he leaned closer, his maddened eyes assessing me as he finished what he'd lured me here to say.

"She will always belong to me."

The thin thread of composure I'd had snapped in two.

I didn't remember pulling my piece and training it on his head.

Didn't recall wrapping my angered fingers around his throat and squeezing until he pled for his meaningless life.

All I saw was Emberly. Her face, littered with horrid bruises.

Her eyes, fear filled and lifeless. Her trembling body, as she cried against my chest. Her pleading with me not to go after her attacker, afraid of losing me.

Fight to the death. That's what it was.

Laws ceased to exist.

The chains of society's rules didn't stop me. I was doing this for her.

I would do anything to ensure her safety.

I love you, Emberly.

Darkness.

EMBERLY

*T*he subtle beeping of the machines in the small, dark hospital room enticed me to open my eyes and I felt the hand in mine twitch, the large hand that engulfed mine suddenly tightening. It had been a whole forty-eight hours since the accident that put Tristan here. Well, maybe *here* wasn't really the word to describe him, but I could practically feel a fierce will to live emanating off of his sleeping form. He was a fighter, I knew that. He had too many people who needed him in this life to leave it just yet.

He knew that, didn't he?

Squeeze. His large, pale hand gripped mine, much tighter this time, and I knew it couldn't be just a twitch like some of his doctors had warned us of.

He was waking up!

"Oh my god...Tristan? Can you hear me, can you squeeze my hand again?"

I stood by his bedside, moving away from his grasp only to push the button that would notify the hospital staff he had woken up at last.

"Not a child, Emberly. I can hear you just fine." A burst of laughter bubbled up and out of my chest at his gruff statement, his eyes opening just enough to look at me and when they did, a faint, humored smile graced his pale face.

"You're awake." I said dumbly, not believing it quite yet.

"Seems that way. Where's my woman?"

Looking behind me to the slightly open door of his room, I shook my head, trying to recall where I'd heard Ashlee say she was going. I think the cafeteria.

"I'm not sure."

His thick, black eyebrows instantly drew together, agitation covering the playful look that had been present in his eyes only a moment before.

It could have been the pain medication heightening his mood, I wasn't sure.

I knew just how much he cared for my best friend and how fiercely protective he was over her. Almost as much as my Hudson was.

"She should fucking be here. Go find her."

"Tris-" I placed a gentle hand on his shoulder to stop him from doing what I was sure he wanted to right then: going to wherever she was.

"Where the fuck is she? I wake up from God knows how long in this stupid place and she's not *here*? Wait- how long has it been?" I saw the devastated need for her in his dark, wide eyes and swallowing hard, I backed away just a step - giving him some space.

Twisting my hands in front of me, I wasn't sure how much to tell him.

He'd been through so much already, and I didn't want to add to that only mere minutes after he'd woken up from his coma.

"Do you remember the accident?" Tristan's eyes widened at my words and slowly nodding his head, he raised an agitated hand to move through his hair before responding.

"Yeah. How long, Emberly?"

"2 days."

"And she's been here?"

"Yes, of course. I'm sure she's just grabbing some food..."

"*Babe?*"

The word was spoken so softly, I barely heard it, but with one look at Tristan, I knew he could have heard it in the middle of the loudest room.

Turning my head toward the voice, Ashlee stood with her arms wrapped around herself, a brown bag from the cafeteria hanging from one of her hands as she stared across the room at the man she loved.

The man she almost lost...

"It's okay, Ash. He's okay."

She didn't budge.

I was betting that her emotions were overwhelming her and that she just needed some space and time to realize that what she was seeing, truly was real. The energy in the room seemed to shift as Tristan reached out for her hand from the hospital bed he was attached to, his eyes pleading with her as he spoke for the first time since she'd entered the room.

"I'm right here, Gorgeous. Come here, fuck, come here."

Ashlee looked from his face, etched in concern and annoyance of the situation, to his hand and back again. Nonetheless, she just shook her head, backing away from his grasp.

It wasn't like her.

She was fearless and kind and loving, showing compassion to every single person that she met.

She didn't have a mean bone in her body.

From the visible shaking of her shoulders and the rigid way she held herself, I thought she was in shock. I stepped toward her just as a loud, ripping sound permeated the air and heavy footsteps landed on the laminate floor.

"Tristan! What are you doing, your injuries..."

He'd torn the I.V. and sensors from his arm and was standing beside the bed, his massive frame shaking with the effort I knew it was taking him not to pull her into his arms and shield her from whatever was running through her mind, halting her from moving toward him.

"She's my everything, Emberly. How am I not supposed to go to her?"

He damn near growled the words at me and I nodded, stepping back as he quickly made his way to her, stopping only a foot away from where she still stood, frozen. I don't think she realized who was standing there, not until his hand gripped her chin and moved up to hold her face in a gentle, yet firm grasp.

"Look at me, Ash. Fuckin' feel me. I'm okay, pretty girl."

It took a minute for her eyes to dilate and her tremors to subside, but when they did and her eyes looked up at him, you could have felt the connection they had hanging in the air.

"Tristan!"

Her arms quickly wrapped around his neck, his hands lifting her up his body so her legs could wind around his waist and as he held her there, comforting her and murmuring how much he needed her, how he would never leave her, something inside of me broke.

Because as I watched my best friend reunite with the man she loved, all I could think about was Hudson and how he'd left to find Brad after I'd begged him not to. He was a stubborn man and his protective instincts were motivating his choices. What I wanted didn't matter in the face of the danger Hudson felt I was in. I couldn't help the sinking feeling in my gut that told me something would go wrong.

Please come back to me, Hudson.

"I'm going to, um find your doctor."

I mumbled before closing the door behind me, leaning on it for support for several long minutes until finally my legs felt steady enough to walk to the nurse's desk, around the corner of the hallway.

"Is he awake?"

Ellie was standing behind the counter as I approached, but as soon as she saw my face, she rushed over, engulfing me in an embrace I hadn't known I needed until that very moment.

"He's okay, Ellie. He's okay."

She didn't release me as she exhaled a heavy sigh of relief against my shoulder.

"Thank God. Ashlee..."

"She's in there with him. I thought I'd give them some time before letting family in to see him."

Nodding, she pulled away, looking at me with concern, but I shook her off.

"I'm fine, I promise. Can you page Doctor Sinclair to his room? I think I'm going to go into the chapel for a bit."

Understanding softened her gaze as she looked at me and when she nodded, I slipped past her and moved quickly down the hallway, eager for some distance from the reminders of Hudson that I saw around every corner.

If something happened to him...

I pushed open the heavy, wooden door to the chapel, refusing to think like that.

He'd been in danger every day, chasing bad guys and putting them away.

This was no different, I told myself.

No, it was.

This time, he wasn't putting his life on the line for his job, or his badge, or his shield.

This one was for me.

"Hi Mom," I said, forcing the words through the lump in my throat, emotions I had refused to feel for so long after her passing suddenly resurfacing, and I felt them all:

Anger, for the man I'd thought of as my father, when really all he'd ever been was a monster and an abuser.

Pain, for the woman who was taken too early from this world, before she found the strength to leave him.

Regret, for all of the times I could have done something, *anything* to stop his abuse and cruelty towards my mother, but I hadn't.

But most of all, I just missed her.

I missed the way she would sing when she thought no one was listening.

I missed the beautiful songs she'd soothe me with when I was young, lulling me to sleep with promises of a better life.

In a lot of ways, it still felt like just yesterday that I had learned the news.

I was in school at the time when a guidance counselor pulled me into her office, and my grandmother met me with one of her long, comforting hugs.

I was too young to truly understand that the injuries which caused the bleeding of her brain, the injuries that took her life, were caused by my own father's hands.

She'd told the doctors that she was clumsy; she had fallen down the stairs while doing laundry that morning.

Mom had lied.

It wasn't laundry day, and she wasn't normally clumsy or careless like that.

No, it was him.

He killed her.

My hands were clenched into fists in my lap as I tried to reign in the hopelessness that sent chills down my spine. The same way it did every time my thoughts returned to my childhood, and to the darkness that I had lived in for so many years.

Looking up at the ceiling, I closed my eyes tightly.

I didn't have to live like that anymore.

I had love and happiness and safety in my life now, and something else I never would have imagined having:

A man who loved me.

Hudson.

"I know I haven't talked to you in a while. It's not that I didn't miss you, Mom. I do miss you, so much. I guess it's just been hard for me to think about you, because it's not fair. You should still be here. We should be together, making memories that I can tell my children about. Wow, I don't even know if I'll have them, but if I do, I want you to know that I'll try to be the best mom I can be. I just wish you were here to help me."

My hands had begun to shake in my lap as I went on, a weight of pent-up emotions pressing on my chest and I knew I had to get them out, now.

I waited too long, trying to move on with my life, to forget the past.

But I didn't want to do that anymore.

She was my mom.

"I'm happy, now. I have friends, a job I love and I met someone. I think you'd really love him. His name is Hudson."

I swallowed past the tears that clogged my throat as I heard the soft sound of the door to the chapel being opened.

"Emberly?"

Swiping under my puffy eyes, I turned and waved at my best friend, glad to see the light of happiness returning to her face.

"Hey. I was just..."

"I know, Emberly. I heard. I think it's really good that you're coming to terms with everything. It wasn't long ago that I wondered if you ever would."

Nodding, I took her hand as she sat down beside me on the long, wooden bench.

"I think it's time."

Her warm arms wrapped around my shoulders and I sniffed back the rest of my sadness, squeezing her equally as tight before she leaned back, away from me, a serious look crossing her normally soft features.

"Tristan just received a call from his sergeant. It seems that Hudson's car was tracked to an old warehouse up the highway. He thought you should know."

It took a solid minute for what she was saying to make sense, but when it did, it felt like all of the air had drained from my body.

Hudson.

"Oh, no. No, no, no... he was going to find Brad. He was the man that..."

"Oh, babe. I'm sure he'll be okay. He's a good cop."

As if pieces of a puzzle clicked together, my mind suddenly understood the real reason Hudson was so adamant about going after him.

He didn't inform anyone.

He went after him... *alone.*

"Oh my god, I have to go."

Her hands tightened in mine when I attempted to pull away and from the look in her eyes, she wasn't about to let me go anywhere without spilling.

"He said he had to go after him, said it had to be him. I don't think... Ash."

Her face went white when she understood what I was trying to say and then she was the one that was pulling away, grabbing her purse from the bench before running out of the chapel. I followed just steps behind her.

Urgency and dread pumped through my veins and my mind was a mess of worries and *what if*'s.

All I knew was that we had to get to him.

I'd thought he was risking his life by leaving this morning, but I never imagined just how much of a risk it was.

If something happened to him...

"Look at me, Emberly. I know you're scared and I know you're freaking out. I would be, too. But we have to help him. You with me?"

Nodding, I forced my shocked body to move down the hall behind her, only pausing when we reached the open door of Tristan's hospital room.

I didn't hear what Ashlee leaned down and told him but

when his wide, concerned gaze turned to me, I knew he understood.

"I'm going to call the sergeant. He'll have someone come and get you and bring you to the scene. And Emberly?"

I was almost out of the door when he spoke my name, so I turned back until my eyes landed on his.

"Yeah?"

"If anyone asks, you're his fiancé. It's the only way they'll let you go."

The thrill that passed through me barely penetrated the fog of worry I was living in, but I nodded, anyway. Linking arms with Ashlee, we headed toward the entrance and one thought echoed in my mind the whole time.

He has to be okay.

EMBERLY

$\mathcal{T}$he blur of bright flashing lights, police officers and yellow tape made me dizzy as Ashlee stopped her car in front of what looked like an old abandoned building.

"This is it?"

"I think so. It's the address Tristan's sergeant gave him. Are you sure you're ready for this?"

She knew how anxious all of this made me and as she raised a thin, blonde eyebrow, I knew she hated this just as much as I did.

If I walked in to see Hudson hurt...

My heart ached just thinking about it.

An abrupt knock on the car's window pulled me from my fearful thoughts, and the officer behind it gestured for me to follow him.

"I'll see you later. Thanks for coming with me."

Squeezing me to her side, Ashlee hugged me.

"Go find your man."

Smiling through the weight of worry that pressed heavily on my chest, I nodded, pulling away.

"Miss, come with me."

"Okay. Thank you."

We moved into the people swarming around the perimeter of the yellow warning tape in front of the building and as the officer lifted it, an urgency to see Hudson coursed through me.

The large metal door was held open for me and with a shaky inhale, I stepped through.

The dark interior of the room was filled with men in blue... EMT, too.

My stomach clenched in fear, my thoughts instantly going to my Hudson.

Was he hurt?

"Baby!"

I settled at the sound of the voice; deep and growly with an edge of emotion I couldn't place. Searching the room until my eyes landed on his, I saw it. There was a heady mixture of warmth, concern and relief swimming in those sky blue eyes and I was caught in them; frozen as I stared. He dropped his head to his chest, shaking his head roughly, then tore his arms from around his neck and held them wide at his sides. At that moment, my composure shattered and I ran to him.

Hudson.

"Hud, God, are you okay?"

I climbed him like a tree, my urgent, needful fingers clasping his broad shoulders and clinging tightly as his large hands grasped my hips. He planted his face in my neck, and I tightened my arms when I felt the painful relief vibrating off of his large frame, now that I had finally made it to his side.

"Yeah. Fuck, you feel good in my arms."

Kissing his throat gently, I attempted to pull back, to look at him, but he wouldn't have it. Strong, binding arms tightened around my middle and I nodded, knowing what he needed.

"Need to hold you, Darlin'. Could've lost you."

Breathing in the unique, minty scent that is Hudson, I rested my face against his chest and let him do just that.

"What happened? Is he..."

His full lips met my ear and I felt the muscles beneath my fingers clench, as if I'd hit a nerve.

"He's gone, Emberly. It's over."

Able to pull away from his hold at last, I whispered my fingers over his cheeks, noticing shadows in his gorgeous features that I hadn't noticed before.

"Tell me."

"He set me up. Knew I wanted to find him, so he made sure it would all be on his terms. Fucking prick didn't even care when I told him I knew the truth. He knew it was coming. All of this..." His hands flew up and dragged roughly through his hair, agitation and renewed rage radiating off of his body in waves.

"It was a game to him. He set up a bomb to start counting down when I arrived. There wasn't another door in the room so if I wanted to live..."

My audible gasp filled the meager space between us and I felt the blood drain from my face, leaving dread and horrified shock in its wake.

"Y-you had to kill him."

"Yeah, baby." He whispered, then his eyes widened, "Shit, you're pale. Get a chair over here! And an EMT!"

His voice boomed across the warehouse, urgent and determined, and I loved him for the sudden concern crinkling around his eyes.

"I'm okay, Hudson. I promise, I'm okay. Tell me the rest."

Sighing roughly, he grasped my hands and lifted them to his lips, causing my heart to swell as he began to tenderly kiss my fingertips.

"I don't have to tell you, now. We can..."

Quickly pressing my fingers to his mouth, I shook my head.

"I want to know, need to know. Please."

After a long pause, he nodded as I sat down in the chair one of the officers had pulled over for me. Hudson leaned against the wall beside me, linking our fingers in a tight, reassuring grasp.

"I tried to level with him, but there was something in his eyes, he wasn't right in the head. Didn't have another choice."

Reaching up to cradle his face, I nodded, understanding.

He was a monster, a demon from my past.

And just like all my other demons, he'd fought to protect me and destroyed it.

"Are you in trouble?"

He'd killed a man.

Even with all of the things Brad had done in his life, did he deserve that?

I didn't know.

But it was either him or Hudson.

I shuddered at the thought of what could have happened if the events had gone a different way.

This man had tunneled a way into my heart and there was no pushing him out.

And I could have lost him.

"No, Darlin'. Shit, come here."

I was pulled into his lap roughly, though the hands that slowly caressed my back were anything but.

"It's over."

HUDSON

I kept her glued to my side as the EMT checked my wounds and bandaged one of my badly bruised hands. I thought I considered myself to be a strong person, but if the bomb Brad had set for us had gone off, there would have been no escape. I would have died in here, and this beautiful girl in my arms would have been left alone, again.

I'd *risked* that. Because of my fucked-up pride and the emotion clouding my judgment, today I had risked taking myself from her and what for? For vengeance? For some sort of vigilante justice?

It wasn't a choice I would have normally taken. In other circumstances, with a clear head, I would have done the right thing.

Call my superiors. Build a case. Make an arrest.

But with Emberly, I couldn't make that choice to stand down and do what was *right* in the eyes of the law. I just acted on my instincts, the same instincts that had told me to claim this woman, for-fucking-ever. They'd never steered me wrong before. As I drew her deeper into my chest and dropped my mouth to her cheek, I was thanking whoever had been looking over us today. It could have gone so very wrong in the blink of an eye, and it would have been Emberly who'd be left hurting. I couldn't risk that again.

I had to be better, for her. But the fucked-up thing was, I didn't regret it.

Now, she was safe, and the fucker who had hurt her was gone from this world.

If that wasn't justice, I wasn't sure what was.

The barely-there sensation of soft fingers trailing up my bandages pulled me from my inner thoughts and my eyes went to her, as they always seemed to do.

"I shouldn't have let you come here. I could have..."

"Shhh, Darlin'. I'm fine."

Lifting her chin with my thumb, I made sure her big, bright eyes stayed on me as I spoke.

"Let's go home."

Something in her shifted as she heard the underlying meaning behind the seemingly mundane words.

She was coming home with me.

It wasn't as if she'd spent much time away from me in the past month, anyway. Ever since our first date, she'd spent almost every night in my bed, or I in hers. She'd begun leaving little reminders of herself in my house and though I didn't tell her, I loved all of those things. Her makeup bag in my medicine cabinet, her slippers next to mine in the hallway closet, even her favorite ice cream in my freezer. To the naked eye, these were silly, small things. But to us, it was more. Hell, it had always been *more*, with us.

"Please." Was all she said, but I heard it, the way her voice softened with longing and love. *Jesus*, I loved this girl.

I pulled her to her feet and placed my arm around her shoulder, keeping her close as we left the crowded warehouse and walked across the now dimly-lit parking lot toward where I'd left my truck.

"Lennox!"

I turned my head, hearing my name called from one of the slew of P.D. cars lining the lot. My sergeant walked toward us, an expression on his face I'd rarely seen in the past five years I'd worked under him: he was smiling. *That shit was weird.*

"I heard congratulations are in order, son." Begrudgingly releasing Emberly's hand, I nodded, reaching a hand out to shake his.

I hadn't exactly followed procedure today, but I had eliminated the threat to his daughter and I knew he was grateful, even if only for that fact. I was sure I'd have a long, heated chat with him after my furlough was up, but I wasn't too worried about it right then.

I had more pressing things to worry about - like how many times I'd make my woman come on my face when we got home. It couldn't have been more than four or five hours since I'd left her at home in order to track down her attacker, but I had still missed the hell out of her.

I was pretty sure that affliction would never wane.

"Why's that, Sir?"

His narrow, knowing eyes moved from me to Emberly and back again, before a wide grin spread across his face.

"You finally popped the question, didn't you?"

I damn sure was going to. When his statement finally set in, I turned to meet the guarded stare of the woman I loved, confusion filling my head.

Why would my Sergeant believe I'd asked her to marry me, when I hadn't?

Instead of setting him straight though, I let him keep on believing it.

How many times had I thought about the life I'd give this girl, if given the chance?

This was a chance, I told myself and fuck, if I wasn't going to take it.

I knew she had most likely just told him that we were

engaged because she wouldn't be allowed to see me if she wasn't immediate family. I would have probably said the same thing. But now, the seed was planted. How could I let her off the hook for this?

It was time.

"Yes we are, Sir. We didn't want to wait any longer, right, *baby*?"

I could feel her annoyed stare as I spoke with him and after a beat, she chimed in.

"Um, yes."

"Well, I'm very happy for you both."

I cleared my suddenly dry throat as he walked away, my arm quickly winding around Emberly's deliciously curved waist before she even thought about getting away from me.

"Wanna tell me what that was about, Darlin'?"

The bright blush that filled her cheeks was cute as fuck, and I bit my lips in order to hold back the smirk that wanted to paint my face at the sight of it.

Damn, she was lovely.

But before I gave in to my need to ravage her, I had to get the truth out of her.

"About that..."

She looked up at me, those beautiful doe eyes filled with concern as she bit down on her plump lower lip, fucking enticing me with those lips that I craved to devour; right then, right there.

God damn it, she knew I couldn't resist her when she did that.

"Minx," I growled, lowering my mouth to hers at a bruising force, hungrily swallowing her outcry of surprised lust as my tongue slipped along hers and my teeth tortured that lip she'd so easily teased me with. Pure heat filled my veins and drove me to dizzying heights as I slowed the kiss to a mere coaxing of our mouths, and I allowed my hands to roam her lush ass through her pretty little skirt. It was perfection, as it always was with her.

My Emberly.

The thought that filled my fogged-up mind stopped the movements of my mouth over hers, and I just breathed her in as I let it take hold.

My wife...

She'd say it was too soon, I knew that without a doubt.

But now that the possibility of it had been planted, how could I stop myself from asking her the question that teased the tip of my tongue? *I couldn't.*

"Tell me why, Emberly."

Her breath panted from her lips as I released them and she blinked her eyes open, most likely trying to find words after I'd stolen her ability to think by kissing her. *I'd be doing that for the rest of her life, so she'd better get used to it.*

I didn't say that out loud, though.

Baby steps.

I actually scoffed at the thought of going slow with this woman.

We'd almost lost each other today.

There were no more *baby steps* for us.

"Tristan told me I had to say that we were engaged. It was the only way they'd let me see you. I mean, it's not that big of a deal. We can tell him we're not really..." Her voice dropped off as I raised one thick eyebrow, daring her to say the rest of her sentence. But my smart girl knew better, closing her perfect mouth before she could say the rest. Moving my hands to cup her cheeks, I lowered my forehead to hers, just breathing her in for a while; needing to remind myself that she was really *here* with me before I said what I had to say.

I wasn't entirely sure if she was ready for this, but I couldn't keep it inside anymore. I needed to make her mine, in every possible way, before it was too late. Facing Brad and seeing the pain in her eyes earlier today had taught me that I couldn't take those sort of risks with my life anymore.

I had her to think about now, and if I had my way? *Forever.*

Her eyes damn near bulged out of her head when right there, in the middle of the parking lot, I dropped to my knees and grabbed her hands in both of mine, making sure she couldn't get away.

"You wanna marry me, Darlin'?"

HUDSON

*H*er wide eyes tracked me intently as I lowered to my knees in front of her and let a smirk play over my mouth, knowing it would soften her up for the question coming her way.

"Look at me, Darlin'." I demanded, my voice harder than intended as I waited for her to look down at me with those big, beautiful lavender eyes. As she did, I grabbed hold of both of her hands, needing to hold on to her as I said this.

"Marry me."

Two fucking words. Just two words shouldn't have meant this much, but they did. I could feel the ground shaking from beneath me as they penetrated the thickened air between us. I felt as if I were hanging from the highest cliff, needing my woman's hold on me to keep me from falling, from breaking right here; in front of her.

Her voice was all breathy and sexy as fuck when she opened those pretty lips for me and I was a starving man, hanging on to the annoyed words I knew she'd utter.

"No! I mean... God, I don't know."

My grin widened as she squirmed in front of me, her eyes

filled with a mixture of confusion and hope; the look was shattering my resolve. And so I tightened my hold on her slender, smooth skinned fingers, struggling to find the words I'd held in the back of my mind from the second I laid my eyes on her. I knew I wanted her to be mine that day and had just been biding my time, not wanting to scare her away with the strength of my crazy feelings for her.

"Which is it? One I can work with, the other... *not so much.*"

Her eyes darted away from me as she frowned, pouting her lips in the cutest way, weakening my resolution to get an answer out of her. But this shit was important. I didn't care if it was too fast, or if she was scared of getting hurt. She knew by now that I would *never* hurt her and I would *always* protect her.

Always.

"What are you doing Hudson? Get up! This is... this is crazy..."

Trailing my mouth over the knuckles of one of her hands, smiling at her in the way I knew she loved.

"I'm just asking a question, Darlin'. You had to know this was coming sooner or later. It was just a matter of time."

Huffing heavily, she threw her hands in the air, causing a deep growl to fill my throat when she inched away from my hold.

"You're crazy, you know that?"

Shaking my head at her, I settled back on my haunches, getting comfortable because I damn sure wasn't moving anytime soon.

"Noted. Marry me, baby. I'm right here and I'm yours. Just say yes."

I watched the mask shielding her expression slip away as I gentled my voice, pleading with her to just say yes because the longer I was made to wait for her answer; the more I worried I wouldn't be able to convince her.

I wasn't taking no for an answer.

"Been wanting to do this for a long time now, just wasn't sure when the right time would be. I knew you would think we were too new, too fresh and I didn't want to push you into something you weren't ready for, but baby, this is us. We're ready for this. We're ready for forever. Just say yes."

"No," The word was a breath - a lie - a feeble attempt to avoid the inevitable and I let her have it, because I knew she needed it. She needed to claim her happiness on her own terms and as much as I hated to admit it, if that meant being without me, then I would accept that.

I damn sure hoped it would be with me, though.

"Y...you don't have to do this, Hud. I'm not expecting you to ask me this just because I told your sergeant that we were engaged. We just met! This is too soon."

Jesus, she was stubborn.

"But it isn't. I can't imagine living my life without you in it. I can't even think about what it would feel like, living in a world where I couldn't see your pretty smile and hear your addicting laugh. You've been mine to protect since the start. Mine to love since we kissed. Mine to fucking cherish ever since. Don't you feel this? Feel my *love* for you? Because I swear by every star in the sky that it won't end, won't go away. Not until the last breath leaves my lungs."

Her hands shook as I grabbed them roughly, needing to have a part of her in my grasp as I pled with her in the only way I knew how. I wasn't too proud to beg her and that was just what I did. *The first time I saw her, I'd staked my claim. Now I was begging her to claim me, too.*

"We have time, Hud. We don't need to rush this."

I had the sudden desire to shake her when she said that, because this *was* me going slow. I wanted to ask her a long time ago, but I'd controlled the urge.

"This is gonna happen, no matter if it's today, or a year from now. Longer, I don't care." Stopping to take a deep, much-needed breath, I tightened my fingers around hers and made sure her eyes were on me while I continued my plea.

"Do me a favor. Think about your life before us, Emberly. Think about our life, now. Can you imagine ever going back? Tell me that you can and I'll get up off this hard ass ground and forget about it all together."

"Hudson-"

"Marry me."

"No!"

I was up off my feet and on her before I could think better of it.

Selfishly pulling her mouth to mine, I bruised her lips, biting into her flawless skin and greedily swallowing down her moans of surprised delight.

"Fucking. Marry. Me."

"We can't..."

"For fuck's sake, why are you so stubborn?"

Smiling cheekily, she reached up and lightly bit my nose.

"I learned from the best."

"Emberly, I'm going to ask you one more time, got that?"

She nodded slowly, eyes softening as I reached in my pocket and pulled out the box I should have shown her the first time I'd asked the question.

"I love you more than anyone has ever loved anything. Crave you like the most addictive drug. Need you like the air I breathe. Please, Darlin'. Marry me."

Smiling, she reached between us and took hold of the box that encased the ring I had long been waiting to place on her finger; *where it would stay*.

"Put it on me, Hud." I did, my damn hands shaking the entire time. When her arms were wrapped around my neck and her lush curves pressed to my waist, I soaked in the feeling, afraid this was the end of us.

I lied. I wouldn't stop asking her. I'd ask her for the rest of our lives, even if she refused to hear it.

"Yes."

Yes!

"Fuck, you just made me the happiest man alive. Kiss me."

And she did.

EMBERLY

My gaze fell to my left hand, taking in the beauty of the ring that had been placed on my third finger not even a few hours before. My heart was still racing from the thrill of it and, putting my hands against my chest, I could feel the rapidly-thrumming beat of my heart within its chambers. God, was I dreaming?

I was engaged.

Engaged!

In a sense, it felt so final; so real.

But it was only a formality, really. I'd known for a while now that the intensity I felt for the man, never far from my mind, would most likely never go away. In the beginning, my need for the protective, stubborn man I now loved had been terrifying. He made me want, made me *feel*, after living most of my life merely getting by. I had let so much time go by, avoiding getting hurt or making any attachments other than my close friendship with Ashlee and the girls I worked with at the hospital. It just seemed easier. As I heard the sound of heavy footsteps approaching, I smiled, knowing that I'd never have to worry about heartbreak again.

Not with Hudson with me.

He not only loved me, but he shielded me; against any threat, even the smallest ones.

God, I loved him.

"The nurse said he's sleeping, but we could go and sit with him for a few minutes."

"Okay. Do you want me to go with you? I know..."

His much bigger hand gripped mine in almost the next second, holding me fiercely, yet softly.

"No, Darlin'. I want you with me." He tugged me close, grasping my wide hips in his loving hold and I sighed happily, curling my fingers through his ashy brown hair. The smooth, short strands were soft against my skin, such a contrast from the hard, determined man he could be.

"I'm with you."

His eyes gleamed with emotion as he looked at me, those ocean blue eyes seeing straight to the very heart of me. My fingers pressed even deeper into his scalp, gently massaging and eliciting a low, sexy groan from his lips.

"Good," His mouth brushed mine, sending electric sparks over the surface of my skin and I moaned against the warmth of his reverent kiss.

"Let's go see him."

Nodding, I kissed him one last time, stealing a nip of his full, lower lip before pulling away.

"Woman," Hudson said on a low growl and I grinned, escaping his grasp before he could pull me close again. I heard his following footsteps behind me and I didn't have to look back to know he was shaking his head at me.

I saw right through him.

A few minutes later, I softly knocked on the door of the room Tristan had been placed in, then turned the knob, opening the door. Hudson's grasp tightened around my hand as we stepped inside the hospital room, but when he saw his best friend sitting up in bed, the color returned to his features and his mouth firmly planted on Ashlee's, it was like no time passed.

The pale, lifeless man that had laid there a few days ago was stronger than ever and as I raised my eyes to Hudson's, I felt the sting of tears beneath my lids. He was so dedicated to those he cared for, those he loved. The idea of losing Tristan had all but broken him.

Thank God he'd managed to pull through.

Roughly clearing his throat, he stepped into the room with me and moved toward the bed, the tension in his shoulders evident from the hard set of his large, seemingly intimidating body.

"Can I have a minute, Ashlee?"

Her near bleach-blonde head moved from Tristan's shoulder as she nodded, moving from his side while concern crossed her pale face.

"I'm fine, pretty girl. Just go talk with Emberly and don't go far."

Her face lit up with another, nearly blinding smile and she nodded, turning her attention to me and leaping towards me with the energy for life she'd always had.

"You okay?"

I murmured into her hair as we embraced and felt her quick nod against me.

"I am now. If he wasn't okay..."

My arms tightened around her as her voice trailed off, the familiar pain that we had all felt after his accident rapidly rising to the surface again.

"He is," My eyes flitted over to where Hudson and Tristan were talking and there was no doubt in my mind that they were brothers; in every way that counted.

"Look at them, Ash."

Hudson had lowered his head, sitting in a chair near Tristan's bedside and both men had their heads pressed together, one of Tristan's large hands clasped around Hudson's neck.

The stance was intimate, telling of how close they'd both come to losing the closeness they'd had for one another; beyond friendship or the bond between colleagues. My heart stung for them both, but I knew it would all be okay, now.

Tristan was okay.

"Fuckin' gave me a scare, man."

"I know. I'm good now."

Pulling away from one another, Hudson nodded gruffly.

"Let me know if you need-"

"I know. I've got my girl, she's all I need right now."

How sweet was he?

Soon enough, my man was back with me, his strong arms circling my waist and his stubbled chin tickling my nape.

"Tonight, you're mine."

Shivers flew down my spine as his voice heated my neck, where he placed a hot, open-mouthed kiss.

"Yes," Was all I uttered, but it must have been enough because he spun me toward his hard, muscular chest and secured me with a dominant hand holding tightly to my hip.

"Now."

EMBERLY

*H*e was everywhere.
His hands.
His mouth.
And God, that tongue of his.
"Hud, baby..."
"Anything, Emberly. What do you want?"

His mouth tortured my neck as his hands moved over the zipper of my sundress, giving a sharp tug until the billowy fabric gave way and fell to my ankles. The cool air of the room pebbled my nipples against my bra, causing shivers to slide over my prickling skin. The rough texture of Hudson's hands moving across my body was heavenly, and I never wanted the sensations to end.

"You," I exhaled the word, my heartbeat racing within my chest as my breaths slowed into quick, anticipatory pants. The soft nip of teeth around the shell of my ear caused a pleasured whimper to fall from my parted lips and a shudder shook my body, almost as much as the man looming behind me had rattled my heart.

"Where? Where do you want me?"

Before I could utter a word, I was spun within his hold, my

bra-clad chest pressing to his bare torso and his firm, sure hands cupping my chin with a tenderness that brought the threat of tears. But instead, I was smiling because the sadness I'd felt for so long was gone now. These were tears of sheer, unrelenting joy.

"Everything, Hudson. I'm yours."

A mischievous smirk lit up his face and he lowered his mouth to mine, leaving the whisper of a kiss in his wake.

"It's forever, Darlin'."

God, yes.

I arched up just as his mouth swooped down, capturing a taut, aching nipple through the frilly lace of my barely-existent bra. Searing me with the intensity of his mouth.

"Naked. Now."

The faint click of the front clasp of my bra was the only warning I had before the fabric fell away and his warm hands took its place, pressing and loving and brushing against my oh-so-sensitive skin, taking each nipple between his calloused fingertips, giving the pointed mounds just a hint of roughness against the way he touched me. I felt my core tightening between my legs, swelling with the desire I held for him - only him.

"Hudson," My hands moved from my sides to his jaw, my needful fingers feeling the whiskers of his beard as I waited for his eyes to find mine, the warmth and emotion they held warming me all over.

"I love you."

It wasn't that I thought he didn't know the truth of the words. He did. He'd known of my feelings for him before I'd ever realized them, before I could face it.

For so long, I had thought I would always be alone. Aimless, adrift, floating through my life rather than *living* it. I'd thought I wasn't enough, unworthy of the love and adoration I saw in the world around me. But this man, this beautiful, determined man had seen right through my walls and my excuses for why we couldn't happen. I refused to let him into my heart, even after I saw how deeply he cared for me, wanted me. He didn't let me get away, though. He knew we were right for each other, before I ever did.

The past week was hard for us. Between the danger of being watched by an unknown man, then Brad and Tristan's accident, we'd been tested more than I would have thought we could withstand. I had been sure I would lose him, whether from the hands of the sick man who'd taken me from the hospital, or from the bomb that had almost taken Hudson from me, forever.

"Fuck, Emberly. Please don't do this to me."

His fingers wiped at the hot, stinging tears that made their way down my face and I shivered, remembering all of the ways he could have been lost to me. Wrapping my fingers around his wrists as he gently held my face, I knew he'd become so much more than my protector.

He was my savior, my soul, the owner of my heart and all of its love.

"It's happy tears. It's okay. I'm just," Pausing to breathe, I moved my hands to his stoically set face, softly rubbing my thumb over his bottom lip the moment he bit into it. Just as I had known he would, as he always did when he was uneasy or worried.

"I'm just realizing how close I came to losing you, Hudson. I know I haven't always made it easy for us to get here, and I'm sorry..."

The crush of his warm, rough kiss stopped my words short, and a moan slipped out of me the instant I felt his teeth graze the lush flesh of my lips, ravishing me and loving me all at once.

"I was talking." I breathed against his full, devilish mouth, but he only kissed me deeper, licking at my lips and stealing my breath as his kisses always had. That was, until he released me, leaving me shaking in the aftershock of his ardent assault and I swayed into him. Easily catching me by my waist, he held me where he wanted me.

"Do you really think I would have given up on you just

because you made me wait a while? You're the woman I love, Emberly. Fuck, you're my world. It wouldn't have mattered if I'd waited a year to have you, Darlin'. It would have been worth it."

"Hud," I pulled his head down to mine, letting our foreheads press together for a long moment, taking the time to thank God for bringing him into my life: a life that I'd refused to risk until I found him. His mouth skimmed my cheek as I kept my eyes firmly closed, letting the flow of overjoyed, persistent tears slip free while in the safety of Hudson's arms.

"I know, baby. I know."

And as he made love to me, well into the early hours of dawn, I knew he was right.

This was forever.

HUDSON

"*W*ake up, darlin'."

I laid the tray of food beside her as I whispered in her ear, letting my fingers trail over the soft, pale skin of her cheek. It seemed I couldn't go long without touching her, somehow. I craved closeness with her, even in the smallest of ways. She stirred beneath me, a cute-as-all-hell yawn parting her mouth as she stretched.

"Come on, baby. I brought us breakfast."

"Mhmm." Her little moan of protest was both maddening and endearing and I dropped my head to hers, rubbing my lips over the top of her head before telling her something that I knew would perk her right up.

"And coffee."

"Oh!" Her eyes popped open, the colorful irises illuminating with excitement as she bolted up, holding her hands out for the drink I'd picked up for her at her favorite cafe. My girl loved it sweet and strong, and she wouldn't have anything less. I grinned at her, bemused that I could make her happy by a gesture so small. I placed the white paper cup into one of her outreached hands, then took the other in my own, lifting it to my mouth. Her little moans of pleasure hit my ears not long after

AMANDA KAITLYN

and, though I knew she loved my kisses, I was sure those sounds were because of the coffee. My chest heated with a sense of possession I'd only ever felt for her and I ground my teeth, wanting those moans to be because of *me*. Only me.

How the fuck was I jealous of a beverage?

Crazy.

She made me crazy.

"Did you just growl?"

I snapped my eyes to hers, slowly releasing my fists so that she didn't see how absolutely crazy she was making me. Good thing she had my ring on her finger. *She couldn't get away, now.*

"No," Moving my mouth from her little fingers to her full, lush lips, I groaned against their softness. As my hands found purchase in her honey blonde hair, my knees nudged her legs open so that she could wrap them around me. *Jesus*, I loved her body.

Fucking perfect.

It made me crazy that she thought of herself as anything but the beautiful woman I knew her to be; the perfect woman I was holding right then. There wasn't one flaw on her that I could see, and even if there had been, I would have loved her all the same.

Mine.

"You did it again, baby."

I felt her pulling away from me, propping her chin lightly against my chest and her eyes seared into mine, filled with a raw love that locked my chest in an almost painful vise, one I withstood because it meant this was real.

We were real.

"Did what?" I said the words against her mouth before lowering my kisses to her jaw, then the soft line of skin just underneath her chin, her collar bones and then her neck. Something primal inside of me was sated when she began mewling low in her throat, sounds of *more, more, more* meeting my ears as I trailed my mouth to her earlobe. I bit her lightly, nibbling on her supple skin. Like I planned to do to her sweet pussy once I was

220

done teasing her. I wouldn't ever tell her, but I loved teasing her. Those little noises of pleasure she gave me were dizzying, and I found myself craving them as I loved on her.

Claimed her.

Ravished her.

Owned her.

"You growled."

A wide grin spread over my face at her little quip and I bit her again, catching the skin of her lobe between my teeth, giving no mercy until I heard her sweet laugh in my ear. *God*. That sound. I wanted to listen to it for the rest of my life.

"I'm crazy for you, Darlin'. Don't you know that by now?"

I lapped at her neck, circling the soft spot I knew she had just behind her ear and I kept at it, wanting to hear her beg for me to stop; for me to keep at it.

"*God*. Hud, please. You're making me..."

"Crazy?"

God knew I had that affliction myself.

"Hudson, please..."

My hands moved to the button of her slim-fitting jeans as her plea filled the room and I smiled wider, wanting to savor it. Though, with a low chuckle, I realized I didn't necessarily need to. She was wearing my ring and soon enough, we'd be bonded in every possible way. We'd been in love for some time now and I think we had both known all along where it would lead: *Marriage.*

I couldn't wait.

"Off." I growled; *yes,* growled. My insatiable need for her was in every beat of my heart, in every thrum of my pulse.

"Yes," She shimmied her curvy hips, pushing the denim fabric down her wide, creamy thighs and over her knees before letting them fall to her ankles. My mouth met her ear again and as I tortured her some more, I let my always wandering hands find the hem of her tee and I lifted it off with a quick tug, dropping it to the floor, then lifted her off her feet in the same motion.

"Hud, baby. What are you doing?"

"Bed."

"Now?"

I sucked one of her tight, plump nipples between my teeth and tugged, groaning my protest when she pulled sharply on my hair in response.

"Yes, now. Lay back, Emberly."

Her body fell away from me, save for her legs that were still wrapped snugly against my waist. I just stood there, ravaging her with my eyes; I couldn't stop myself from looking at her.

"Jesus, baby. Look at you."

Her face pinked at my adoring words and though I knew she was learning to be confident in her beauty, in her skin, I knew a part of her still wondered if I'd ever see her the way she did. As anything less than the angel she was. And it didn't much matter to me, because I would get to spend the rest of my life reassuring her. *Loving* her.

"What?" Her voice was small, but those wide, violet eyes of hers were full of emotion. The same emotion I felt for her, mirrored back: *Love.*

"You're spread out for me like a fucking feast, baby. How am I supposed to resist these legs? They're a damn dream." I ran my hands over her milky thighs, knowing the roughness of my skin, earned by the combined years of working with my hands as a teen and then with the force, would have her coming alive beneath me; she always did.

"And these hips. These little love handles. Makes me crazy with wanting you." I dropped my head as my fingers curled around her waist, letting my lips linger on her smooth, pale flesh for a moment, then I continued my journey up her curvaceous body. Emberly was chanting my name, arching and moaning and *needing me* and I kept going, letting out a hearty moan of approval as I finally filled my hands with her pert breasts, the lithe flesh molding perfectly in my hands. My mouth took one pointed nipple and my hunger for her was boiling over, not to be ignored, and I feasted on her.

I ravished her.

"Ah, God, baby. So tight. So damn snug for me."

An uncontrolled groan left my lips as I gave a harsh thrust of my hips, rooting myself in her depths with just one motion. My eyes closed at the sensation of her hot, wet channel as it grasped me in the tightest vice; holding me captive, right where I wanted to be. I dropped my face to the nape of her neck, gently planting my lips along her moist skin, kissing her everywhere my mouth would reach as my body showed her how badly I wanted her; needed her.

Needed her sweetness, her innocence that I'd been drawn to from the very beginning.

Wanted her hot pussy, cradling me and owning me; in a way no other women ever had.

Craved the way she was looking at me, holding onto me as if I were her world.

I knew that sentiment was true, since I felt the same exact way.

I'd never thought I would want this.

Love.

Marriage.

A family.

It was her: my sweet, sassy girl. With the most beautiful eyes I'd ever seen and a full, loving heart that had captured mine and hadn't let go.

It was a good thing, too, since it was hers.

I would never want her to give it back.

"Oh my god, Hud!"

Her hot breath wafted over our joined mouths as she panted against my ardent kiss. And I smiled, giving another thrust of my hips against hers, twisting a budded nipple – swollen from kisses - at the same time. Savoring the way she yelled my name, with a fervor I craved, a desperation I would quell for her as soon as she gave me what I wanted. Her hot pussy was tightening around my cock, leaking its essence all over me, and she hadn't even come yet. God, I loved her like this.

So eager.

So mine.

"Please, baby. I need..."

"What do you need, Darlin'?"

Her mouth parted from mine and her breath came out in heavy, exaggerated sighs, telling of how I was teasing her.

"I need to cu-"

She didn't get the chance to finish her dirty words, because I chose that moment to bury myself to the hilt inside of her, pressing against the swollen bundle of nerves of her clit, no longer needing even one more second to tease her with the orgasm she wanted so badly.

I needed to feel her fucking come for me.

Now.

"Oh!"

"Yeah, sweet girl. Give it to me. Come all over me."

And she did.

EMBERLY

*M*y body was still buzzing from the intensity of his love-making as Hudson gently pulled out of me, his mouth leaving a lingering kiss over my closed eyes before I felt him move off of the bed; most likely toward the bathroom to throw away the condom. I stretched then, feeling exquisitely and undeniably sated, a deep, aching reminder resonating between my legs only adding to the afterglow I always felt after he loved me.

My sweet, over-protective, beautiful man.

God, I loved him.

"Shit, Emberly. Why didn't you tell me?"

A deep, roughened voice pulled me from my joyful thoughts and I frowned, opening my eyes to see Hudson leaning against the wall at the foot of the bed, an agitated hand tearing through his dark brown hair and a line of anger hardening his full lips. I sat up against the headboard, curling my arms around myself as a slight chill slid over my skin. *What was wrong?*

"Tell you what?"

He moved closer, taking a seat on the bedspread next to me before he lifted a large hand to cup one of my breasts, his cracked fingertips ghosting over my nipple as he spoke.

"I was rough with you, baby."

My mind immediately rebelled against the thought of it and I shook my head, letting my eyes move from his pale blue irises to my chest, where I noticed a few deeply red bite-marks littering my otherwise pale skin. And I smiled.

He was so possessive of me, so viral and fierce and loving.

And I loved him that way.

I'd spent so much of my life feeling unloved, unwanted; alone in every sense of the word. I loved that he didn't let a moment go by without showing me, in some way, how he felt for me.

How he'd felt for me, all along.

He *loved* me.

With everything he was.

I wouldn't want him any other way, he had to know that.

Right?

I got up from my spot on the bed, moving quickly into his lap before he could protest. Cupping his cheeks, I looked into his now-dark eyes, which were filled with self-loathing and doubt, and I hated seeing those emotions marring his face.

"I love you, Hudson Lennox. Any way I can get you. Gentle and sweet; rough and intense. It's all the same for me because I'll take you no matter what. If I didn't like what we did together, I would have told you. Okay?"

His mouth moved, the hard lines of his angular jaw working, yet no words came out.

He wasn't letting it go, I realized.

"Hud," I moved in, disregarding that he seemed to want to distance himself from me, to punish himself for something I would do with him, again and again.

My mouth brushed over his and I licked against him, begging him with my kiss for him to stop; to let me in. And I swear to God, my soul soared as he did. The feeling of one of hands as it cupped the back of my head was the perfect prelude to the hard press of his mouth over mine, capturing and searing and burning and loving me and I let him. God, did I let him.

Gentle and rough, it didn't matter to me.

Because it was Hudson.

My Hudson.

"Sorry, Darlin'. I lost my head." His words imprinted upon my lips and I nodded, or at least, I thought I did. I was losing my head in an entirely different way, losing myself in the heat of his tongue as it glided over mine. In the bruising, yet oh-so-soft way he kissed me. In the subtle brush of his stubble against my still singed skin.

"I know. But, I love you. Remember that. There's nothing you could do that would change that. And if there was, I'd forgive you, anyway."

His smile rocked me to my core and I corded my fingers through his hair, loving the way he held me, adored me.

I never wanted to live without it.

"When can we get married?"

His mouth moved away from my throat at my blurted question, but I didn't regret it. I felt a sudden urgency to seal the deal, to marry this wonderful, crazy man who I knew I couldn't live without.

He was everything I wanted and nothing I would have ever expected.

The knowledge of that only made the reality of us sweeter.

"Whenever you want."

"No, a date, Hud. I want to set a date."

An amused grin spread over his face as he looked down at me, lowering his head until our foreheads pressed together; as one.

"I'd marry you tomorrow, in jeans and a tee-shirt, Darlin'."

I frowned at his answer, wanting so much more for us.

I wanted the big event.

Family.

Friends.

A dress in white; him in a suit and tie.

"I'm not getting married in jeans."

The chuckle he let loose curled through me like the warmest embrace and I smiled, leaning into his thick, muscled arms and the effortless way he held me.

"Well, it normally takes at least a year to plan a big one, baby. You want us to wait that long?"

A shudder ran through me at the thought, and I immediately rebelled against it.

"God, no. Six months, that's all I'm willing to wait."

"So, Christmas?"

I smiled, liking the idea of a holiday wedding. Most of his family would be coming in for Christmas already anyway, and I knew he would want them there.

I wanted to give him that and *more*.

Smiling wide, I nodded, leaning in to brush my lips over his as I muttered my agreement.

"*Christmas.*"

EMBERLY

*T*he large house came into view and I gasped, my eyes widening at the estate-like grounds that housed a three-story home. It was painted a rosy pink color, its matching window shutters and double-glass paned doors giving the place an unexpectedly quaint feel. I heard the deep sound of Hudson chuckling from beside me, but I couldn't peel my eyes away from the car window as he neared the driveway that led to a spacious garage that undoubtedly fit three, or maybe even four, vehicles.

"This isn't -"

"Baby, it's not that big."

My eyes narrowed as they moved from the house to Hudson's amused blues, and I frowned.

No wonder I hadn't met his parents before now.

They would have most definitely scared me away.

"Did you grow up here? This is..."

"Nah. We lived a few towns over in Haven. We moved here when I was a teenager."

He threw me one of those sweeping, disarming smiles he so often did, before climbing out and moving around the hood, all the while running a hand through his hair in that sexy way of his. Squeezing my legs together in an effort to ebb the sudden sparks of lust I was feeling, I inhaled one deep, cleansing breath before taking his hand and allowing him to pull me from the truck.

"It's just unexpected. I didn't imagine this when I thought about meeting them today." I twisted my fingers in front of me and looked down, unsure if my simple black jeans and flannel, mid-sleeve shirt were okay to wear when meeting his parents. I knew how important first impressions were, and if they didn't like me...

"Stop thinking, Emberly. They are going to love you."

"I didn't exactly dress up or anything. What if..."

I didn't get to finish my sentence before Hudson dove for me, his mouth ravishing my own as it crashed over mine; sending my body into a sudden myriad of sensations. My breath was swept away by the hungry rasp of his teeth over my swollen lips and the flick of his expert tongue as it met mine.

My hands grappled for traction as they clenched into his dark hair, threading through its strands and I swayed against him, needing the stability of his thick, muscular arms that bound my waist, and the reassurance of his kiss.

"You're my woman. My world. My soon to be wife. They. Will. Love. You."

Each word was blunted by a soft kiss on my neck, the line of my jaw, even the tip of my nose.

Oh, how he could swoon me, this man.

"Is that her?"

The voice came from behind us and, drawing in another cleansing breath, I let Hudson's strong, steady hands turn me around to face the music.

"Oh, honey! She's beautiful."

I was grateful for his hold on me as I listened to his parents as they approached us. I could feel Hudson shaking with silent laughter at his mother's appraisal of me.

"She better know how to cook. I wouldn't want him going hungry like..."

"I feed you just fine, Daniel!"

A tall, older man with salt and pepper hair and broad shoulders, just like my Hudson's, leaned his head back and laughed; low and hearty and deep.

He must be his father.

"Homemade pasta and canned sauce is not just fine, woman. A man needs meat. Steak. Pork. Chicken. How am I supposed to protect you when I'm old and gray if I don't have proper nourishment?"

An annoyed sigh was the only response I heard and I bit my lip to stop the giggle that wanted to escape. After seeing the house, the expanse of land, the garage-

I wasn't expecting this.

They were *normal*, whatever that was.

And it was *wonderful*.

"You're ridiculous. I'm committing you, I swear..."

"When was the last time you made me meat, June?"

His terse reply was filled with amusement and affection, reminding me of how Hudson would tease me whenever I was having a bad day.

It was his way of lifting my spirits, even before we'd been a couple.

It seemed to me that he'd gotten that trait from this man: his father.

"Last Friday." Another sigh, this time from Daniel, and the arch of his brows said it all.

He was teasing her.

"Ah! That was last week, babe. I'll be skin and bones before you know it."

His eyes landed on mine as he smiled at his wife and they sparkled with warmth, the tepid blue color nearly identical to the irises of the man I loved, and I smiled as his parents continued to banter, back and forth, as if I weren't standing there at all.

They were trying to make me feel at ease, welcoming me into the fold of their family without a second thought, and I was stunned because I had never felt acceptance like that before.

Family, for me, had always come with ulterior motives and agendas.

But this, this was what family was truly about.

Love.

Laughter.

Easy.

And now, I'd become a part of one, like I'd always wanted to be.

I felt the stinging of moisture in my eyes as I watched Hudson's father roll his eyes at his wife, who threw up her hands at him as if he were crazy.

If he was anything like the man behind me, he probably *was* crazy.

"For God's sake, Ma, you're scaring my bride-to-be."

Hudson's voice boomed through the warm Texas air, and suddenly it was as though time had frozen.

You could have heard a pin drop for how silent it was.

And then I heard Daniel's deep, rich laughter again. followed by the sound of his wife slapping him on the arm.

"Go inside and start the salad. You're annoying the heck out of me, you silly man!" Her hands were on her hips, her long, brunette hair swept over her slender shoulders as she stood there, waiting for him to follow her orders.

Just from observing them, I could see that Hudson's father was the type of man who valued family above all else and used humor to lighten the deeper moments of life

From what Hudson had told me of his parents, I knew that his mother had stayed home to raise him from the day he was born. Retiring with a small pension from the law firm she'd worked for before her pregnancy, she'd never gone back to work after he was in school, choosing instead to be there for every moment of his life, even the small ones. While she'd stayed home, his father had worn a badge and shield, risking his life every day in order to keep those around him safe. Just like his own father, Daniel had chosen to dedicate his life to helping people above all else, and he had passed those morals on to his son, who followed in his footsteps.

I craned my neck to look up into the clear blue eyes of the man holding me and found that he was already looking at me.

It didn't matter what I was doing or who I was talking to, Hudson always had his eyes on me.

Always the protector.

"Emberly?"

I begrudgingly moved my focus back to his mother, who was now standing a few feet away from me, her hands outstretched. I smiled softly, hoping she didn't see the nerves that were pumping through me: *I was finally meeting her.*

There had been so many things I had wanted to say - to do. But when I found she was finally here in front of me, I couldn't think of a single one. So instead, I just stepped closer, then grasped her hands in my own and told her what was in my heart.

"He's everything to me."

Her sharp intake of breath was audible and she pressed her hand over her mouth for a minute, her brown eyes wide with understanding and awe.

"That is all I could ever ask for."

She said, and I heard her voice tremble as she spoke, as if she were just as nervous for this moment as I had been.

Was that even possible?

I didn't get to think much more on it before she gently pulled me into her arms and rested her cheek against mine, just holding me. The warmth of her embrace was that of a mother's; an embrace I hadn't known I'd needed until it happened.

"Thank you for loving my son. He's my only child and I've

worried that he wouldn't find what I now see you both have. It's beautiful, as you are. I couldn't have asked for more from the woman he loves."

Don't cry, don't cry.

I chanted to myself in my own head, not trusting my voice as her words registered and instead of speaking, I nodded against her shoulder, relief spreading through my limbs as she hugged me just a bit tighter.

"I didn't expect him. He was a curveball I never saw coming, but I love him. More than I can express, honestly. I wish I knew how to show him, but I'll spend the rest of my life trying." My voice was shaky, as I'd expected it to be.

But she didn't let go of me, only leaning away from me in order to see my face.

"Trust me, Emberly. He knows."

"Thank God," Daniel said around a bite of the chicken cordon bleu I had made us for dinner. On his insistence, I'd joined June in the kitchen to make the men a special meal to celebrate our engagement. From the appreciative look in his eyes, I was pretty sure he was liking what we'd made.

"She can cook!" He boomed, raising a fist into the air as he took yet another bite. I smiled widely around a giggle I failed to cover with the back of my hand, and I turned my gaze back to Hudson's, which was filled with warm amusement.

The guilt and anger that I had seen in his eyes for the past few weeks was now long gone.

How had we gotten here?

I honestly didn't know, but God, was I grateful for it.

The haunting darkness that followed me after leaving my home and all of the pain that went along with it, at last was nothing but a memory. Though there were moments when I still doubted my worth, I had this amazing man by my side to remind me what we had; what he'd never lost sight of.

We faced so much and somehow, we'd come through it all.

Together and stronger than ever.

"What are you thinking about, baby? I can see those gears turning."

"I've never had this." I said, my voice little more than a murmur.

"What's that?" The rugged touch of his thumb brushed the rose of my cheek triggered a sensation that warmed my chest. I leaned closer, pressing my face into his palm as he caressed me, both gently and assuredly.

"A family like this. I never thought it could be so easy, so good."

I pressed a grateful kiss to his hand, nestling my cheek deeper into his skin before allowing my shoulders to shake lightly in a slight shrug, hoping he understood what I was trying to say.

"I know it's new for you, but it's all yours. What is mine is yours, now."

My heart sang within its chambers at the underlying meaning of his words and I nodded, smiling, before wrapping my arms tightly around his neck and just holding him, needing the contact to know that the moment we were sharing was real. I knew it was.

The way I felt for this man was so very real.

Real, beautiful, meaningful. And I was so lucky.

"Thank you." I mumbled once I'd found my voice again, and I felt the wide set of his grin against my hair before his thick, strong arms tightened their hold around my waist. Never letting go, never losing his grasp.

"For what?" His lips brushed over my ear, sending shivers of needful lust down my spine. I rested my back against his chest, then laced my fingers with his and tipped my face back to meet his curious blue eyes.

"For giving me this. Love. Life. Family. I'll never take it for granted."

With the buffer of his parents' easy chatter and the steady, never-wavering beat of Hudson's heart next to my ear, I felt content and safe: the way I always felt with him.

Nothing could hurt me because he wouldn't stand for it, and I loved the security he gave me, without question.

Did I give him the same?

I really hoped so.

"You don't ever have to thank me, Darlin'. You're my world, now."

I lifted my lips to his, pouring all of the love in my heart into the kiss, knowing the feelings I had for him would only grow with time.

"I love you, Hudson. So much."

He grinned against my kiss, biting gently at my lower lip before pulling away with another soft, reverent kiss on the side of my mouth.

"I love you, too, Emberly. I'll never stop."

The words warmed me all over and I knew they were true.

Our love was everlasting.

"So, when's the big day?" June asked as we cleaned up the kitchen after dinner, her warm amber eyes landing on me.

"We were thinking Christmas time. I want everyone to be able to make it and between my schedule at the hospital and Hudson going back to work soon, it just seems like the perfect time." The broad, beaming smile she gave me told me she must have agreed with me. A shocked - yet happy - gasp escaped me when she set down the dish she'd been drying, and she quickly took me into her arms, her embrace tight and her hands soothing as they rubbed up and down the length of my back. I breathed in her sweet scent: a mixture of a light, fragrant perfume and the flour that stained her cooking apron. My chest felt tight as I let her hold me like that, knowing that she considered me one of her own now.

I just wished I could have had moments like this with my own mom.

God, I missed her.

She wouldn't be there to attend my wedding, or see me in my dress.

She wouldn't get to meet our children, or be a part of their lives.

The sting beneath my eyes worsened at the very thought of such missed memories and I swallowed thickly, forcing the renewed sense of loss into the farthest corner of my mind, where I'd revisit it at a later time when there weren't prying eyes and sympathetic glances.

"Oh, honey, what's wrong? Am I smothering you? I'm sorry..."

"No! No, please, June. You've been amazing." I pulled back from her and smiled, my eyes stinging and nose tingling - tangible signs of the emotions that had been growing inside of me. But I pushed them back.

I wasn't going to let my past ruin that moment.

"I guess I'm just not used to..." My voice trailed off, unsure of what to say.

I wasn't used to the affection, the family, the kindness I knew she felt for me.

I wanted to melt into it and be a part of it, but it was scary, too.

I'd already lost so many people.

What if I lost this, too?

I was getting a chance to be a part of something bigger than myself, part of a family who truly cared and wanted the best for me.

I didn't want to mess it up.

The sensation of hands cupping my face caused me to open

my eyes, not realizing I had closed them in the midst of my inner struggle.

"Hudson told me about your mother, Emberly. I'm so sorry, and I know those words aren't enough. But, I love you already, honey. I hope you'll let me get to know you and maybe one day you'll think of me as a mother, too?"

My heart melted at her question and I knew she cared. She was such a good and kind woman, and wanted nothing more than to get to know the woman her only son would marry. I had never really thought I would have a second chance at a family; one that didn't come with conditions or painful revelations.

This was my second chance and I was grabbing onto it with both hands.

"I would love nothing more, June."

The smile that spread over her face reached her eyes as they sparked with an acceptance I wasn't sure I had ever felt from my father.

He hadn't really been much of a father, though. But at the time, it was the only thing I had that even resembled a family. It was only in that moment in the kitchen with Hudson's mother that I realized family was so much more than what that man had given me.

June, Daniel and the rest of Hudson's relatives were my real family.

"Come on, now. I think I have some of my old wedding planners upstairs. Let's plan us a wedding!"

I smiled so big I was sure I had cracked my cheeks, but damn, did it feel good.

HUDSON

I have to go, baby." I loosened my arm around Emberly's shoulders and tipped her chin up with my thumb, wanting her beautiful eyes on me.

"I know." She nodded, lifting up to meld our mouths together, and the sweet softness of her full lips was nearly enough to leave me wanting to stay at home with her. It had been a few weeks since I'd taken leave from the department and my time off was about up. If I were being honest, I'd missed the beat; the challenge of the job and the rush of chasing a collar. *It was time.*

I was going to miss the fuck out of my girl, though.

"How about a late dinner, I'll pick something up on my way home."

That seemed to perk her up as she shifted in my hold and reached up to caress my jaw, the prickle of a beard I hadn't bothered to trim bristling under her adorations. I took one last, greedy taste of her before pulling back and moving my mouth to the top of her head.

I hated fucking leaving her.

"Be careful."

"I always am, Darlin'. I love you."

A bright, blinding smile spread over her face as she leaned in, her arms hooking around my neck as her lips ghosted over mine in a barely-there kiss that left me craving even more of her.

"I love you, too. Now go."

And against my better judgment, I did.

EMBERLY

"Something's bothering you, isn't there?" Ashlee sat at the kitchen island, a steaming cup of coffee between her hands and her big, knowing eyes trained on me. I twisted my fingers in front of me from my place across from her, then dropped my face into my palms. A spreading sense of dread tightened in my lower stomach and was spreading further through me as more and more time passed since he'd left for work.

I had known it would only be a matter of time until he would go back, and I thought I would be prepared. He was a cop. I knew that. He thrived on helping people and protecting those he loved. I knew that, too.

But...I'd almost lost him.

"I don't know, Ash. We're in such a good place and if something happened to him..." My words trailed off as emotion clogged my throat and I closed my eyes, trying to get a hold of myself. It wasn't just worry that was bothering me, and I had a suspicion my best friend knew that. It was the fear of the unknown. I'd never had to worry about losing people before, because except for Ashlee and my Mom, I had never truly had *loved ones*.

Family was a foreign concept to me. The idea of having people in my life who cared for me, wanted the best for me, just because they cared... that was all new for me. Knowing Hudson had changed everything. Suddenly, I had this whole family who cared for and loved me, simply because I was the girl their son loved.

It was amazing and scary and a little crazy, and I was latching onto it with both hands. It's what I'd wanted for so much of my life. *To be loved.*

The mere thought of losing any of them scared me.

Ashlee grabbed my hands in hers and implored me with her eyes, a clarity in them I must have needed because once I realized she understood, something inside of me calmed. The undercurrent of anxiety for him, however, remained.

"He's smart, Emberly. You have to believe that he'll be okay. You believe that, don't you?"

How could I?

A maniac from my past had trapped him in a room and set off a bomb that would have undoubtedly taken him from me, forever.

Forever.

"You don't understand, Ash. I almost lost..."

"I know that. He knows that, too. Do you think he'd ever risk his life if he thought there was a chance he wouldn't be able to come home to you? He wouldn't. He loves you way too much to risk that."

I pulled my hands from her grasp and shook my head, pacing the length of the tiled kitchen floor as my concern for the man I loved continued to grow.

She just didn't understand.

"He risks it *every day*, Ash. Every day he'll go to work and he'll do his job. A job I know he loves. He wears that badge with pride, and I know how much it means to him, to follow in his grandfather's footsteps. He had other choices, but he chose the department. It's all he's ever wanted to do with his life. What kind of person would I be if I took that away from him?"

I curled my shaky fingers through my hair, still gathered in a messy up-do since I hadn't gotten in the shower quite yet. I was a mess, but I couldn't seem to snap myself out of the feelings I was fighting against.

I loved how protective and loyal Hudson was to those he loved and cared for. It was a trait I was sure he'd inherited from his own father, and even his grandfather, who'd been shot in the line of duty, much too young. *Was that what awaited us?*

Would I lose him too soon?

Was my worry warranted?

Would he understand why I felt like this?

I didn't have any answers and as I moved back to the counter and took a seat next to Ashlee again, I realized I didn't know where I would find them.

"You should tell him you're worried."

I shook my head, not willing to take away something I knew he loved.

I would rather experience worry and fret every day, than to wake up one morning to find that the man I loved despised me for taking his livelihood away.

"He loves his job, Ash. I'm not doing that."

"He loves you more. Don't tell me you believe he'd choose his job over you, because he wouldn't."

I turned on her then, my constant anxiety over Hudson's wellbeing morphing into annoyance with her incapability of understanding why I felt that way.

She was dating Tristan. Didn't she worry, too?

"Can you say the same for Tristan? Don't you worry that he'll..."

I hated even saying it, because it felt as if I said it, I would speak it into becoming a possibility.

I didn't want to lose anyone I loved.

Was that so much to ask?

"Of course I do. But I know he takes every precaution to ensure that he's safe with the missions he does go on. When he's on the beat, it's unlikely he will even draw his gun. The rest, I just have faith, Emberly. You will, too."

I exhaled heavily, unsure if this faith she talked about was something I could ever learn to have. Faith hadn't kept my father from hurting my mother.

Why would I rely on it now?

"I don't think I can do that."

"Talk to him."

Nodding, we stood and hugged for a few minutes. She whispered reassurances in my ear and I desperately wanted to believe them, yet I knew I most likely wouldn't.

When she was gone, I sat back down and sipped my coffee, hoping it would give me enough liquid courage to talk to Hudson about my fears when he came home. God knew I needed some.

"It's good to have you back, honey. How is Hudson?"

"He's good, Linda. He's really good."

Linda pulled away from our embrace and smiled, and I wondered how we'd gotten here. After the assault, I'd decided to take some time off from work. I needed some time to recover and I think Hudson had needed the time with me, too.

To reaffirm our bond. But it had been a few weeks since everything happened, and I was missing the babies something fierce.

So, I was back.

"It's good to be back, Linda. Thank you so much, for everything."

"We've missed you, Emberly. Go on up and I'll have someone come cover you in a few hours, okay?"

Nodding, I hugged her one last time before heading toward

the elevator that would lead to my floor, where the infants - who I'd seen on a near-daily basis before my leave of absence - waited for me. I was sure most of them had been discharged by now, but I would see them again during their quarterly visits and I was excited for that. Going back to work was what I had needed.

"Emberly, is that you?"

"Ellie! Oh my gosh!"

I rushed over to her and engulfed her in a hug, excitement bubbling up inside when I saw the slight bump protruding from her yellow scrubs that were the bright color of a canary. She was pregnant, and she radiated with the glow I often noticed shining from the faces of mothers who visited the unit before their babies were born. Often they would stand outside the baby unit and just sigh at the sight of so many new lives, and the dreams they had for their own child would grow as they watched from behind the glass.

I had left for just a few weeks and I'd missed her big announcement, it seemed.

"You have to tell me everything!"

Her laughter in my ear was light and airy, and I could tell she was happy.

I had known she'd been dating someone new before my leave, but I'd had no idea it was so serious...

"It's not like it was planned or anything. Darren and I..."

I pulled back, smirking at his name. A security guard in the hospital - of course he was. We often worked twelve to twenty-four hour shifts and after that, who had time to date?

I knew I wouldn't have, if it weren't for the insatiable and persistent man I was going to marry. He wouldn't take no for an answer, not even in the beginning.

"When did you find out?"

"Last week. I told him, thinking he'd be upset with me for forgetting my pill, but he was so happy, Emberly. So happy."

I grinned widely and hugged her again.

God, this was just what I had needed to get out of my own

head after my melt down this morning. Maybe I'd just been cooped up for too long first in the house, then in the hospital after Tristan's accident, and perhaps I'd begun to go a little stir-crazy.

"I'm so damn happy for you!"

"I'm so nervous."

"You're going to do great, Ellie. And I'll help you."

She was the one to pull back this time and her haunted eyes met mine. I could still see the excitement in them, but now they were masked with worry.

I knew the feeling.

"You're going to be an awesome mother."

She nodded quickly, only looking around when eyes of the other nurses were on both of us.

"I'm really glad you're back. How's that sexy cop of yours?"

I felt my cheeks blush at her words and I grinned like a fool again, only this time it was all for my Hudson.

"He's amazing. We're engaged."

"Oh my gosh! The ring is just beautiful, Emberly. I'm so excited! I'm invited, right?"

I laughed at her, shaking my head in amusement.

If I had my way, the whole wing would be invited.

"Of course you are! I'm going to put my things away and then we can figure out the schedule. Is Ash here?"

"I'm here! Just late."

I turned to see my best friend running up the stairs, her face red from exertion and her arms full of bags from the local market.

"Let me help you. Why didn't you use the elevator?"

"Well, I didn't get to the gym this morning."

She was a nut.

Taking four plastic bags from her, we headed to the break room where I busied myself with stocking the cabinets while she set to reorganizing the fridge.

"Did you talk to him?"

At the reminder of our conversation this morning, I deflated.

There was no dismissing my worries for Hudson and what he did for a living as figments of my imagination.

They were living, breathing, masses of emotion inside of me and at the mere mention of them, the dreadful chill of nerves returned.

I had a sudden urge to snap at my friend, but refrained.

"No, he's working until ten."

"Is he picking you up tonight? If not, I can drive you home."

I narrowed my eyes at her as I shrugged on my scrubs, fixing my hair into the low ponytail I always sported at the hospital.

"You don't have a car, Ash."

"Yes, I do." She pulled out a pair of keys to what I was guessing was Tristan's sleek, new Lexus. *Nice.*

I'd sneaked a look at it during the house warming party we'd had last week. Tristan bought it straight out, and it was brand new, too.

"Oh! We're going to have fun."

"It's so smooth."

"I know, right? I already told him it's my car. He just doesn't know it yet."

That was just like Ashlee. She loved the finer things in life.

As I ran my hand over the brand new, leather seats and smelled the distinctive *new car* smell, I couldn't say I didn't enjoy it.

It was *nice.*

It was just the thing to take my mind off the talk awaiting me at home. After Hudson proposed, I hadn't wanted to wait to live with him until after the wedding, and he'd had me moved in that night. Thankfully Ashlee and Tristan were looking for a place of their own and were able to take over the lease for me, so

I hadn't had to worry about breaking it. And I loved coming home to Hudson. He was my everything.

But between the day I'd had and the overwhelming feelings I'd dealt with that morning, I wished I could avoid him, at least for a little while.

"He'll understand."

I looked over at Ashlee, and she must have seen the war I was having within myself. Her eyes were wide and knowing and I nodded, though her words hadn't really registered with me. Not when my own mind was going hopelessly in circles.

A part of me wanted to just ignore what was happening, because that's what I normally did when I was scared or upset about something in my life.

I always just ignored it, in hopes it would sort itself out.

I had a feeling this wouldn't resolve itself, though.

"I hope so. I love him so much."

"Babe. He *knows* that."

We pulled up to the house quicker than I thought we would, and I reached over to hug my best friend before closing the heavy car door behind me.

Steeling myself, I took a deep breath.

Here goes nothing.

HUDSON

*W*hen I heard her key in the door, I immediately headed that way, eager to place my greedy hands on her again. I hadn't realized how much I would feel her absence when I went back to work, but fuck, I had. It had been only a mere day since I had last seen her, but it felt so much longer.

My eyes swept over her as she walked in the door, her flats barely audible against the hardwood floors of the entryway.

My Emberly was a cute little mess of wild blonde hair and worn, wrinkled blue scrubs, and I couldn't breathe at the sight of her.

Even though she was dragging from her shift at the hospital; though her normally pale face was flushed from the sun and her lips were chapped from biting at them as she often did when she was nervous, she was exquisite.

My woman.

God, I'd missed her.

"Come here, Darlin'."

I tugged her into my arms and planted my face into her blonde locks, inhaling her unmistakably decadent scent, allowing the essence of her to overwhelm me.

"Hud," She breathed, all sweet and airy in the way I knew meant she was needy for me. If I had it my way, she'd always sound like that. I would keep her tied to my bed, naked except for a pair of her high heels and those frilly ass panties she liked to tease me with. She'd stay there all day, just waiting for me to ravish her. She was a real-life fantasy, and even the eight and a half hours I'd been away from her since this morning were too long.

Her whimper leaked from those pouty lips of hers and I withdrew, slipping my hands around her upturned face and dropping my mouth to ghost over hers. When her hot tongue came out to touch mine, I couldn't resist. Reaching for the bottom of her scrubs, I pushed them up her stomach until the fabric reached her chin. Reaching down, I tweaked one of her rosy nipples, diving in for a taste of her; groaning when she whined against me, like a cat in heat.

God, she made me crazy.

"I missed you so damn much."

Her small hands grabbed at my shoulders as she looked up at me with bright, warm eyes, and I felt that warmth all the way to my bones.

After a day filled with darkness and uncertainty, criminals and danger, she was my peace.

"Take me to bed, Hud."

"Off, Darlin'." Emberly's eyes blazed with heated lust at my roughly spoken words and, nodding eagerly, she slipped her shirt over her head and let it drop to the floor. Her hands went to the sides of my jacket, easily pushing it off my shoulders to join the quickly-growing pile of clothes behind us.

My hands scooped under her lush, perfect ass and then I was lifting her up my body, heading quickly toward the nearest flat surface in order to love her right.

"Wrap those legs around me." She did, her face rooted in my neck, planting hot, needful kisses over my buzzing skin.

How was it possible to need her this much?

I didn't have an answer to the question that whispered in my head.

All I knew was that I was lost to this woman, this beautiful, sassy girl.

Mine.

She was all mine.

"*I love you.* I love you so much."

Hearing her feelings for me would never get old, I realized. As I pulled her pants down to her ankles, removing first her flats and then her socks from her small feet, the words she spoke weren't what caused me to pull back and look up at her as an ache in my chest formed, right in the deepest parts of my being.

It was the little cracks in her voice that was normally smooth as velvet.

"Baby. I know you do."

Her eyes opened, glistening with such love it was like a noose wrapped around my neck. I forced a breath from my lungs, finding it hard to breathe at the sight of such consuming emotion.

The knowledge that it was aimed at me and only me?

It made me deliriously happy.

I curled a firm hand around her waist, lowering my head to press against hers. Letting my words whisper into her ear, I wanted her to hear them and believe they were the truth.

"*I love you* doesn't seem fitting for these feelings, Darlin'. I'm fucking crazy without you and sane when I'm with you. I missed you from the second I left this morning and didn't calm down until now."

Her hands wrapped around my neck, holding steadily and when her bright eyes found mine, I saw the reflection of my desperation for her mirrored right back to me. There was something else there, too, however. It made me pull back, concern bubbling up inside of me. It looked as if she had something to tell me, but kept stopping herself.

Before I could ask, she was arching up against me, her bare

body pressing against me and tempting me to take her like I so craved.

"Then make love to me, Hudson."

She didn't have to tell me twice.

37

EMBERLY

ABOUT 6 MONTHS LATER

I'm getting married today.

The promise of that one, simple truth had my eyes opening happily to the day that awaited me and I stretched, excitement spreading through my well-rested body. Even the bright sunlight of the early morning that streamed in through the blinds I'd left open the night before didn't sour my mood. Reaching over to Hudson's side of the bed, I wrapped my fingers around his pillow and breathed in his lingering scent, my eyes closing at the bliss it gave me.

"God you're weird. Are you sniffing my pillow, baby?"

"No, of course I'm not." Blushing from head to toe, I dove under the plush, warm covers of our bed as his teasing chuckle filled the room. His footsteps approached the bed, then he knelt beside me and spread his limbs until they wrapped snugly around my waist. His large, rough, always-greedy hands squeezed my ass under the thin sheet, eliciting a hearty moan from me. He'd always loved my ass.

"Don't be ashamed, Darlin'. I know I smell good." He mused, cocking one of those heart-stopping grins I loved so much and, burying my head in his chest, I breathed him in. *Oh God, bad idea!*

"No, oh my god, no, you don't, Hud! Go shower." Pushing

both my hands against the mass of his rock-hard chest, I made a feeble attempt to push him away, feigning disgust. I didn't know why I'd tried it, though. My man was built like a truck.

And those muscles...

"Are you kicking me out of my own bed?"

"No. I'm kicking you out of *our* bed. And technically, we're on my side. So up you get. We have a wedding to get ready for." I felt his deep laugh against my hair before he pulled back, strands of my hair surrounding us as he did. I was giving a whole new meaning to *bed head*. I grimaced as he attempted to tame the crazy hair I was sporting, watching an amused smile spread over his handsome face.

"A wedding, huh? Who is gettin' married?"

"Us, baby. So get up!" Laughing again, Hudson pulled me up with him and lifting me against his chest. I quickly wrapped my legs around his wide waist, grinning when he groaned.

"You're not wearing any panties, are you?"

"No, why would I? You'd just rip them off me."

His hand came down, suddenly, on one side of my ass, eliciting a low moan of surprise from my sassy mouth. *If that was my punishment, I'd have to remember to be sassy more often.*

"Shower sex?" I asked against his lips, smiling cheekily.

"Hell yes, shower sex. Get in there, vixen."

Raising a hand in mock salute, I earned myself another playful slap.

"Yes, sir!"

"Are you nervous?"

After our long and oh-so-steamy shower this morning, Hudson dropped me off at Ashlee's place (i.e. our old apartment) and headed to his parents' house, where he would get ready with Tristan and the few groomsmen who were coming today. I knew Tristan, who was his best man of course, but I hadn't met his other friends at the department who would be standing beside him at the altar, waiting for me. I'd be meeting them soon enough, though. Ashlee was doing my hair up in some fancy, twisty braid thing she had said I'd love, and since she'd always been the more stylish of the two of us, I'd told her she could do whatever she wanted with my makeup as well. As long as it wasn't too crazy.

"No. I'm so excited. Is that weird? Should I have cold feet right now?"

Her face softened, her eyes filling with understanding and awe.

She was my best friend. Pushing the chair back a little, I looked up at her, smiling.

I couldn't do any of this without her cheering me on.

Did she know that?

I hoped she did.

"You're messing up all my work! Geez, woman!"

She complained, mussing with my hair again as if I'd been running in circles instead of slightly moving my head to look at her while we talked.

"You know I love you, right?"

"I know that if you mess up your makeup once it's done, I'll cut you."

But, I had heard what she really wanted me to know.

I love you, too.

Sighing dramatically just for her, I let her continue to complain.

"Now, we couldn't have that, could we?"

"No, we can't! So shush and let me finish making you pretty."

Rolling my eyes, I let her get back to work, even though I had a feeling that if I did ruin my makeup, the man waiting for me wouldn't mind.

I couldn't wait to marry his sexy ass.

"Fine, Ash. Do your worst."

It took another hour before she was done getting me ready after I had messed her up. Her words, not mine. Ashlee smiled as she appraised me, contentment lifting her lips and warming her gaze. *I must have looked damn good!*

"You ready for the dress?" She asked, leaving to enter the adjoining room where we had placed the garment bag earlier. For some reason, I couldn't follow her. My feet suddenly felt as heavy as lead and my legs shook furiously, as though the carpet had just been pulled from under me. Dropping down onto the mattress behind me, my face went between my hands and, pulling in a ragged breath, I tried to breathe through the panic attack that I knew was on the horizon. I would get them every once in a while, when my anxiety got to be too much for me to handle. In hindsight, I had been getting them much less frequently this year and I knew there was one, singular reason for that fact. *Hudson.*

"Oh my god! You okay?"

"*Hudson.*"

Pushing his name through my dry throat, I felt the weight of grief-stricken sadness settle within my chest. As we'd been planning our wedding, there had been times when I had felt my mom's absence, when I'd wanted her there with me more than anything. But, it was my wedding day. It was my wedding day, the day when I would give myself, wholeheartedly, to the man I loved and cherished and would spend forever with...

My Mom wouldn't be here to witness any of it.

God. How hadn't I expected this? Why was it hitting me so hard, now?

Useless, stinging tears slid from my eyes and landed on my shaking hands as I heard Ashlee scurry from the room beside us. Her hurried footsteps sounded urgently as she returned, her hand clasping one of mine gently: it was as if she were afraid I would break.

I was surprised she wasn't mad at me for messing up my makeup, but I couldn't get the apology out of my lips before she was pressing my phone to my ear. I grabbed it as she urged me onward, focusing on simply breathing, in and out.

"Hey, Ashlee. What's up?" His deep voice, so smooth and so rough at the same time, slid through me like the smoothest of whiskeys and I sagged with the calmness he gave me, just from the sound of his voice. I hiccuped through the soft, grateful sob that broke painfully through my chest. He must have heard it because his once cheerful voice became tight with concern when he spoke once more.

"Fuck! Darlin', it's me. Listen to my voice, you hear me, baby? I'm going to marry you in a few hours and nothing will hurt you, ever again. Nothing. Now, tell me what's wrong." In just a few sentences, he calmed my panic and quelled my reminiscent sadness. I missed my mom so much, but I knew she wouldn't want our day to be ruined by tears or the pain of my dark past. Hudson and I were meant to find one another, to heal each other from the losses we'd both felt in our pasts and most of all, to build a life together that would be filled with love, laughter and such hope. Hudson had given me a love I had never dreamed I would have, and if I let anything get in the way of that, I'd be a foolish woman.

"I'm okay, baby. I'm sorry, I was just missing my mom."

"Fuck, I wish I was there to hug you right now. I love you, Emberly."

Smiling through my tears, I knew he meant it with everything he was.

He always had.

"I love you more."

"I was just about to text you, it's weird that you called before I could."

Frowning, I looked up at Ashlee's worried eyes and nodded, letting her know I was okay. She helped me out of my jeans and held the opening of the beautiful white dress, which was made of lace, sleek and simple. The moment I had seen it, I had known it was *my* dress. It was perfect.

Stepping into the garment, she took the phone from me and put it on speaker so that I could slip my sweater over my head. Adjusting my strapless bra before she closed the zipper in the back, I finally turning around to take a look in the mirror. When her jaw popped open on a soft squeal, I knew she loved it as much as I did.

"God, you're beautiful, girl! So pretty." Blushing, I heard my sexy man's voice coming from the phone and laughing, I picked it back up, somehow having forgotten about our call.

"You forget about me, baby?"

"I was putting on my dress, Hud."

"Shit, I can't wait to see it." Sitting carefully on the bed, I smiled at the thought of his reaction when he saw me. One tradition we'd kept was that he hadn't seen the dress before today. I had wanted it to be a surprise and, judging from his fervor, I was sure it'd be worth the wait.

"Why were you going to text me?" I asked, wondering if something was wrong if he was willing to distract us so soon before the ceremony. He had tried to say that I had fifteen minutes to get my ass down the aisle, but what could I say?

I liked making him wait. And the braid thing took a while.

"There's a raid I've been called in for at the station. We've been working on it for a few weeks now and we finally have a location for the shipment."

My heart dropped into my stomach as he explained how important it was, but all I could think was: *he was leaving our wedding for work?*

What the hell?

"What?"

"I'm sorry, Darlin'. I won't be long."

"Hudson, I don't think-"

I heard some voices in the background and then his voice took on an urgent tone.

"I have to go, Emberly. I'll be back before you know it."

"Hud-" The dial tone hit my ear a moment later and frowning, I pulled the phone away, sure he hadn't hung up on me.

On our fucking wedding day, no less!

My stomach curled as worry filled my clenching gut, the same worry I felt when he went to work every day. The worry that until now, I had stayed quiet about.

What could be so important that he'd leave, now?

Now of all times? *God*, I was going to be sick.

"Emberly! You okay?" No, no I wasn't. I didn't say that though. Swallowing thickly, my stomach rolled again and squeezing my eyes shut, I whispered.

"Please unzip me." Ashlee frowned, but quickly undid the zipper at the back of my wedding dress and as soon as she had it over my head, I rushed into the bathroom next to her bedroom, losing my lunch in the toilet not a full minute after my knees hit the floor.

Worst. Feeling. Ever.

"What's wrong, babe?"

"He's going into work. Some drug raid. I don't know."

I didn't have to turn around and look at her to know that she was frowning in disapproval. She'd told me to talk to him about my worries. But had I?

Nope.

38

HUDSON

"*M*other fucker!". Cursing under my breath, I rushed through the front door of Ashlee's apartment, my annoyance at the whole situation only worsening when I noticed she'd left the door unlocked. *Damn stubborn women.*

The message she sent me wasn't like her. Not like my sweet, beautiful Emberly.

12:13 PM: I see where your priorities are, Hudson. Have fun with your raid.

In the two hours or so that I'd been gone, Emberly had sent me one text message. It wouldn't have bothered me, if it weren't for the utter defeat that her message left me with. She was upset with me, even mad. I wasn't dumb, so I got that shit.

But, what I didn't understand for the fuckin' life of me was, *why?*

She'd never had a problem with my job. If anything, it was what drew us together. If I weren't a cop, we never would have met.

Fuck. The thought of that left a sour taste in my mouth.

260

Dragging my hands through my hair in aggravation, I spoke through the locked bathroom door, knowing my girl was on the other side. Ash's car wasn't there when I arrived, so she must have already left for the church. My girl was all alone and under the obvious anger she was feeling, there was something more bothering her.

And I was about to figure that shit out.

"Open the door, Darlin'."

"Did you have fun?"

Rolling my eyes, I leaned my hands against either side of the door, ready to break down the wall she was putting up between us. We were past this, I knew that.

Whatever she was upset about, it was enough to scare her into shielding herself from me, again.

What had scared my beautiful girl?

"It wasn't fun, Emberly. It's my job. I thought you knew that."

Dead silence met my terse response and after a few minutes, I heard the lock slide free and I slammed it open, bounding inside the bedroom without another thought.

I needed her back in my arms. Then I would fix whatever was broken. *Whatever I'd unintentionally broken...*

"Hudson!" She squealed in surprise as I hoisted her in my arms and took her to the bed, making sure my grip on her was nice and tight before taking one hand off her curvy waist and tucking it under her chin, lifting her face so I could see her eyes.

She could run and hide from me all she wanted, but when her violet eyes looked into mine, I saw her heart. I saw everything she was feeling, clear as day.

It was one of the things I loved about her: that when it came to us, she was an open book. You just had to take the time to read between the lines.

"I'm so mad at you."

Finally! An answer.

"Why? Explain this shit to me, because I don't get it. This is my job."

It was what I'd always done. Protect and serve. Catch bad guys. What else did she expect from me when I went in to work every morning?

"It's our wedding day!"

"And you know I wouldn't miss marrying you for the world. I know that's not what you're upset about. Ash told me you've been upset. What's that about?"

Biting her lip, she nodded.

"Ever since you went after Brad, I've known how easy it would be for you to be hurt. God, or worse. I don't know how I would handle that. I just... worry. I don't want us to lose each other. We've come so far..." Her voice began breaking and then it was breaking me.

Where was all this coming from?

"You've felt this way all this time, Darlin'?" I hoped to God she hadn't. These secrets were behind us. Or, at least, that's what I thought.

"Y-yeah." She whispered, her eyes closing tightly as the words slipped from her quivering lips.

"*Fuck.*" She'd been feeling like this all this time and I didn't even have a clue. At that realization, I let her go, pacing the room in front of her. I tried to get a handle on the emotions that bombarded me. Anger, confusion, regret for all the worry I could have shielded her from if she had only just *told me.*

But, she hadn't. My girl kept all this from me. *Again!*

"Are we back to this? You're scared, so you keep shit from me."

"No, baby..." Her voice was pleading with me, but I couldn't fucking hear it.

I was finished with the omissions, when all I'd ever done - from day one - was be honest with her. This was supposed to be the best day of our lives. How had it gone to shit so fast?

"Tell me I'm wrong. Tell me you haven't kept your feelings

about my job from me. For *weeks*!" Her face crumpled into tears and shaking my head resolutely, I threw up my hands. *I was done with this shit.*

"I'm done with this, Emberly. I would have quit if it would have made you happy. I would have done anything to make you smile." Stepping forward, I got right up in her face, blinding, unrelenting anger taking away every protective instinct I had in me.

I was at my boiling point.

"And you never gave me the chance to do that."

Walking away from her, I may as well have ripped my heart out and left it in her hands. Because the minute the door closed behind me, I felt empty.

39

HUDSON

"She's coming, right?"

The tension gathered in the stiff set of my shoulders, keeping me on edge as I waited at the altar, Tristan standing beside me with a reassuring hand clasped on my shoulder. Some of our closest friends stood behind him as my groomsmen. It felt like I'd been waiting forever for this day to get here. It was the first day of the rest of my life with my beautiful girl. It should have been the happiest day of our lives.

Ever since you went after Brad, I've known how easy it would be for you to be hurt.

Her tear-stained face and wide, sad eyes flashed through my mind and tightening my hands at my sides, I forced myself to stay where I was instead of giving in to the instinct to go look for her. Seeing the pained desperation in her eyes right before I walked away from her fucking gutted me. I never wanted to be the cause of her pain.

Hell, I'd done everything in my power to take it away from her.

My girl had seen so much pain in her young life, more than anyone should ever have to face. And she'd faced it alone.

She was so damn strong.

Ever since I laid my eyes on her, nearly a year ago, I had done everything I could think of to ensure that she felt safe. In the months when I was detailed to the hospital, I had become addicted to her. I wanted her with me, even if that meant just looking at the night sky with he, or watching one of those cheesy chick flicks I knew she loved. I craved closeness with her, beyond the physical aspect I normally pursued women for. With Emberly, just spending time with her was enough. The minute she told me she wanted more, I knew I would never her go. I needed her too fucking much.

When I asked her to marry me, it hadn't been done lightly.

Laying my heart at her feet, I told her I loved her and wanted to spend every waking moment with her, for the rest of our damn lives. I told her I would always protect her, love her and keep her. Pacing back and forth in front of the minister, and all of our friends and family members, I realized how badly I'd fucked us up.

I'd promised to never let her go and the second shit got rough, I'd walked away.

Aggravation and panic tightened my chest, making it difficult for me to breathe. Swallowing down the emotions that blocked my suddenly dry throat, I looked over at Tristan, knowing he'd give it to me straight.

"She's coming right?"

"Yeah, man. She loves you too much to let your dumb ass go."

Letting loose a hard, forced laugh, I nodded my head.

Well, thank fuck for that.

EMBERLY

"Ready, sweetheart?" Looking up at Daniel, I nodded, though I felt anything but ready to walk through those doors. Was he still waiting for me?

Had he left, already? Were we over? Had he finally seen how unworthy I was and decided to cut his losses? My heart was hollow, barren in the wake of his final words before he'd walked out on me; not even able to look at me after how I'd hurt him.

Hudson was my protector, my savior, my vice. He came into my life, rocking it on its axis and changing me, forever. I never thought love and family could be the way it was with him and his family. He cared for me more than anyone ever had in my whole life and though I had been terrified of letting him into my heart, I did. It was the easiest thing I had ever done, letting him love me.

It was like breathing. Loving him, and being loved by him in return, were the most beautiful and rewarding things I had ever witnessed and even if this was the end for us, I wouldn't have wanted to go back and change anything. Meeting him, being with him- it was everything to me.

If this was the end for us, I didn't think I'd survive it.

I'm done with this.

When he'd said those words, they'd sounded empty, resigned. Like he really had given up on me. Blinking back the stinging tears in my eyes, I bit my lip, hoping to stop the break-down that I felt humming just under the surface of the mask I'd donned before leaving Ashlee's and coming to the chapel, certain that the day wouldn't end the way I had hoped it would. Instead, I had been expecting a happy day, filled with laughter and some tears, ending with a wedding band on my finger and a honeymoon on the horizon.

The thought of losing those dreams was almost as painful as the memory of how he'd walked away from us. *Forever.*

"Emberly?" The deep voice, so much like his son's, pulled me back into the present moment and nodding, I quickly wiped away my tears. He probably thought they were tears of joy, of happiness. I just didn't have the heart to tell him they were of anything but that.

"We had a fight." I whispered, tears continuing to leak down my stinging cheeks.

"He's hard-headed. Just like me, unfortunately. But my boy loves you with all of his heart. You know that?" His voice was clear, but his eyes were warm, understanding.

Maybe there was hope for us yet?

I was afraid to hope and as the double doors of the chapel opened, I felt my heart still from it's frantic pace when I saw a dark head of hair, a bearded jaw and a strong set of shoulders I knew all too well, covered in a gray suit jacket. *Hudson.*

My Hudson.

A soft, yet powerful sob slipped from my heaving chest and I stepped forward, my arm looped into one of Daniel's as we began our walk down the aisle. I closed my eyes, intent on making it to the altar without breaking down at the sight of my sexy man. His back was still turned to me and, breathing through the pain of knowing he couldn't bear to look at me - even now - I told myself I could still fix this. We'd been through so much to get here, and if I had to spend the rest of my life making up for how I had once again pushed him away, I gladly would. As long as he'd still have me.

"Darlin'."

Wide, pale blue eyes, wet with unshed tears, trained on me, causing my feet to falter and my bent arm to fall to my side.

Would he walk away now?

Would he forgive me?

Too afraid of the first possibility, my eyes fell to the white floor of the aisle, which was covered in rose petals, while my eyes closed tightly in preparation for him to end us. He'd given me so much and when I could have trusted in him, in *us,* I'd failed.

Why would he still want to marry me after that?

"Look at me, Darlin'. Please just look at me."

He was closer to me then, his shiny loafers only a foot away from my white, open-toed heels. Shaking my head, I lifted a tentative hand to his chest, feeling his heart as it beat strongly and quickly, just as mine was.

It was something I often did when I felt uneasy or nervous. I would lay either my hand or my head across his chest and listen to his strong, loving heart beat. It would calm me, instantly. His heart loved me when I was too scared and too broken to love myself and, through the small amount of time we'd known one another, it had given me the strength to open up my own heart in order to love him back.

If I'd lost him...

"I shouldn't have left like that, Darlin'. I was angry at myself and disappointed that you felt you couldn't come to me with your fears, but not for one second did my feelings for you change. They never will." I sucked in a startled breath at his words and the second I lifted my eyes to his pained blues, I could breathe again.

We were going to be okay.

"I'm so sorry, Hud. Please don't-"

His mouth sealing over mine stopped my apology and holding onto him for dear life, I prayed this kiss wouldn't be our last.

"It's over now. Just be honest with me. I don't want to fight with you, baby. Never."

Nodding, I cupped his handsome face, relishing the sensation of his stubbled jaw and warm, tanned skin.

"I will. But you have to promise me something, too."

Hudson tilted his head against mine, tucking his face into my neck and breathing me in, then finally nodded.

"Isn't that what the vows are for?" He whispered, teasing me.

"I'm serious."

"Anything, Emberly. Tell me."

"Don't ever walk away from me again. If you're mad or upset or *anything*, you talk to me. Please don't just walk out like that. I couldn't take that."

"Fuck, I know, Emberly. I know. I'm sorry." He hovered over

me, peppering my face with kisses and I sobbed in relief, rejoicing in the fact we hadn't lost each other, after all.

"It's okay. It's all okay now." His head dropped to mine and I lifted my mouth to close the few inches that separated us, sealing my mouth over his in a kiss that I hoped would describe what my words failed to explain.

He was my whole world, and the thought of being without him had torn my heart in two. His large, firm hand pressed to my nape as he slowly guided our kiss, licking and nipping at me in a way I felt in my bones. Drawing back enough to let me up for air, he smiled wide before pressing his mouth to my ear. I knew whatever he would say didn't matter, because I felt his love for me in every mending piece of my heart.

"I love you more, baby. You still wanna be my wife?"

Was the sky blue?

"That's a given, Hud. Marry me."

"Gladly." Kissing me again, his mouth swept over mine like a whisper of the wind and my toes curled in response to the heat that one small kiss had engulfed me in.

His warm, calloused fingers slid through mine and he lifted his head to the shocked, yet smiling faces of the people we loved: our friends, our family. He just shrugged his broad shoulders.

"You all knew I was crazy for her before this. It shouldn't be a surprise."

Amused laughter and words of agreement surrounded us, and he tugged me quickly down the aisle. I noticed his father standing beside Tristan, speaking to him low enough that their conversation didn't carry in the crowded church.

"Sorry to steal her, Dad." Hudson clapped his father on the shoulder, but the look of contentment in his eyes told me he was anything but apologetic.

"No need to be sorry, son. Just take good care of each other."

Placing a kiss first on my cheek and then on the top of his son's head, he stepped back, joining June and the rest of Hudson's family, then took his wife's hand and kissed the back of it. Looking at the love they obviously still had for each other after so many years of marriage made my excitement to marry the man in front of me only grow more.

This was the first day of our forever, and I couldn't wait for whatever came next for us. If it was anything like the last year, I'd be a lucky woman.

"Who here gives this woman to this man?" The minister, a tall, slim man dressed in a finely pressed black suit with a navy blue tie asked, and Daniel rose from his seat, his warm gaze landing on us once more.

"I do."

I was so blessed to be part of such a beautiful, loving family and, dabbing my eyes with the tissues Ashlee had handed to me, I smiled through my tears.

Family had always been a loaded word in my life and for the first time, I was surrounded by people who truly loved and cared for me. I wasn't sure what I did to deserve them, but I was grateful for whatever had brought them to me. Looking up into the wide pools of a pair of pale blue eyes, I realized it was him.

He'd given me so much more than he'd ever know.

"We are here this afternoon to join these two people in holy matrimony. I've been told that you two would like to recite your own vows. Emberly, why don't you begin."

Nodding, I linked my shaky fingers within Hudson's much larger ones, feeling the callouses glide over the back of my hand; a reminder that this was real.

I was about to marry my best friend.

"I never expected you." I muttered, earning a bout of laughter from those in attendance. Does anybody ever expect to fall in love? I most definitely never did. Of course, I had hoped to find someone who would accept me, even with all the emotional baggage I carried with me from a young age, and I had hoped that person, would learn to love me not because of my broken pieces, but despite them.

Hudson loved me wholly, never letting me feel alone or unworthy of him.

"I had thought love wasn't possible for me. Growing up, I watched what loving my father did to my mom. If that was love, I didn't want it. But you made me see how wrong I was, Hudson. You didn't let me hide behind my walls and when I finally let you in my heart, I knew it would be safe with you. It always will be." When I saw the thick tears gathering in his gorgeous eyes, my own spilled over and onto my cheeks again. I swept a hand over his rough, stubbled cheek and smiled when he kissed my hand, leaning into my touch with the warmest of smiles spreading across that mouth of his that I loved so much.

"I vow to always love you and to never shut you out of my heart again. I promise to honor, protect and keep you, for the rest of our lives. I love you, baby, and I can't wait to see what our future holds." Concluding my vows, I raised his hands to my lips and kissed his fingers, smiling when he groaned roughly, my tongue sneaking out to taste his skin. His cheek pressed to mine as he leaned forward a few inches, a possessive arm holding tight to my waist. Feeling his hot, minty breath on my neck, I shivered at the sensation. *God*, he smelled good.

"I'm going to fuck you so good tonight, baby. But first, let's get married."

Sighing heavily, I grinned up at him in disbelief that, in just a few short minutes, he would be mine. *Mine forever.*

"You drove me nuts from the second I saw you outside the hospital. You were this little bombshell, with those pretty eyes of yours and legs for fuckin' miles."

My eyes widened at his curse, though to be honest, I wasn't surprised.

My man was a sweary one.

"Sorry, sir." He muttered to the minister, who nodded, amused at my soon-to-be husband. Hudson's warm gaze slid over mine again.

"The second I saw you, I loved you. I know it sounds crazy

and impossible to love someone from just a look and one simple touch, but that was it for me, Darlin'. I was so done for. I knew if I wanted you, I'd have to go slow with you and I did. Or at least, I tried to." Winking down at me, my mouth popped open in surprise.

He had told me he loved me only weeks after we met, and had told me I was his long before that.

That was slow?

"That was slow to you, Hud?"

Frowning, he nodded, his eyes heating up when I bit my lip in order to stop the laugh that threatened to slip from me. He was crazy, and I loved him all the same.

"You're crazy." I whispered.

"For you." Leaning in, he feathered light kisses over my hair and the sweetness of it warmed me all over.

"I hate fighting with you and I love taking care of you. I'm a selfish man when it comes to you because I want you all to myself. So, I promise you this. I'll never walk away from a fight again. I'll love you more every day and I'll put you first, above all else. If you need to cry, I'll be the one holding you. If you need to swoon, I'll watch a chick flick with you, the ones I know you love. And baby, if you need me, I'll be there. Always. I love you, too, Emberly Logan. I love you so much."

I smiled so big I was sure my cheeks would crack with the force of it, but I didn't care.

This was the happiest day of my life. *I love you,* I mouthed and when he gave me a wide, lopsided grin, I knew he had heard me.

"Please place this ring on Hudson's finger and repeat after me. I, Emberly Logan take you, Hudson Lennox, to be my husband, from this day forward. Take this ring as a symbol of my love and fidelity." Taking the wide, golden band I'd picked out for him, I slipped it onto his finger and said the words with conviction, meaning each one with all of my heart.

After Hudson did the same, placing a beautiful, simple band

on my finger with his husky, emotion-laden voice repeating the minister's words, I looked up at him, giddy with anticipation for the words that would seal the deal.

I was so ready to be his wife.

"I now pronounce you..." I didn't hear another word as strong arms banded around my waist and lifted me off of my feet, while firm yet soft lips crashed against mine; stealing my breath and branding my soul with a passionate, warm, all-consuming kiss.

"Congratulations, honey. I'm so happy for you both."

June engulfed me in her warm arms soon after Hudson begrudgingly released me and hugging her tightly, I looked at my husband over her shoulder.

Husband... God, that sounds good.

"He's everything to me, June. I'll love him forever." She drew back, hearing the evident emotion in my voice and, looking at me with genuine love in her eyes, I knew she believed in how much I cared for her son. I wanted her to know that he'd saved me just as much as I'd saved him and, though I was hesitant at first, I was all in with him now. I would never doubt his love for me again.

"I know that, Emberly. And more importantly, he knows that. Go take some pictures with him and we'll talk at the reception, okay?" Nodding, I kissed her cheek and claimed Hudson's big, warm hand just as he reached for me.

"I'm so fuckin' happy, Darlin'." His mouth pressed to my ear as he muttered the words and smiling softly, I wrapped my arms around him, soaking in the moment as our relatives and friends began exiting the church, ready to celebrate with us at the reception.

"Me too. Thank you for never giving up on us."

His teeth nipped at my ear as he shook his head, admonishing me.

"Never, Emberly. Never."

40

HUDSON

"*P*ush that beautiful dress up to your waist, Darlin'. I'm gonna fuck you in it."

Grabbing her curvy little waist, I buried my face in her neck, licking my way to her lush lips as she lifted her dress like I'd asked. She climbed into my lap, wrapping her long, sexy legs around me. She was plastered to my bare chest and her scent filled my lungs: sweet flowers and a light perfume she often wore when we got out. She smelled like heaven. My greedy hands loosened her braids and once they were free, I swept my fingers through her long, smooth hair, loving the feel of it as I made it to her lips and dove in for a taste.

Jesus, she tasted good.

"We only have a minute, Emberly. This is gonna be fast." Grabbing her chin, I made sure she was looking at me before saying the rest.

"But make no mistake, I'll make slow, easy love to you all night long. I just need you first." Her hands cupped my face as she nodded, her eyes heating as she slipped the top of her dress down and unsnapped the front clasp of her white, lacy, sexy-as-fuck bra, letting her perfect tits press beneath my chin. Unable to contain myself, I dipped my head to take one of her taut nipples between my lips, groaning when she began to grind down on me, her panties scraping against the roughness of my slacks.

My dick was hard as stone and if I didn't get into her heat soon, I would embarrass myself. Quickly shedding my slacks, boxers and shoes, I lifted her up and against the wall, kissing her hard as my need for her damn near overwhelmed me.

"Ready, baby?"

"Take me." Emberly breathed and, though I'd heard it many times before, it still drove me crazy for her. My hands grabbed her perfect little ass and my mouth lightly nipped at the side of her neck. With one jab of my hips against hers, I slid home.

Mother fucker, she felt good.

"Hold on tight, baby." Wrapping her legs back up around my waist, she did just that, kissing me wherever she could reach, while her hands slid around my tensed shoulders to hold herself up against my chest. As I dove into her with slow, measured drives, my thumb worked her swollen nub in small circles, earning soft, mewling cries from her full lips.

"Hud, baby. Faster!" Grunting in agreement, I slid into her with another quick thrust, followed by a twist of my hips that I knew drove her crazy and hit her sweet spot, every time. Screaming my name, my perfect little wife convulsed around my aching cock as I fucked her with everything I had. A few hurried thrusts later, I followed her over into mindless ecstasy. Dipping my head, I kissed her forehead, smiling when I realized I'd just claimed her as my wife; in her dress, no less.

"Damn baby. You wreck me." Pulling her face from my throat, she smiled so big my knees felt weak and I had to lean against the wall behind her in order to remain standing.

She held so much power over me with just one smile, one look, one touch. And she didn't even know it.

"I love you." Rubbing my lips over hers in the gentlest of kisses, I grinned like the sap I was. She was finally mine.

My girl.

My world.

My wife.

Shit, that sounded good.

"I love you, Emberly. So much. Now, let's get down to the reception before my mom sends out a search party." Laughing softly, she nodded her head.

"If we have to."

EMBERLY

"It's time for the first dance! Get your sexy butt up there, girl!"

Laughing at Ashlee's signature toast, I blushed, taking Hudson's firm hand in mine as he led me to the center of the makeshift dance floor. We had chosen his parents' back yard for the reception, only inviting our close family members and friends to attend. I hadn't wanted anyone having to drive far from home and, since the holidays were so close, it just made sense to have everyone celebrate here. When the song began playing through the speakers located at each corner of the yard, I stopped short and looked up into the clearest blue eyes I'd ever seen. *The Fighter* by Keith Urban and Carrie Underwood was the song he'd chosen for us and even though we hadn't discussed it, I realized how perfect it was.

We had fought so hard for this moment and somehow, we'd come out of the other side, stronger than ever. We were and always would be worth fighting for and, wiping away my tears, I wrapped my arms around Hudson's thick neck and laid my head against his chest. The sound of his strong, steady heartbeat only made the moment sweeter and even more special. This was us. This was who we were, and though I had experienced my doubts in the past, my head was clear and my heart was now full. I was ready for our forever.

"It's perfect," I whispered.

"You're perfect. I'm just sorry it took us so long to get here,

Emberly. I'm so sorry I walked away, baby." Raising my head, I brushed my lips over his jaw, smiling when he bent his knees so that I had more room to touch him.

"I never should have kept you in the dark about how I was feeling. It was so wrong of me, Hudson. Forgive me?" Lacing my fingers through his dark locks, I pled with him with my eyes, needing him to know how sorry I was for hurting him today.

I had never meant to hurt this beautiful man.

"There's nothing to forgive. I love you."

The words healed my soul and swelled my heart, but when I heard someone clearing their throat through a microphone, I frowned. I didn't think the speeches would start just yet. Turning in his protective arms, Hudson dropped his chin to my shoulder while his hands snagged my hips, keeping me right where he wanted me.

"What are you *thinking*, Emberly?"

That voice.

Oh, god. It couldn't be.

Closing my eyes, I tried to will away the memories of a past I'd long forgotten as they bombarded against my thoughts, but they were relentless as the pain of hearing the voice that had taunted my nightmares continued to speak.

You're nothing to me. You and that brat upstairs are only disappointments to me and the sooner you learn to do what I say, the easier this will all go for you. Now make my dinner again. And this time, don't burn it, bitch.

It was the last thing he'd said to my mom before beating her to a bloody pulp. It was the last, horrid beating she was given, in which she received the blow to the back of her head that killed her. He'd killed her, but because he'd had connections and lied through his teeth, forcing me to do the same, he never faced the consequences for that crime. My father killed her and had lived to tell the tale. Clenching my eyes shut, I shook like a leaf, the edges of my vision blackening as he spouted something about being proud of his little girl, though he was sure the man behind me could do better than worthless trash like me. The last thing I felt before I passed out was Hudson's insistent hands shaking me gently, his deep, worried voice begging me to stay with him. But I was already slipping away.

"I need you to wake up, Darlin'. I just got you to marry me. I can't lose you now."

His voice was cracked and broken, like splintered glass and, opening my heavy eyes, I combed my fingers through his hair as he rested his wet face against my arm.

"Fuck, baby!" He sprang into action so fast I could barely keep up with him, and only when he rubbed his rough palm against my cheek and pressed a kiss to the top of my head did I notice he was holding a small cup of water to my lips. As the cool water slipped down my dry throat, I took a deep breath and looked around me. I was in a hospital.

And then it all came back to me. Everything did.

The wedding, the reception... *him.*

"Where is he?" When the frown crossed his face, I realized he didn't know.

"Who, baby?"

"That man that was speaking was my father."

A myriad of emotions flitted through his eyes, but when he roughly fisted his hair in his hands and cursed loudly, I knew he had put the pieces together.

"We had thought he was just some drunk. Fuck!"

Before I could anticipate it, he was bounding toward the door of the room, his feet loud and his steps unwavering.

No, not again.

He'll kill him.

"Don't, Hudson. Baby, it's not worth it." I begged him softly, struggling to reach him from my spot on the bed. His back tensed at my words, but as he swang the door open and stepped through, I realized he wasn't going to stop. *I had to stop him.*

Desperate to get to him before it was too late, even the pain in my head and the fog of the medicine they must have given me couldn't stop me from going after him. Ripping free from the I.V. that had been in my arm, I ran to the door and shakily opened it, his name flying from my lips as the panic inside of me rose.

"Hudson!" His back was to me as he stood in front of the elevators and, running to him, I crashed into his hard back. Wrapping my arms around his waist and burying my face between his shoulders, I just held on for dear life.

"Come back inside, Hud."

"Go back to your room. You need to rest. I'll be back before you know it."

"You promised you would always be there when I needed you. Baby, I need you to stay with me." It was a low blow to use his vows to make him stay, but I was past the point of caring. Something deep inside of me, instinct, intuition... something was telling me that if he left right now, he wouldn't come back. And I wouldn't let him go this time.

"Darlin'..." He gripped my hands against his chest, but still didn't face me. Swallowing down the hurt that filled my chest, I held on tighter, not wanting to let him go for fear of what would happen in an altercation with the monster that was my father.

"You promised." As a heavy sigh left him, he turned around and looked down at me, his eyes so dark, it was like looking into the eye of a storm. Cupping his cheek, I begged him, one last time.

"Please don't go. Please don't let us go."

Hudson bent his head in defeat and grabbed my waist firmly, his forehead pressing against mine before his mouth brushed over my temple.

"I'm sorry, baby. I love you so much." His lips continued to brush over the top of my head and, hanging onto him like a lifeline, I swallowed down the sob of relief that threatened to slip free.

"You'll stay?"

"Yeah, Emberly. I'll stay."

Those two words calmed me like nothing else ever had and, sagging against him, I rocked my head against his shoulder; grateful he'd listened to me this time. He gently raised me in a fireman's lift and, holding me close to his warm chest, Hudson carried me back to my hospital room, where he held me for the rest of the night.

41

HUDSON

*M*y throat felt like sandpaper as I forced a heavy breath through it, the rawness of my simmering rage keeping me constantly on edge. Peering over Emberly's sleeping head, I tightened my locked jaw, feeling like a fucking dick for how I had acted before our wedding and, wanting to make it up to her, I'd enlisted my mother's help; together, we'd planned a honeymoon that would sweep my beautiful girl right off of her feet.

If anyone deserved it, this girl did.

Closing my eyes, I tried to stop my thoughts from turning to the reception and everything else that happened last night. Just the idea that her dick of a father had been there, right in front of me - saying those things...

And I'd done nothing.

Nothing!

"Hey," Warm, slender hands glided over my jaw. Opening my eyes, I hoped she couldn't see the emotion in them, because right then I felt too raw to put these fucked up feelings into words.

"Stop it, Hud." Admonishing me, she shook her head gently; her eyes holding me captive like the vixen she was. The love I saw in them was almost enough to make me forget everything else - *almost*.

"It wasn't your fault. He's gone now."

"I should have done more, Darlin'." I muttered, tipping her head back until her pouty, parted lips were merely an inch from my reach.

"You made sure he wouldn't come back."

If that wasn't an understatement, I wasn't sure what was. Once she'd told me who he was, or rather, *what* he was, I'd made sure to call my sergeant and explain the situation. Her father was a monster, a vile human being who had dared to hurt not only my Emberly, but her too-forgiving mother. He wouldn't be coming within even a mile from her unless he wanted the Austin Police to re-open his wife's murder.

Sergeant Reed said her father had tucked tail so fast, he'd barely seen him go.

Good fuckin' riddance.

I also took the opportunity to let him know that I would be giving my notice, effective immediately. Two birds with one stone and all that shit. Of course, I'd miss my job and the guys I had worked with, but my woman came first.

That was my vow to her and above all else, I intended to keep it.

"I should've castrated him for even breathing, babe. He's not even human." I gritted, instinctively tightening my hold around her waist as I considered the subject of her father and all the horrible crimes he'd skated on. It wasn't fair. Not to her mother, not to justice, and certainly not to the angel in my arms.

"And then you'd be in jail. Look at me."

Had I ever denied her anything? So, I did what she asked. Turning my head I met her intense stare; the softness her colorful eyes normally gave me was replaced by such fierce devotion, I was rocked by it.

"You couldn't have known who he was. I do not blame you, Hud. Now tell me you'll stop blaming yourself." Her voice was shallow and weakened from the high dosage of sedatives I'd insisted the doctors give her in order for her to rest properly; but I heard her as clear as fucking day. She was my little fighter, my woman and my saving grace. Resting my head against the top of hers, I thanked God for leading me to her.

My Emberly.

"I'll try, Darlin'."

HUDSON

"*C*an we get out of here, Hud?" Her voice was all raspy as it whispered in my ear, still thick with sleep from the sedatives her doctors had given her. Taking the time to swipe her blonde hair from her pale, smiling cheek, I nodded. Had I ever been able to deny her anything?

"Let me go find the doctors, Darlin'. Rest." A wide, fucking beautiful smile spread over her face as she reached up to brush her dry lips over mine, but hell, I didn't mind one bit.

"Hurry back."

Smiling like the sap she'd made me, I kissed her one more time before slipping from the stiff hospital bed and making my way down to the nurse's desk in the hopes of finding her release papers awaiting me.

"Mr. Lennox. I was just coming to go over Ms. Logan's results with you. Would you like to follow me back to her room?"

Why did it suddenly feel as though there were a knot lodged in my throat?

"Yeah, sure. Is something wrong?"

Hell, she was healthy... happy. I'd seen and felt that shit by my own hand. So why did it feel as if he had grim news for us? It was plain as day in his dark eyes.

"Mr. Lennox..." His voice dropped low in a tone of dread I had feared and, lowering my head to my hands, I tried to prepare myself for what was to come.

Nothing could have prepared me, though.

"I think it's best to tell you together, son."

Fuck!

"Okay. Right behind you."

It felt as if I were following him to my execution as he turned the corner of the hallway and entered Emberly's room, setting his medical chart on the small table at the end of her bed before closing the door with an effortless, yet ominous click. I reached her bedside in three strides, scooping her suddenly cold hand into both of mine before resting my chin over her hair and soaking in the last moment of peace I would have for weeks to come.

"Hud... are you okay?" There was my girl. Always caring for others.

"Yeah, baby. The doctor has your results is all. I need to make sure you are okay because I don't plan on ever leaving your side again." Feeling her eyes on me, I lifted my head and grasped her chin in a sure, yet gentle hold, waiting until I had her attention.

"Never, Darlin'. You got that?" She gasped at the intensity of my declaration but quickly nodded her head in agreement.

"I got that, Hud." Satisfied by her answer and the comfort of her little head resting against my chest, I turned my eyes to the doctor, nodding once as if to say, go ahead. With ease, he pulled a chair from the wall and sat down directly in front of us, what I presumed to be her test results resting in both of his pale hands.

"When a patient is taken in after losing consciousness, for whatever reason, I like to run a few tests to rule out the larger causes. Now, I didn't have to do these tests, they weren't required given your condition. But I did because I'm concerned about your care."

"Do you want a fucking award for doing your job, Doctor? Get to the point!" I roared, fisting my now shaking hands at my sides in hopes of taming my anger, my confusion at what the hell was happening.

"Hudson! Stop it." Her warm hand was against my cheek, her eyes - so bright, so full of life - trained on mine, her little body pressed to my side serving as my very own source of solace. Grinding my teeth together, I heaved a breath from my lungs and worked to calm my nerves, knowing my emotions would only make this worst for her.

And she was all that mattered to me.

"I apologize, Mr. Lennox. I didn't mean to upset you."

Fucking prick.

"Spit. It. Out." I said, barely-contained control splicing my voice.

"Alright, then. I hate to tell you this, Ms. Logan, but it seems that you were pregnant when you were admitted."

Silence; complete and utter silence met his admission and it was only when soothing, yet urgent hands grazed my locked jaw that I realized I'd been holding my breath.

"A baby." Emberly whispered against my cheek, her hands wrapping around my tightened shoulders in a way I had always done for her during times she felt the weakest. Except, this time, it was she who was giving me strength.

My girl.

Fuck, I loved her.

"A baby." I wondered aloud, suddenly overcome by the joy of the news the doctor had so poorly given us. As if we would have been anything but happy about this shit.

"Fuck, Emberly. I didn't think I could love you more when I said those vows, but right now? I do." Palming her flat lower stomach over the thin hospital gown she was wearing, I tucked my face into her neck and shed a few tears for the precious, little baby I hadn't met yet; but I knew I would give my life in order to protect her.

Or *him*...

"I love you, too." There she went again, piecing me back together in the way only she could. She was perfect for me: always had been.

"I'm so sorry, Ms. Logan. I hate giving news like this, knowing the pain a miscarriage can be. Me and my wife have..."

"*What?*" It was my voice that resonated through the air, but to anyone on the receiving end of it, I was sure it sounded more like a growl. He wasn't making any sense. This was a miracle.

Our baby...

"M-Miscarriage?"

"Yes, Ms. Logan. The shock of your ordeal caused you to miscarry sometime between your admittance and now. We aren't sure when to be exact..."

The quiet, yet powerful sobs that broke through the room tore my heart out of my chest as I watched in disbelief as my strong, beautiful girl broke to pieces in front of me at the news that she'd lost our baby.

Clenching my eyes shut, I wanted to will back the blissful moment of only a few seconds before, and somehow make this one to disappear. For the love of God, just let me be dreaming.

But when I heard her audible gasp and felt her hands close into tight little fists, hitting my chest, my eyes flew open and just like I had feared, I realized this moment was all too real.

"No! No, let me go! I don't want..." I grabbed onto her thick hips and, for once in our coupling, was not hard for her instantly. The sadness in her eyes showed that something inside of her had broken, and I was afraid, bone-chillingly afraid that no matter how much I loved her, I wouldn't be able to fix it for her.

"Your fault...your fault..." She kept mumbling her anger to me and I just kept holding on tighter, even as her words penetrated the very soul of me.

She fucking blamed me and I know, I know, she had every right to.

I failed her.

43

HUDSON

TWO WEEKS LATER

*I*t had been two weeks since the wedding. Two long, silent weeks of *supposed* married bliss. Except they were so far from bliss, I wouldn't know how to describe them without gritting my fucking teeth. I knew without a shadow of a doubt that this was my fault. The pain in my beautiful girl's eyes when she looked at me; the sadness that she wore like a well-used mask on her face; the indent in her side of the bed from the days on end she spent there, staring blankly at the ceiling of our home as if it held the answers she said she needed.

Shortly after Emberly had woken up in the hospital, we learned why her doctors were so intent on keeping her overnight for observation. Hitting my head against the leather steering wheel in front of me, I closed my eyes and remembered the moment that had taken my angel's light. Fuck! Why hadn't I insisted on an exclusive guest list? Why hadn't I hired security for the wedding? Why had I gone to that stupid drug raid beforehand?

So many fucking what ifs.

So many unanswered questions.

Looking up at the house in front of me - our house - I told myself to be strong. In the two weeks that had passed since our lives had changed, Emberly had barely looked at me, never mind anything else.

I didn't know what to do, how to make this better for her. She'd lost so many people in her young life and asking her to forget our unborn baby and move on wasn't what I wanted to do. Hell, I couldn't even sleep without dreaming of the life we could have had - would have had, if it weren't for the miscarriage.

It wasn't meant to be. That's what we'd been told over and over again, in hopes of helping us move on from our loss. But they were dead wrong, I had realized. Emberly was meant to be a mom. She was so beautiful, so kind to everyone she met. She was a nurturing soul, a nurse by day and a loving person at heart, even when she wasn't required to be.

If our baby had lived, I truly believed that we would have been happy.

Nah, scratch that. We would have been fucking content because we were together. Her, me and any kids we may have gone on to have.

Had we lost that dream in the face of the one we'd lost?

"Fuck," I muttered, noting the time on the dashboard of my Lincoln. My parents were coming to stay with us for the weekend and I knew it meant a lot to Emberly that we all spend time as a family. My girl had never had that growing up and if it was the last thing I did, I would give her the family she had wanted for so long.

I locked my car and bounded up the steps of the porch, opening the front door before letting Brat, our little Pug mix, out for his morning run. Thankfully I'd picked a house for us that had a fenced in yard, so he had as much space to play as he wanted. Looking down at his jumping legs and happy face, I couldn't help but smile.

I kinda loved the little shit. When we'd come home from the hospital, my Emberly was so quiet, so sad that it broke my heart - not knowing how to help her. That's when Tristan's brother,

Alex, asked the guys at the station if anyone was looking to take in a stray pup he'd found. His landlord wouldn't let him and his wife keep it, but he had promised her a good home.

That day, I had brought Brat home and ever since then, my girl was happier. Not completely healed from what she'd gone through, because I knew that would take more than a puppy and a few week's time. I think having Brat follow her around gave her a sense of peace, someone to care for that wouldn't ask her if she was okay; if she was *over it* yet.

Would we ever truly get over losing our baby?

"Hud, you're home." Her soft voice found me in our bedroom and, smiling as much as I could, I nodded.

"Yeah, Darlin'. Where are my parents?" Her eyes raked over me and if I didn't know better, I would have thought she was looking at me, instead of through me, as she'd developed a habit of doing since coming home.

Not that I blamed her...

"They went to get us breakfast. Sit down with me?"

Reaching her hand out for mine, she had asked me softly and something in my heart loosened, knowing this was the first time in weeks that she'd voluntarily touched me.

Maybe there was hope for us, after all.

A few days ago, I'd gotten word from Tristan that Emberly's father was being held at the precinct awaiting charges. He hadn't only violated the restraining order by coming close to my girl, but he'd also been evading arrest on an outstanding warrant for some time now. It seemed his shady dealings in business had finally caught up with him, and I didn't have a lick of fucking sympathy when it came to him.

The man was a monster. Through and through. If I had my way, he'd never see the light of day again. But, Tristan also told me that he'd requested a meeting with his daughter and as a condition of a pending plea deal, that was his one wish.

Fuck. Even thinking about it made me angry.

Every instinct in me had told me to keep it from Emberly, to protect her from the evil man she'd shed too many tears over. But I knew my girl.

She was a fighter. She was a survivor. And she was stronger than this, than *him*. Though it would kill me to see her walk into that room with him, I knew it was what she'd needed in order to move on. *Closure.*

When she'd walked out of that interrogation room, I had known - against my better judgement and my hatred for her father, a man who had hurt so many, with no remorse - that I'd made the right choice. Because she was finally at peace with her past. She was finally free to live her life, free of the weight of all the pain that she'd born for so many years.

She was finally free to be *mine*.

44

EMBERLY

a baby.

Holding in yet another pain-filled sob, I reached over to the nightstand for a tissue in the hopes of cleaning myself up enough to look okay when Hudson's parents came back. They had gone to the coffee shop down the street for coffee and bagels, promising to bring us both something as well. Hudson must have told them what happened because the moment June saw me, I didn't have to say a word. She'd engulfed me in her arms and whispered mournful condolences in my ear. I didn't know what to say or how to feel, knowing that I was the woman who had lost their first grandchild.

God. Everything hurts right now.

Clenching my eyes tightly shut, I reached my hand out on the bed until I found his large, shaking fingers and quickly wrapped my hand under his; needing the connection in order to continue breathing through my living nightmare. It didn't seem real. *God.* How could any of this be real?

We had finally found our way through the darkness; Only to be, once again, brought back underneath it by yet another loss.

When would it be enough? When would the universe give us a break? Why us?

"I love you so fucking much." The words slipped into the tense air between us and, as if the noose had been loosened from around my neck, I crumbled in on myself.

The sadness, the pain of what we had lost - it all came rushing to the forefront of my mind and no matter how much I tried to staunch it, to ignore it... it was there. His arms, big and strong and harboring, circled my waist just as the first soul-crushing sob climbed up my throat and in those very same arms, I lost myself.

"I- I'm sorry, Hud. I'm so sorry I lost our baby." I whispered, in the hopes that he could still love me after I'd failed him.

"Christ," He muttered roughly and curling in on myself, I tucked my knees under my trembling chin, knowing we would never be the same.

How could I have been carrying his baby and not realized it? How could I have let my father's presence strip me from such a beautiful, innocent life? How would he ever forgive me?

The questions bombarded my mind and closing my eyes on a shuddered, struggling breath, I prayed for peace that just wouldn't come.

"Look at me, Darlin'." His voice was closer then but stubbornly, I shook my head and burrowed my face deeper into my knees; unwilling to face the anger I was sure would be in his eyes. I'd seen it before, when the doctor told us what had happened.

"Baby, I need those pretty eyes on me. Please don't deny me." He pled with me and I gasped, the thought that he had to beg me for anything tearing at another fractured piece of my heart. Opening my eyes, I reached out and grasped his face; letting him see the tears in my eyes and the loss that caused it.

"I'm not mad at you, baby. I'm angry that I could have avoided this, could have protected you but for whatever reason, I didn't see it coming. I fucking failed you and that sweet little baby we made together." The tears I had tried to keep from falling did just that as soon as I heard how much pain my strong, beautiful man was in, and it didn't matter what walls I had tried putting up in order to be unfeeling against what we were facing. I couldn't push him away anymore.

"I wish..."

"Fuck, me too, sweet girl. Come here." His voice was rough and deep and filled with the emotions that swarmed in my own heart, too, and with a sharp tug of my waist, he surrounded me. His hands cupped my jaw lovingly as his mouth swept gently over mine, a whisper of a question, if it was okay, before I whispered his name, allowing him to taste me in the way only he ever had.

"Missed... I missed you." I whispered, my voice shaking and he dipped his mouth to the slow trickle of my tears and lapped them away with his tongue, healing me with a gentleness that calmed me for the first time In weeks.

"You're my whole world, Emberly. Never forget that."

45

EMBERLY

"*H*oney?" My head moved to the doorway where June stood, her soft, kind eyes crinkling with an emotion I had become accustomed to since my miscarriage.

Worry.

Concern.

Pity.

God, I hated that look.

"Can I come in for a minute?" Nodding my head numbly, I tightly folded my hands at my sides, hoping that by doing so, she wouldn't see how they were shaking. I felt as if I were standing on the top of the highest hill, waiting for the harsh wind to blow and inevitably push me over the edge. I kept waiting for someone to blame me for causing all of this, for losing the one good thing I'd been given, and I almost wished they would, that way I'd be able to stop waiting for it. Hudson had calmed my fears so much, but those worries still remained. Was it time that would lessen them?

I'd never felt this... It was more than hurt or pain, fear or self-doubt. It was this emptiness inside of my heart, one even Hudson's forgiveness hadn't outweighed.

"Oh, sweetie. You're so pale. Are you feeling alright?" *Yes.*

I'm fine. The automatic response came to the front of my mind, ready to be uttered yet for some reason, I couldn't make the words slip free. She had been so supportive of us from the very beginning and even now, she was beside me, silently telling me that it would be okay. I didn't want to pretend I was fine anymore.

"No," The word was barely a whisper, but she heard me.

"And that's okay, Emberly. It's really okay to not be okay right now."

"I'm sorry, June. I'm so sorry." The tears I had expected began to drip from my heavy eyes and closing them, I braced myself for her to blame me, to look at me with contempt instead of concern, anger instead of motherly love.

A love I'd never had before then.

"It wasn't your fault, honey. Please believe that." She whispered to me once I'd calmed down, never releasing me from her warm, harboring arms. Moving my head from her shoulder, I looked into her soft, understanding eyes and for the first time since losing my baby, I believed those words.

"You in here, Darlin'?" His deep voice caused a rush of excitement to pulse through my chest and turning toward the sound, I smiled.

And it felt good.

"Right here." He was leaning his large frame against the closed bedroom door, his pale blues trained on me and his arms wrapping that beautiful chest of his, as if I would ever forget to look at it. My smile widened when he raised a thick, dark eyebrow, catching me in the act of checking him out so openly.

Almost a month after our wedding, I still wondered how it was possible that he was mine.

My man.

My husband.

My savior.

Before him, I was content to be alone, walking through the motions of my life on my own, but never really seeing it for what it was. It was lonely and empty and just a facade for the pain and loss I'd been dealt as a girl.

With Hudson, though? I was *happy*.

Even over the past days since we'd found out about our little one, I never truly felt alone. He was right there, always keeping me in one piece; no matter what it cost him. I knew he was hurting, too, seeing it right there in his eyes, each and every time I looked at him. Even now, I could see the remembered pain that our loss had crippled him with. He was such a strong man, and not in the way many assumed. Hudson Lennox was a caretaker, a protector, a leader. He carried those he loved on those big, burly shoulders of his and even when he felt the weakest, he always stayed true to those who counted and believed in him. His parents, his friends and, most of all, *me*.

"You good, baby?" Skimming a kiss over the top of my head, he wrapped an arm around my waist and, nestling into his embrace, I nodded against his chest.

"Now I am." Looking down at me, something flashed between his eyes - an emotion I couldn't place, and before I could try, it was gone.

"Good," He uttered lowly and my heart twisted at the sound that was somehow wrong coming from my big, strong man.

"What's wrong, Hud?" His hands flexed against my lower back, a tell-tale sign that something was weighing heavily on his mind and I reached up to gently skim my fingers over his jaw, strong and tight with iron-gripped control. I wanted him to tell me.

To confide in me, trusting me with the weight of his burdens as he once did. Treating me like a partner in our life, instead of a damsel in distress; too weakened by the loss of our beautiful little girl to handle even the smallest battle.

Sighing heavily, I implored him, looking deeply into his icy blues, hoping that just this once, he'd trust me to be strong enough to handle whatever it was that was hurting him.

"Baby," I melted against him as his large, calloused hands cupped my cheeks with a sense of care that one wouldn't expect from a man of his size, strength. He was always so delicate with me, so sweet. And I treasured every second of it.

"We made it through this together, Hud. Please tell me you know that." I told him, letting my sentence float between us, knowing neither of us could handle the words I'd left unspoken.

"Seeing you so sad has been killing me, Darlin'. I may be a strong man but seeing you hurting is something I'll never fucking get used to." His head fell to my shoulder and the moment I felt his warm tears fall against my skin, I realized just how much he had been hurting, right alongside me. He'd done so in the shadows, quietly, not wanting to burden me with his own pain when I'd lost so much, so soon.

This man, this incredibly strong man - he had been protecting me, all along.

"Oh, Hudson." Digging urgent, needful fingers through the dark hair at the back of his head, I pulled him down to me, the need for closeness outweighing the distance that the pain of the last weeks had placed between us.

"I'm sorry, Darlin'. I'm sorry I didn't protect you both from this. I'm fucking trying to be what you need, Emberly, and it feels like I'm swimming against the tide. I'm failing you and for the life of me, I don't know how to fix it."

My heart ached as he bowed his head down low and whispered the last few words of his deeply-felt apology. Cupping the sharp edges of his jaw, I prayed my love would overshadow the pain that was shining in his pale blues.

He deserved me to be strong for him. He was always my safe place, protecting me so effortlessly and in this moment, he needed the same from me.

"No, baby look at me." Grabbing his face, I pressed my forehead against his, refusing to let him go, even when he locked his jaw and sighed deeply.

"I miss her too, Hud. She was ours and it just hurts that we didn't even get to meet her, hold her, love her..." as my tears fell freely, Hudson suddenly gripped my hips in his hands and crushed his chest to mine, giving me the warmth and comfort I'd been craving from him. I didn't have to say a word, though. Because this man was made for me, knowing my needs before even I had recognized them.

God.

I was so lucky.

Our world was shrouded with a loss I'd never felt before, let alone imagined, and yet with Hudson so close like this, I knew we'd be okay.

Maybe not today. Maybe not tomorrow, even.

But we still had something to fight for.

Something beautiful.

Something honest.

Something unending.

We were unending.

Him and I.

EPILOGUE

HUDSON

One Year Later

"You're home." Her sweet voice met my ears mere seconds before long, slender arms wrapped around my neck and the soft, lush lips of my wife lifted to ghost over mine.

Damn, I thought to myself as I bound her to me with one arm while the other rested over her stomach, where I could feel the slight bump of her little belly beneath her sundress. Smiling against her teasing kisses, I grinned like the fool she made me.

We were having a fuckin' baby.

We'd only found out a few weeks back, when my beautiful girl got car sick on the way to my parents' house for Christmas dinner. She said it was nothing, that it would pass, but something inside of me - I wasn't sure what - had me insisting on making a stop at her doctor's office to be sure she was okay. Thank God I had, because if not, I was sure we wouldn't have caught on to her pregnancy until her next missed period. And we wouldn't have this happiness like we had now.

"I love that smile, Hud. Am I the one that put that there?" Her mouth was on my ear, teasing me with the warmth of her chest against mine and her sweet, vanilla scent wrapped around me, calling me home. Nodding, I dragged a hand through her short, blonde hair, loving the feel of the soft strands beneath my fingers. Shortly after finding out about her pregnancy, I'd finally done what I'd intended to do since the fight we'd had shortly before our wedding ceremony Instead, I decided that I would stay home with our little babies, being a stay at home dad

I remembered having my father at home as a boy and how he'd been there, every day. Never missing a moment. Never failing to show up when I'd needed him to. And seeing how driven my beautiful girl was in her nursing career, I wanted to give her the freedom to pursue it, even after our baby was born, and any others we were blessed to have.

Thankfully, Emberly agreed to my plan and had even told the hospital of her goal to return to work full-time at the hospital after our little baby was born.

"How's mama feeling today?" I asked lowly, tugging her hair back with one hand, letting my other splay over her cheek, needing those pretty eyes on me again.

"Better now." She sighed the words and frowning, I knew what that meant. Ever since we found out, she'd been having what one would normally call *morning sickness*. The thing was, it wasn't just in the mornings that I'd find her sick and frail, in the bathroom that connected to our bedroom where she'd normally just tell me not to worry; that she'd be okay. I found her like that at all times of the day, and I hated it. Everything inside of me told me to do something in order to stop her sickness, no matter what it was.

I wanted to march her to her doctor's office and demand that she be given something to stop the nausea and the recurring headaches she was plagued with. I wanted to protect and shield her from anything, absolutely *anything* that caused her even a little discomfort, but my stubborn girl wouldn't have it. And so, I just shook my head, bewildered, and held her that much closer, thanking my stars that I'd found a woman as strong as her; knowing that no matter what laid ahead for us, we were blessed.

"Love you, Hudson." She whispered in my ear, her head resting in her spot against my chest, right where she belonged. *Forever.*

"Love you, too, Mama. Now let me get you fed, yeah?"

Looking up at me with those bright, shining eyes filled with the love I never thought I'd be capable of having, she just nodded.

Fuck, how I loved her.

HUDSON

Eight Months Later

"I can't wait to meet her." Emberly said as I rubbed slow, little circles on her pregnant stomach, hoping it would help calm her nerves, even just a little.

"You mean him, Darlin'. You know I'm right." Teasing her about the sex of our little baby had become my favorite past time over the length of her pregnancy, and watching the spark of fire in her eyes made it well worth any sass she'd throw back my way.

"Don't you start, Hudson. I know it's a girl, I dreamed it."

"And if you dream something like that..."

"It comes true. Exactly." She smiled widely as she finished my thought, something we'd started doing recently and though she thought it was cute, I just thought it cemented us that much more. We had been meant for each other from the very beginning and I was just grateful that my girl finally got it.

About damn time, wasn't it?

"Where is he? I feel like he should've been in by now."

Her eyes strayed from mine as she looked toward the opened

door to her hospital room. The nurse had just left in order to find Emberly's doctor, Dr. Vale. We'd been here for most of the night, after her water broke during dinner and I'd rushed her to the hospital, sure it was time. And do you know what my wife had done?

She'd laughed at me.

Damn woman.

"I'll go see what the hold-up is, baby. Just relax and do your breathing for me, okay?"

Nodding, she closed her eyes as I quietly left the room and headed toward the nurse's desk, hoping for some answers. When I spotted her doctor speaking in low tones with the same nurse that left our room, I frowned. I might not have been a doctor or known much about medical practice, for that matter, but my instincts were screaming that something was wrong.

"Doctor, what's going on with my wife?"

At my curt words, Dr. Vale turned his head toward me and I could see how my size and demeanor had him shrinking into himself just from the look of me. Cursing internally, I forced myself to calm down enough to talk to him, not wanting to delay Emberly's treatment any more than it already had been.

"I was coming to see you, Mr. Lennox. It seems that your wife won't be able to deliver her baby naturally."

What the fuck?

It was then that the petite nurse standing behind him chimed in.

"I'm sorry, Mr. Lennox, I didn't want to upset Emberly until I spoke with her doctor. It seems the baby is in breech. We'll unfortunately need to perform a cesarean to ensure a safe and healthy birth." All the blood drained from my face as I listened to her explain what would happen in the next few hours, but none of it made a lick of sense. We'd had a healthy pregnancy and my beautiful girl had taken all of her vitamins as asked. Why was this happening to us? Why now?

"Will she be okay?" The question was spoken so low, I was

sure neither of them would hear me, but her doctor did. Placing a warm, firm hand on my shoulder, he merely nodded.

"Yes, your wife will be just fine. Let's go speak to her together."

Nodding, I followed him inside of the room, unsure if I was ready to watch her go under the knife, even if it was for our baby.

EMBERLY

"Hud?"

"I'm right here, baby. I've got you both." He was leaning over one side of my hospital bed as I was wheeled toward the E.R. where I'd meet my baby for the very first time.

God. I'd dreamed of this moment. I had wanted it for so long, so deeply and now, here I was, mere moments from meeting a little baby that was part Hudson, part me.

And I was scared shitless.

What if I messed this up?

What if something went wrong and we lost her?

Could we survive losing another baby that we loved so much?

Tears trickled down my cheeks at the thought and when I felt Hudson's lips skimming their tracks, kissing away the evidence of my fears, I melted inside.

He wouldn't let anything happen to us.

"I'll be right there with you, Darlin'. I swear to you, I won't let anything bad happen."

Looking up into his eyes, I knew he meant every word. Squeezing his hand as tightly as I could muster, I turned my head toward Dr. Vale.

"I'm ready."

HUDSON

1 Hour Later

"Something's wrong, man. I can fucking feel it." The weight of Tristan's hands on my shoulders seemed to be the only thing that grounded me as my heart splintered, the deeply ingrained instinct that something had gone wrong with my beautiful girl churning my gut, ripping me apart from the inside out.

Emberly had gone into surgery more than an hour ago and ever since then, the waiting room had been dead silent. *Shouldn't I have heard something by now?*

Fuck! I was coming apart at the seams without the presence of my girl to calm me down.

"Calm down, man. She's going to be fine."

"Don't fuckin' know that." I growled. In hindsight, I knew it wasn't his fault. He was just as worried as I was. Hell, maybe even more so because he considered Emberly to be the sister he'd never had. He was a protector at heart and as our relationship had grown over the past year, Tristan had stepped up in ensuring her safety when I couldn't.

"Hudson-" He began to admonish me and, clenching my fists, I was ready to lay him a new one before the sound of a door closing down the hall halted my protests all together.

Emberly.

I needed to focus on my Emberly.

Creak. Creak. Creak.

The white linoleum floors beneath Dr. Vale's feet creaked and moaned as he approached us, a grave, almost stricken look crossing his pale face.

No. My mind screamed, the fear of bad news coursing through my veins like the worst of poisons.

I can't do it, baby.

I pled to Emberly silently, needing her to hear me from wherever she was. Don't you dare leave just yet. We have so much to do, to experience together and I'm not even close to having enough time with you...

"Mr. Lennox, your wife pulled through the C-section just fine. Mama and baby are strong and healthy." Relief soared through me the second his words registered and if Tristan hadn't been there to grab my arms and keep me from falling to my knees in gratitude, I was sure I would have ended up on the floor.

"Oh, thank god. Can I see her? Can I see my wife?" Firing the questions at him, it was only when he solemnly shook his head that I realized something was, in fact, wrong.

My heart began to race at that moment, the prospect of something being wrong with my angel threatening to stop its pace entirely.

"Spit it out, Doctor."

"There was a complication, Mr. Lennox. After we delivered the baby, she began to hemorrhage and as we worked on getting the bleeding to stop, she unfortunately went into cardiac arrest." His voice was so flat, so emotionless, I had trouble understanding that what he was saying was *true*.

Hemorrhage.

Bleeding.

Cardiac Arrest...

Fuck! No no no no...

Not now, Emberly. Fuck, not yet; don't leave me yet.

My hands gripped the sides of my head as my world shattered, my eyes closing of their own accord in hopes that it was all some sort of fucked up dream.

"She's resting now and her vitals are all normal, Hudson. She's going to be fine just like I said, alright?" It was Tristan's voice then that spoke news of her condition, and it was only when he pressed his head against mine that I could breathe again.

She was going to be okay.

She had to be okay.

Right?

"Doctor, when can we see her?" I gritted the words through clenched teeth, the last shred of composure driving me forward. Once I saw her, I knew I would be okay.

If anyone could make this all okay, it was her.

"Follow me. One at a time, please." Nodding, I didn't have to look over my shoulder to know Tristan would let me go in first. He knew how I loved her, after all.

I'm coming baby. I pled to her within the dark, pained recesses of my mind, knowing somehow, someway, she'd hear me.

EMBERLY

48 Hours Later

My body felt like dead weight as I forced a strangled cough from my throat, the sensation of a breathing tube blocking my airways causing panic to rise.

What happened?

Was my baby okay?

Oh my god...

"My baby!" My voice came out as a whisper of anguish and, opening my eyes, the first person I saw was the very one my heart called out for.

"Shh, shh, Darlin'. I'm right here. I'm right fucking here." In the time it took me to blink my swollen, tired eyes, he'd engulfed me in everything that was my husband, my love, my Hudson. His thick, muscular arms wrapped around me as much as they could with the wires that covered my hands and arms while his lips covered mine in the softest, sweetest and meaningful kiss we had shared yet.

"She's perfect. She's so damn perfect." Gasping against his ardent kiss, I pushed at his hard chest, needing his eyes on me when he told us about her.

"She's okay? Are you sure?" Grasping his shoulders with desperate fervor, the fear for our tiny baby girl sung through me like a living, breathing thing.

Oh my god.

I'd been right.

We had a girl!

"I'll bring her in in just a few minutes, baby. I swear. I just wanted a little time with my girl first." Smiling widely, I laughed when he bathed my upturned face in sweet kisses, not stopping until I slapped at his chest in protest. *God, I loved him.*

"I was right, you know." I whispered some time later, looking up into his pale blue eyes that were filled with so much love, I was sure he was consumed by it.

"Yeah, baby, you were." Hudson whispered into my ear, moving his body over mine until he had his hands on either side of my head and his mouth mere inches from mine; teasing me with anticipation of another soul-binding kiss. But before I could lift my mouth for a taste of him, he lowered his head to my chest and clasped me to him in a tight, almost painful hold.

"I was so fucking scared." The roughly murmured words were muffled into the hospital gown I was wearing, but as soon as I heard them, the fear that I'd awoken with rushed back to the surface. We had come so close to losing one another over the past few months, between Brad and my father... even Tristan's accident had shaken us to our core.

I thought we were strong before, but now?

We were unbreakable.

"Hud, baby look at me." Shaking his head against my neck, I felt warm wetness against the skin there and it hurt my heart like nothing else before.

Hudson was so self-assured, strong and protective in so many ways. Both aggressive and sweet in the bedroom, and kind-hearted to those around him; his friends, his family, me. But at his core, he was just as human as the rest of us.

"Please, Hudson. I need you to see, baby. I'm still here. *We're* still here. You haven't lost me." Dragging my fingers through his dark locks, I waited until he looked at me and when he did, I saw the unshed tears he'd been hiding from me.

"Don't cry," I whispered, feeling my heart slow its beat as sadness for him permeated its walls. He'd always been the one to protect us from everything and anything that threatened to tear us apart, but right then, I knew he needed me to be the strong one.

"Can't lose you, Darlin'."

"You won't." I vowed.

We'd gone through hell and back together.

We'd fought together.

We'd loved each other.

And we'd finally won.

THE END

BREATHE WITH ME PLAYLIST

Naked by James Arthur
Impossible by James Arthur
Blue Ain't Your Color by Keith Urban
What Lovers Do by Maroon 5
Don't Let Me Down- The Chainsmokers
Kiss Me Like A Stranger by Thomas Rhett
End Game by Taylor Swift
Bad At Love by Halsey
Perfect by Ed Sheeran
Thunder by Imagine Dragons
Break On Me by Keith Urban
Beautiful by Christina Aguilera
Body Like A Back Road by Sam Hunt
Never Alone by Lady Antebellum
First Love by Lost Kings, Sabrina Carpenter
Marry Me by Thomas Rhett

Dear reader,

We hope you enjoyed reading *Breathe With Me*. Please take a moment to leave a review, even if it's a short one. Your opinion is important to us.

Discover more books by Amanda Kaitlyn at
https://www.nextchapter.pub/authors/author-amanda-kaitlyn

Want to know when one of our books is free or discounted? Join the newsletter at
http://eepurl.com/bqqB3H

Best regards,

Amanda Kaitlyn and the Next Chapter Team

BOOKS BY AMANDA KAITLYN

The Beautifully Broken Series

Finding Beautiful

Breaking Lucas

This Beautiful Love

Dare To Love: An LGBT Romance

Saving Tayla (Coming 2019!)

Remembering Us (Coming Soon!)

Loving Elsa (Coming Soon!)

The Black Harts MC Series

Until Us

Broken In Us (Coming Soon!)

Redemption Of Us (Coming Soon!)

Standalone's

Breathe With Me

Lyric's Law (A F/F Romance)

Love, Unashamed (A F/F Romance)

ABOUT THE AUTHOR

Debut author of bestselling novel, Finding Beautiful, Amanda Kaitlyn is an incurable romantic. A lover of fairy tales, just a tad dirtier than the ones she used to read as a child. In her free time you can find her reading, writing or walking her 3 dogs, Sable, Bella and Princess. Amanda likes to keep her stories real and her characters relatable and in the pages of her books you can find angsty, emotionally driven romance and alpha men that will do anything for the women they love.

www.romancebyamandakaitlyn.com
facebook.com/amandakaitlyn
instagram.com/amandakaitlyn_author

Amanda Kaitlyn's Lovely Readers
https://www.facebook.com/groups/amandakaitlynslovies

Breathe With Me
ISBN: 978-4-86750-816-9

Published by
Next Chapter
1-60-20 Minami-Otsuka
170-0005 Toshima-Ku, Tokyo
+818035793528

22nd June 2021

CPSIA information can be obtained
at www.ICGtesting.com
Printed in the USA
LVHW110321060721
691957LV00002B/113